# SWORD & THISTLE

S.L. ROWLAND

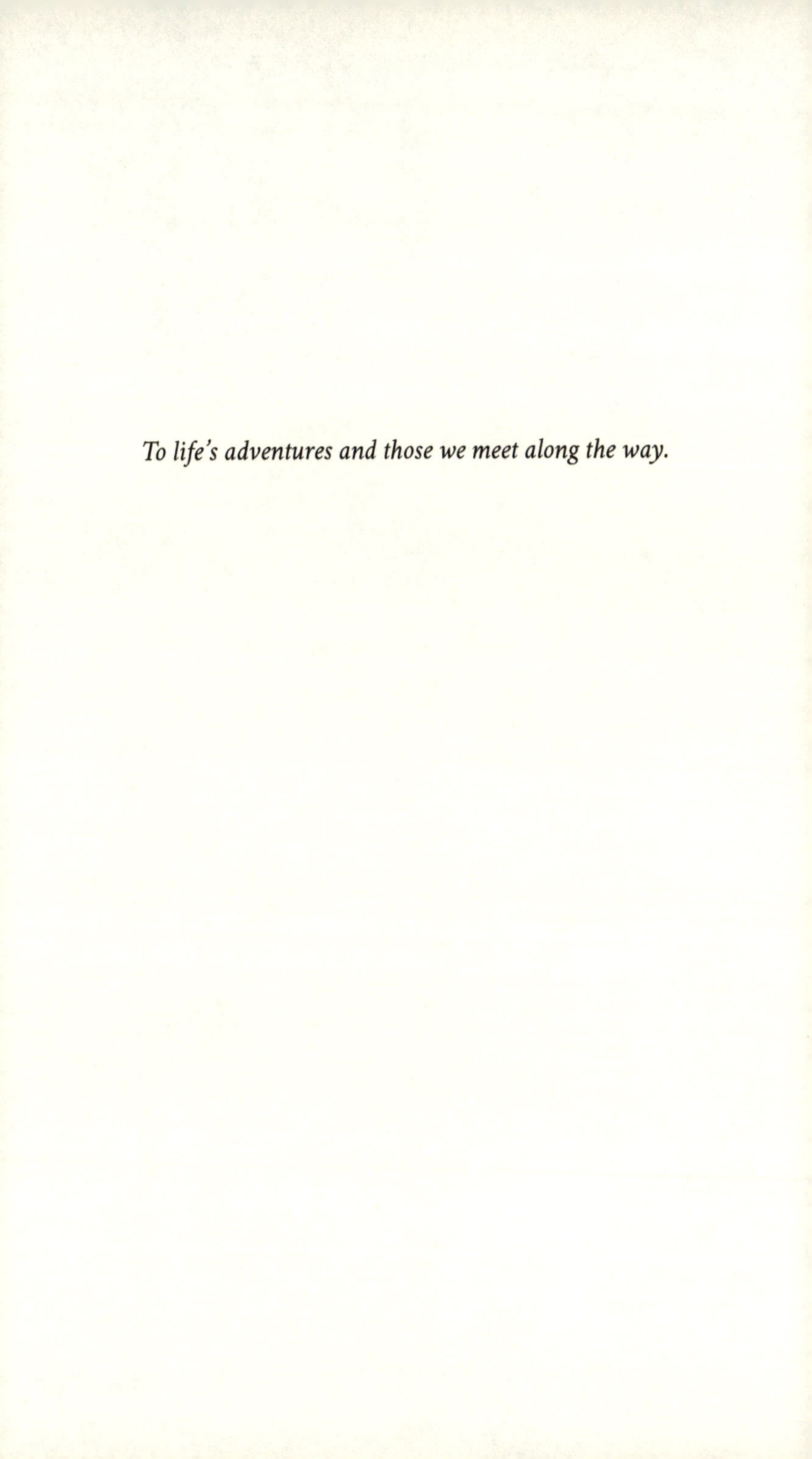

*To life's adventures and those we meet along the way.*

CAPITAL CITIES
NOTABLE SETTLEMENTS
THE BOUNDLESS SEA
T H
STORMREST
AETHERVALE
COGWALL
REVELIA
BARROWSTURM
NARTHWICH
WARMINSTER
WOLFWATER
GANNETT
CROWHOLD
TIBERIA
NELDERLAND
THE VAST LANDS OF
AEDREA

FROZEN NORTH
NORTHPASS
MOUNT TOR
DURENDREG
HOLLOWTON
CASCUS
SANGUIN
DRAKE CANYON
ROCKDALE
VERPEAK
HELLS' CRAG
WHITEHAVEN
DARM
BEARMOUTH
SHIVERDAWN
HILLSIDE
WHITBLOSSUM
NIA
HONEYDALE
TYNE
VUSORA
GREENBRIAR MARSH
ASTBORNE
ICRAMEL
ERMMIR
WASTELANDS
TO THE WILDS

# PROLOGUE

*500 years ago.*

---

Hells' Crag lay in ruins, and Raglan watched as the dwarven city smoldered.

The architecture had been a testament to dwarven craftsmanship. They'd built a city that seemed to rise from the surrounding lake like a monument to the gods. Now, it was nothing more than a fiery tomb of stone and metal.

Raglan's gaze lingered on what remained of the windows carved into the cliffside of the crag. A thousand windows overlooking the lake. They had been beautiful. On a clear night, the glow from within would reflect on the still water like a thousand fireflies.

Now, molten stone poured through many of the windows and spilled into the water below. A dense blanket of steam rose from the lake, and dead fish speckled the deep-blue surface.

On the far side of the crag, the once-lush valley disappeared into mountains that raged with dragon fire. The city had outgrown the crag itself long ago and spread into the nearby mountains. It all burned.

Smoke had billowed on the horizon for three days. The mages of both Darm and Mount Tor were far away in Drake Canyon, holding a council in the hopes of ending the war that had persisted between the mountain and lowland dwarves for over a century.

Raglan leaned against his staff and sighed as a roar tore across the lake, its hatred amplified by the waves as the dragon continued its rampage on the dying city.

The city was defenseless, and Raglan had arrived too late. Now, a fiery graveyard sprawled before him, a necropolis of what had been one of the dwarves' most prized achievements. There was nothing to do but wait and see where the dragon turned to next. Hells' Crag may be lost, but Raglan the Magnificent would not let this terror continue.

The last time a dragon had attacked a city had been hundreds of years ago. Most were content to lose themselves among the highest peaks of the north or deep within the wilds. What had provoked this one to unleash such wrath?

Dwarven architecture was sound, built from the very earth itself. Any other type of dragon and the city might have survived, but the flames of a red dragon spared nothing.

A massive head arched above where the keep had once stood, jaws agape as it spewed fire against the sky. The dragon's burgundy scales told of its age, darkened by the passage of time. Golden scales speckled its body, shimmering in the sun.

The fire abated, and the dragon roared with a fury that shook the leaves of the surrounding trees. Raglan stood transfixed by the majesty of the creature. *Gods, dragons, it made no difference. Everywhere there was beauty, destruction followed.*

The dragon took to the air, wings unfurling like sails meant to blot out the sun. With each flap of its wings, smoke shifted with the force of god-like bellows.

For hours, the dragon circled the crag, burning the landscape until the lake simmered and the trees surrounding Raglan had all withered from the heat.

Still, the mage waited, almost trance-like in his patience. The day faded to twilight, and the glow of the burning countryside cast the world in hues of amber. After all this time, Hells' Crag had finally earned its name. Nothing would grow there again. Scorched earth and barren countryside would mark the landscape for centuries, if not longer.

The dragon took flight once more, its titian underbelly mirroring the blazing terrain as it turned its eyes to the west.

Raglan stood from the fevered bark of the tree he leaned upon and whispered, "No."

He raised his staff, and the opalescent stone embedded within the gnarled wood flashed yellow. Lightning ripped through the sky in a single bolt, white-hot and powerful with dozens of tendrils that grasped for purchase. Arcane energy collided with the dragon, immobilizing it momentarily and sending it plummeting toward the earth.

The resounding thunder echoed through the night, drowning out the crash of the monstrous creature as it cratered into the forest. Moments later, the dragon took flight again, scanning the area until its golden eyes fell upon the storm mage.

# 1. STRONG DRINKS AND OLD FRIENDS

Dobbin took a deep breath, holding it in and closing one eye as he focused on the target. He felt the weight of the metal against his fingers and released with a practiced motion ingrained by years of repetition. The coin bounced off the grime-covered table with a thunk and flipped end over end in a high arc. The rowdy tavern grew silent, and there was an intake of breath all around as time seemed to slow. The gold coin gleamed in the dim candle-light before it sank into the shot glass with a splash.

Cheers erupted around the tavern.

Dobbin made eye contact with the dwarf sitting across the table. After twelve rounds, his eyes were glazed over, and he swayed like a flag in a gentle breeze. The muscled dwarf wobbled as he reached for the glass with a shaky hand. His first attempt missed, and he nearly toppled from the chair. Dobbin sat back, crossing his arms as he grinned. The dwarf's second attempt knocked the shot over, and he fell face-first onto the table.

"Another round on me!" Dobbin shouted above the laughter, twirling his finger in a circle.

The taverngoers celebrated their free drinks, and he enjoyed the bustling chaos. After a month in the forest, it was good to be back around his people.

A pair of slender hands gripped Dobbin firmly on the shoulder and squeezed. "It's always good when you return to Eastborne, old friend."

Dobbin recognized the alluring voice, a voice he hadn't heard in quite some time.

The woman let go, wrapping a tattooed arm around him and tugging playfully on his fiery beard. Her blonde hair trailed down his shoulder as she stared at Dobbin with a wide grin, one gold tooth flashing in the candlelight. "Come on, share a drink with your old pal."

Dobbin chuckled as he shook his head, still unable to believe his eyes. "Alina, you bastard. I was beginning to wonder if I'd ever see your face again. Last I heard, there was a bounty on your head."

"All in the past. All in the past." Alina brushed at the air as if banishing the idea. "Since you're buying, I'll grab a pitcher. Anything for you?"

Dobbin laughed. "Make it two."

He found an empty table in the corner while Alina grabbed their drinks from the bartender. The dwarf who'd challenged Dobbin snored like a direhog while the barmaid lifted his head to clean the spilled wuiskey. Alina blew her a kiss from across the bar, and the barmaid's cheeks flushed.

When Alina returned, she placed two large pitchers on the table, glancing once again at the sleeping dwarf. "It's good to see you haven't lost your touch."

Dobbin raised his pitcher. "To old friends."

"And strong drinks." The two pitchers clinked as they touched, and they each took a hearty drink.

Dobbin closed his eyes, savoring the sweet, malty ale. When he opened them, he looked at Alina in disbelief. "How long has it been? Three, four years?"

Alina cocked her head, golden earrings flashing in the light of the sconce. "Try seven."

"Damn." Dobbin sighed. "Time flies, doesn't it?"

"Like coin in the brothel." Alina bit her lip devilishly. "So, what brings you back to Eastborne?"

"I could ask you the same thing." Dobbin raised a brow. "Seven years…" He let the words trail off.

"Well, after the whole ordeal with the you-know-what and you-know-who, I had a few debts to pay. I spent some time in Crowhold laying low and keeping my ear to the ground, but nothing panned out. I finally had a score with a band of gnomes in Cogwall. Enough to settle my debts at least. So here I am, back where I belong. Been here a few months, and it seems you've earned yourself quite a reputation."

"Glad to see you're off the chopping block." Dobbin set his drink down, leaning forward as his head swirled from the alcohol. "I'm here to collect on my latest quest and see what other opportunities wait in store."

Alina tilted the pitcher, and half of it disappeared. She let out a loud belch before continuing. "Might be I can help you with that."

"I don't doubt it." Dobbin laughed. "But I've seen the kind of trouble you get into."

Alina reached across the table, tapping Dobbin on the

hand. "There was a time when our paths weren't all that different."

"Don't I know it. But times have changed. I've worked hard to get where I'm at." He let go of her hand. "Besides, I work alone."

There were fewer complications that way. Less to lose.

"Right, right." Alina took another long swallow. "'Dobbin, the adventurer who gets the job done, no matter the cost.' I must say, I am a bit jealous. I lost seven years of my life while you were cementing your legacy. But I always knew you were going places. We all did. You and your damn books. You wouldn't start a job without a trip to the library." She shrugged. "Oh, well. I figured it was worth a—"

"Godsdammit." Dobbin leaned down, crouching his hulking frame near the table and failing miserably.

Alina looked over her shoulder, curious. "What is it?"

"One of Lord Ferant's men." Dobbin slid the pitcher to where it concealed most of his face. "I've been in the city less than a day. How does he already know I'm here?"

The man looked out of place in the grungy tavern, wearing a silken blue tunic embroidered with a ram's head on the chest. Silver and red thread depicted elaborate vines and flowers down both arms. He covered his nose with a kerchief as he passed by the sleeping dwarf. Several patrons laughed and pointed as he made his way through the room.

Dobbin continued to hide behind the pitcher even as the man lingered next to the table.

"Ahem." The messenger cleared his throat. "Master Dobbin. Miss." He frowned as he looked at Alina. "Lord

Ferant requests your presence in the Council District tomorrow evening after sundown."

Dobbin sat up. "Fine," he grunted. "Tell him I'll be there."

"Very well." The messenger spun on his heel, and with head held high, he made his way back across the tavern.

Alina watched him with an amused expression. "What has you hiding like a child from a member of the city council?"

Dobbin tilted the pitcher, draining it by a third. "The man has eyes everywhere. I thought I could lay low in the lower districts for a bit and actually enjoy the city for once before he came calling, but he finds me, every damn time. The jobs pay well, but the man is insufferable. It's always 'my boy, this' and 'my boy, that.' I'm forty-two years old!"

"You could tell him no."

Dobbin narrowed his eyes. "And what, find myself blacklisted? I do quite enjoy it here."

Alina shrugged. "You'd still have the Adventurer's Guild to fall back on."

"Who do you think signs their permits?" Dobbin shook his head. "As long as I'm here, I have to endure the whims of the wealthy. Or at least Lord Ferant."

"There are other cities. Bigger cities, even. We worked them, you know?"

"Believe me, I know. But—"

Alina slammed her hand to the table and the glass rattled. "No? No. Don't tell me that it's been seven years and you're still chasing that woman."

Dobbin's cheeks reddened. "It's not like that."

Alina scoffed. "And I thought I had it bad."

"I'm just looking out for her, Alina."

Alina rolled her eyes. "Seven years, Dobbin. Her husband died seven years ago. By the gods, man, shit or get off the pot."

"Look, she doesn't even know it's me helping her. But I was there when it happened, you know. I just, I don't know. I feel responsible in a way."

"And they tell me I'm crazy." Alina stood. "Next round's on me."

# 2. HONOR AMONG THIEVES

Dobbin's head pounded as he made his way along the cobbled street from the Adventurer's Guild to the Bank of Aedrea. He pulled the hood of his cloak low in an attempt to shield his eyes from the midday sun, but it was no use.

The first night back in a city was always the best. There was something about a fresh ale and the company of others that made it taste all the better, and he usually paid for it. He'd drank too much the night before, catching up with Alina and sharing stories of their travels and adventures over the past seven years.

She could drink a man twice her size under the table and didn't take shit from anyone. Dobbin hadn't realized just how much he'd missed her company until they were standing on the bar, swaying together as they slurred the words to *The Miller and the Maiden Fair*.

Dobbin's cloak jingled with the coin he'd collected from the Adventurer's Guild for completing his latest quest as he stopped in front of the bank. The Bank of Aedrea was the safest place in all the realm to keep one's funds. There were regional and local banks scattered about, but there was a Bank of Aedrea located in every kingdom. Since it was owned and operated by the Order of Clerics, its reputation had remained steadfast even as kingdoms rose and fell over the years. For an adventurer, that meant he could follow the work wherever it led. Coin could be retrieved from any of their branches, but the vaults could only be accessed in person. Dobbin had items scattered around many cities to the point that he couldn't remember them all. That would be a problem for when he was old and gray.

He stepped through the heavy wooden door and took a deep breath. Somehow, the bank always smelled faintly of mint, no matter the location. A long counter of polished stone with gilded accents stretched most of the room, adding to the grandeur. To the left, there was a lobby with plenty of seating.

A gnome with lilac hair waved Dobbin over to the counter. Like everyone else behind the counter, she wore the gray tunic of a cleric. "Master Dobbin, good to see you again."

Dobbin dropped his pouch on the counter. "I'd like to deposit this, please."

"The usual?" asked the gnome.

"Yes." He nodded. "Twenty-five percent should go to the Hargrave family."

"I will see to it." She made a note on a piece of parchment after tallying the gold. "Is there anything else we can do for you today, Master Dobbin?"

Dobbin reached into his cloak, removing an old leather-bound book and placing it on the counter. The title was long faded from the cover. "Can you place this in my vault and pull me another?"

"Anything in particular?"

Dobbin tried to recall which books he kept in the Eastborne branch for a moment but then decided to leave it up to fate. "Surprise me."

"Very well." The gnome disappeared behind the counter toward the vaults. A few minutes later, she returned carrying a black book with silver lettering on the cover and placed it on the counter.

*The Shadows of the City.*

Dobbin smiled. That one was an old favorite about a rogue and her adventures in Tiberia.

"Anything else for you?" she asked with a friendly tone.

He picked up the book, feeling the glossy leather against his skin. "That'll be it."

The gnome scribbled the account balance and details of the transaction on a piece of parchment and handed it to Dobbin. "Have a good day, Master Dobbin. The Bank of Aedrea thanks you for your business."

---

With coin deposited and nothing to do until his meeting later with Lord Ferant, Dobbin stopped by the Premier Market for lunch.

It was the biggest market in all of Eastborne, and farmers came from the surrounding countryside to sell their produce to the city. Wagons parked behind covered stalls that displayed the items each had to offer, and a rainbow of color spread around the square from golden beets to red apples and a dozen hues of leafy greens. There were also booths where local businesses sold freshly baked bread, cured meats, cider, and an assortment of cheeses.

The heavenly smell of roasted meat lured Dobbin to a corner stall where giant slabs roasted on a grill. Jerky and salted meat hung from hooks around the booth, and a wooden sign reading *The Bloody Block* rested against the frame.

A large man, with an even larger belly, waved his carving knife at Dobbin. "Hey there, big fella. You look like you could use a bite to eat. The Bloody Block has the best meats in the city, slaughtered just across the river. Here, try this." He sliced a piece of pork from the grill and skewered it with a carving fork, offering a sample.

Dobbin salivated as he took the steaming piece of pork. The fatty cut had a slightly sweet taste that complemented its savory nature. The smokiness lingered in his mouth long after he swallowed.

"Ydora's tit, that's good!" Dobbin licked his fingers. "You sold me."

"Let me tell you a secret." The butcher leaned forward. "If you grab a loaf from the baker, I'll put the roast on top and it'll soak up the juice. You'll thank me."

The man had the look of someone who knew his way around a dinner table, so Dobbin took heed of his advice, buying a small loaf of bread as it was pulled from the oven. The butcher sliced it in half and filled the center with slivers of thinly cut pork.

"All you need now is a tankard of ale." The butcher winked as he handed Dobbin the food.

Dobbin meandered through the city as he ate, past the

Art District where music carried across the open court-yard and magnificent sculptures surrounded a pond speckled with golden fish. He walked past the university with its tall spires and elaborate architecture, where a hundred gargoyles stared down upon the city streets.

There was a beauty to Eastborne in the way the streets ran along the mountainside overlooking the sea. One could find a view of the harbor from just about every district within the tiered city.

Dobbin took an alleyway that framed the bay like a painting before emptying onto a narrow street. Across the way, a bakery sat sandwiched between a tailor and a fine glassware merchant. The pastel purple sign of Cupped Cakes set it apart from the drab storefronts to each side, and a large window revealed the interior of the bakery, with its half-dozen small tables and display counter showcasing the day's treats.

Somehow, Dobbin always found himself passing through this particular area when he was back in town. He lingered across the street, careful to remain unseen. If Alina knew he was here, she'd never let him hear the end of it.

A woman appeared from behind the counter, her apron covered in flour and smudges of icing as she delivered two pastries to a table. Isabella's dark hair framed her face as she laughed, touching one of the customers on the shoulder. As she chatted with the patrons, Dobbin's stomach clenched, and he found himself moving behind the lamppost that was much too thin to conceal his frame.

Moments later, a young boy joined Isabella, tugging on her apron and pointing toward the kitchen. The boy was the spitting image of his father. He had an easy smile and curly black hair that dangled across his forehead.

The pang of regret stabbed like a hot knife as Dobbin recalled his last moments with the boy's father. *One last quest,* Henrik had said the payout would be enough for Isabella to start her bakery, and then he'd leave the adventuring life behind. That day had been filled with so much hope.

And then everything went to shit.

Those memories faded just in time for Dobbin to see Isabella staring at him through the window with a confused expression. She had the look of a wild animal frozen in shock. The shock faded, and she hurried toward the door, but Dobbin was already backing down the alley.

After all this time, he still wasn't ready.

Dobbin's name echoed through the street as he sprinted away.

# 3. CURSED COCKTAILS

Dobbin cursed the long walk as he traversed the tiered streets to the Council District.

Seven years had passed since Henrik had died, and still, Dobbin couldn't bring himself to talk to the man's widow. After every quest, he had gold deposited into her account, and with every visit back to Eastborne, he stopped by the bakery to make sure all was well. But talking to Isabella, looking her in the eye, and explaining how everything had gone wrong—he couldn't do that.

All this time, and not once had he been spotted.

Until now.

Dobbin fumed with each step. While he was more upset about his blunder earlier, it was easier to place that anger elsewhere, namely on the man he was about to meet. He would collect the quest from Lord Ferant and get out of the city as soon as possible so that things could blow over. Maybe Isabella would forget about the whole thing.

The Council District was located within the walls of

Eastborne's original keep and housed the council chambers as well as some of the city's wealthiest citizens. The imposing structure was a remnant of when Eastborne had been a sovereign kingdom and a reminder of its long history. The walk from the lower levels was tedious, but it gave Dobbin plenty of time to ruminate on just how much he disliked interacting with Lord Ferant.

There was nothing necessarily wrong with the man. He was a good council member, decent and honest by all accounts. But he was prideful, and there was something about his nature that spoke of privilege and having never done a hard day's labor in his life.

Every word out of the man's mouth grated on Dobbin's ears like a sharp blade against rough stone.

He kept the hood of his cloak up as he walked, even though dusk was fast approaching. The cloak concealed the sword and dagger that hung from his hips, as well as a dozen other tools and weapons tucked within the hidden pockets. He'd found early on that the more he looked the part of a rugged adventurer, the more he could charge for his services.

Lamplighters scurried from one lamppost to another as they raced against the night. As Dobbin entered the Trade District, he noticed a new business had opened in the revolving storefront that had previously been a spice shop.

The name caused him to stop in his tracks. *Cursed Cocktails.* The owner was either incredibly bold or naive. Rumor was that the building was cursed or haunted. Dobbin wasn't sure he believed either, but for whatever the reason, it seemed like every time he returned to the city, there was either a new shop or an empty storefront in its place.

One of the food peddlers normally stationed down by the harbor had his cart set up in front of the new business.

Dobbin nodded to the man as he approached. "You're a long way from the docks."

The man shrugged. "Can't complain. Most nights, it's steady business. And these folks know how to tip a man for his troubles." He pointed a thumb toward the building. "This one might actually stick around for a while."

"Is that so?" Dobbin pressed a hand to the window and peeked inside.

There was a man enjoying a glass of wine by the fireplace. A little something to take the edge off might be just what Dobbin needed to keep from murdering Lord Ferant.

Inside, the tavern was warm and welcoming, with a bar that stretched along the right wall, a half-dozen tables, and a few large pieces of furniture in front of a fireplace. The weather was too warm for a fire, but the ambiance was nice. A couple of large tapestries framed the hearth, adding to the coziness, and the smell of cinnamon and vanilla lingered in the air.

At a nearby table, two gnomes played a board game, sharing a drink and laughing as they moved pieces across a checkered piece of wood. Next to them, a couple enjoyed a basket of oysters from the peddler out front. The man he'd seen drinking wine sat by the barren fireplace reading a scroll.

An umbral elf stood behind the bar, his gaze lingering on Dobbin as if sizing him up. His ash-colored skin and red eyes were a strange sight this far south.

Dobbin tapped his coin pouch. "I need a drink. Something strong."

The elf offered a warm smile as he pointed to a menu. "We've got strong drinks, all right."

Dobbin leaned against the bar, eyeing the menu full of drinks he'd never heard of. By the third drink, his frustration boiled over and he dropped the menu on the bar. "Gods be damned, don't you have ale?" He wanted a drink, not a recipe book.

The elf tapped the bottom of the menu with a chuckle.

*Ale and wine list available upon request.*

"We've got ale—some of the best in the realm from Barrowsturm to Rakroft—but we offer drinks you can't find anywhere else in Eastborne. The recipes come from all over Aedrea, passed down to me from my father on his travels."

This piqued Dobbin's interest, and he picked up the menu again. In his experience, both umbral and elder elves preferred their solitude. There were few reasons one would travel the realm. "Your pops was an adventurer?"

The elf shook his head, grinning. "Not in the same sense as you, but he had an adventurous spirit."

Dobbin respected anyone with the courage to leave their comforts for a life of adventure. "Alright, you've convinced me." He pushed the menu forward. "But like I said, something strong."

"Coming right up." The elf began crafting the drink, mixing ingredients in a metal cup and talking as he worked. "What brings you to Eastborne?"

Dobbin looked over his shoulder to make sure no one was listening, but the other guests were all engrossed in their own conversations. "Special business. I have an appointment with a nobleman, and if I don't have a drink before I go, I'm likely to show him the pointy end of my sword."

"That bad?" The bartender raised a brow as he added ice to the container, capped the other end, and began shaking the drink vigorously.

The elf had an easy, disarming personality, like someone who only wanted to listen, and Dobbin found himself venting before he even realized. "Oh, you know the kind. They think the world revolves around them and the rest of us are lucky to be in their presence."

"This should help with that." The elf winked and poured a little extra rhum into the mixture. He shook the drink again until a cool sheen coated the exterior, and then he strained the contents into a glass. "Why do you do it, then?"

"I follow the coin," Dobbin lied, "and I can count on this lot to fill my purse at least once a season."

Although the coin was good, he enjoyed the challenge that adventuring presented. Every quest was different, and he never knew what skills or knowledge it would take to get the job done.

The bartender garnished the deep-red cocktail with a few raspberries and slid it across the bar. "Work is work. I'm not one to bemoan anyone making an honest living."

"Cheers to that!" Dobbin lifted his glass, tapped it to the bar in a show of respect, and took a hardy drink. He drained the cocktail in one swallow, but the sweet and refreshing aftertaste made him wish he'd savored it a bit more. This was a far cry from the swill he drank across the river. He set the glass back on the bar. "By the gods, that's good. One more for the road."

"Be careful." The elf laughed as he rinsed the shaker and prepared to make another. "Those things are stronger than they look."

Whether it was the remnants from the previous night's shenanigans or the drink was in fact stronger than it looked, Dobbin felt emboldened. He winked at the bartender as he played up his persona. "That's what they say about me."

The elf looked Dobbin up and down. "You look pretty strong already."

"Exactly." Dobbin smirked, and his head began to buzz from the drink. "I've traveled all across Aedrea in my time. Whether it be man, woman, or monster, Dobbin has yet to find a foe he couldn't match."

"I believe it. Dobbin, is it? You can call me Rhoren."

Dobbin sipped on the second round a little slower, savoring the beverage. This time, he was able to appreciate its subtle flavors of sweet raspberry and lime. "This is a nice place you have here, Rhoren. I don't remember seeing it last time I was in Eastborne. Just so happens I saw that fellow over there drinking his wine as I was walking down the street."

Rhoren nodded appreciatively as he looked around the room with an air of pride. "We've only been open for a few weeks now, but it's good to know we at least look appealing."

"Here's to hoping you stick around." Dobbin raised his glass and took a drink. He then pointed over his shoulder to one of the tapestries on the wall. It depicted the crest of the Northern Guard over a snowy mountain range. The Guard protected the realm from the dangers of the frozen north, but it was rare to see them referenced in the southern kingdoms. "What's with the Northern Guard tapestry? You don't see those much this far south."

Rhoren's gaze settled on the tapestry. "I served before I moved here."

"You don't say?" Dobbin shifted in his seat. He suddenly found this elf a lot more interesting. "I served in the Warminster military in my younger years. Adventuring is a lot more fun."

Rhoren laughed. "I do not doubt it."

A second drink quickly turned into a third, and Dobbin and Rhoren shared stories of their time in the military. By the end of the third drink, he was convinced these drinks were stronger than they looked.

Dobbin leaned forward, looking over each shoulder to make sure no one was lurking. An elf of Rhoren's skillset would definitely appreciate what he was about to tell. "Want to know a secret?"

Rhoren leaned closer, sporting a wide grin. "Always."

"There's a secret society among the nobles of Eastborne," he whispered. "They call themselves the Eastborne Dinner Cult. A few times a year, they hire me to hunt down rare or magical creatures so that they can eat them."

Rhoren's eyes went wide. "And what, they just eat rare creatures?"

Dobbin nodded. "They believe it brings them closer to the gods."

"Oh, wow. What do you usually bring them?"

Dobbin shrugged, wondering what Lord Ferant might want him to procure this time. "Whatever they want, if the coin is good. Fairies. Wargs. Last year, I traveled all the way to Drake Canyon for slimes. That one took me half the year." He frowned at the memory of spending the entire winter in the mountains. "Who knows what the bastard will ask for this time."

"You keep coming back, so it must not be all bad."

Dobbin lifted his glass, only to find it was empty. He sighed. Probably for the best. "I guess that's my cue. I'll be in town for a few days at least. I'll stop back by and try some of your other offerings." He reached into his pocket, pulling out a handful of silver coins and letting them fall on the counter. "Will this cover it?"

Rhoren laughed. "See you around, Dobbin."

# 4. EASTBORNE DINNER CULT

A pair of guards stood sentry outside of the entrance to the Council District. The ornate gate with elaborate metalwork was the only point of entry, at least officially, sandwiched between high walls that ran the perimeter of the keep. There were catacombs and secret tunnels throughout the city from ages past, but when it came to council members, it was best to play things by the book.

Dobbin flashed his badge from the Adventurer's Guild. "Lord Ferant is expecting me."

The guard sneered at Dobbin's appearance before glancing at the badge. He stepped aside and soundlessly, the gates swung open. Like everything in the Council District, it was maintained perfectly.

Dobbin walked past the guard, catching his reflection in the man's immaculately polished armor. He wondered if the guard had any real-world experience, or if all his training had come against the noble-born and wooden dummies.

He was aware of how his own appearance stood out

among the well-kept streets and pristine facades of the wealthiest houses in Eastborne. But it wasn't his guise that gave him favor among the elite, it was his reputation. The well-traveled cloak and rough appearance only added to the flavor, but he'd wager his sword held a sharper blade than any guard in the city.

His head still swirled from his brief stop at the tavern, but the drinks would make his visit with Lord Ferant more bearable. The conversation with the elf had been a welcome distraction. Former soldiers could almost always find common ground in the joy and misery of their past lives.

The flame of the streetlamp flickered against the night. Straight ahead was the keep, an imposing reminder of the city's history. It now housed the head of the Eastborne Council and all of the council offices.

Lord Ferant occupied the last house on the left. Though it would tower over most other homes in the city, it looked minuscule in the shadow of the keep. Dobbin wondered if that wounded the man's pride at all.

He climbed the steps and waited, staring at the golden door knocker in the shape of a ram head. After a few deep breaths, he rapped it three times. The metallic clank echoed across the empty street.

A moment later, the door opened, and a young man wearing a black tunic emblazoned with the Ferant crest welcomed Dobbin inside.

"May I take your cloak sir?" the young man offered.

Dobbin frowned as the servant reached for his cloak. "I won't be long."

The young man stammered, seemingly frozen for a

moment. "Very well. Lord Ferant awaits you in the sitting room."

He led Dobbin through the foyer, past the marble staircase that led to the second and third stories, and down an arched hallway filled with paintings larger than the walls of some houses. In the sitting room, Lord Ferant stood near the fireplace wearing a tunic of fine quality, complete with an elaborately stitched ram's head with sapphires for eyes. He held a glass, swirling an amber liquid within.

Lord Ferant smiled wide when he noticed Dobbin. "Dobbin, my boy! How good to see you! You should have heard the way the cult spoke of your last procurement. Those slimes you fetched for us—" He curled his fingers and blew a kiss. "—divine!"

"I'm glad to be of service," Dobbin said flatly.

"You never disappoint, now do you?" Ferant took a sip of his drink. "When my little birds told me that you were back in Eastborne, I sent for you right away. You always do have impeccable timing, don't you, my boy?"

"It certainly seems that way." Dobbin clenched his jaw, then massaged it gently before continuing. "What is it I can help you with this time?"

"Always to the point with you, isn't it? That's why you're the best, I suppose. Don't let me keep you in suspense." Lord Ferant's eyes lit up, and he placed his drink on a table. "Lord Sisk assures me his latest request is a real delight. The man loves to read his histories, and he came across mention of a rare mushroom said to only grow in soil that has been touched by dragon flame. As you can imagine, they are quite difficult to procure. If you can track this one down, then it will be well worth your time and effort, I assure you."

"Dragon flame?" Dobbin mused aloud. Dragon attacks were a rarity, and the creatures were difficult to locate at the best of times. Most were said to live high in the reaches of Mount Tor or in the untamed lands beyond the frozen north. To track down areas where one had scorched the earth seemed all but impossible.

"My boy?" Lord Ferant was suddenly standing only a few inches from Dobbin, watching him curiously. When Dobbin made eye contact, he continued. "I'm aware this is no easy task, but if anyone can do it, I believe it's you. You have yet to let us down, and we are willing to pay you handsomely for your troubles. So, what do you say?"

Dobbin loved a good challenge, but there were jobs that even he couldn't do.

He stroked his beard. "What's so special about this mushroom?"

Lord Ferant flourished his drink, staring into the glass as the amber liquid swirled within. "Legend says that the mushrooms grant visions to those who ingest them."

Dobbin raised a brow. "What kind of visions?"

Lord Ferant shrugged. "Therein lies the mystery. The histories are rather nebulous on the subject."

Dobbin grunted. Probably because anyone stupid enough to go exploring within dragon territory didn't live to tell the tale.

Visions could mean anything. There were many ways to alter one's perception of the world, after all. Fairies could enchant with their dust, and there were creatures whose venom caused hallucinations. Numerous potions and elixirs were capable of altering one's state of mind.

Certain mages were said to have truesight and could see beyond the mortal realm. Future sight and premonitions were incredibly rare, and from what he'd heard, they left a lot to interpretation.

There was no telling what kind of effect a mushroom born of dragon flame could elicit, but the Eastborne Dinner Cult were the same people who ate slimes, warg meat, and fairy wings.

"So?" Lord Ferant tapped his fingers on the glass expectantly.

Dobbin took a seat in one of the tufted leather chairs. "Let's talk fees."

"Most excellent, my boy!" Lord Ferant rubbed his hands together. "It will most certainly be worth your troubles. Never underestimate the risks a man of wealth will take to secure his future."

From where Dobbin was sitting, it seemed like the risks were all his.

# 5. THE LIBRARY

The hour was nearing midnight by the time Dobbin arrived in the University District. After enduring Lord Ferant's posturing for an hour, Dobbin wanted nothing more than to stop for another drink on the way back. But he had too many questions and precious few answers regarding his new quest, and there was only one place he could find guidance.

In all his time working for the dinner cult, he'd never known them to be so ravenous for a particular item. Dobbin had used that to his advantage, negotiating a fee that totaled more than his previous few quests combined. And if he returned before Ahtenoght, then the fee would be doubled.

Lord Sisk believed that eating the mushroom at the height of the festival of fortune would increase its mystical properties. With the festival only three months away, Dobbin would need to leave as soon as possible. Especially considering that he'd likely need to travel to Mount Tor in order to find any trace of dragons.

Any hope of spending a few weeks relaxing in Eastborne had vanished as quickly as he'd arrived in the city.

Dobbin stopped in front of the library, admiring its magnificent spires and arched windows in a kaleidoscope of colors. The building was one of the tallest in Eastborne, and the tint of the stained glass seemed to change depending on the time of day. A battalion of gargoyles lined the roof. In the moonlight, they looked almost alive, silent guardians protecting the priceless knowledge hidden within. Dobbin considered the library to be one of the most beautiful structures in the city.

He tugged on the door, but it was locked. After checking the street for any sign of the city watch, Dobbin crouched by the door.

He smiled as he pulled the lock pick from his cloak. Picking locks was a skill that had served him well over the years, a skill he'd learned long before his time in the military or Adventurer's Guild. Growing up in Barrowsturm, he would often sneak into the library at night, spending hours reading old tomes in the restricted section. He'd pored through the handwritten accounts of mages and explorers, imagining what it would be like to go on such great adventures himself. Those were still some of his fondest memories.

It only took a few twists of the pick before the lock clicked.

Dobbin pushed open the heavy oak door. The hinges groaned, and the musty scent of aged leather and parchment washed over him. The smell always put him at ease. He breathed it in.

The door shut behind him with a thud, echoing through the empty library. He flashed his Adventurer's

Guild badge to the vacant front desk. Without an attendant to locate the books, his research would take much longer, but he had a few leads to go on.

The dull luminescence of the glowlamps painted the library in amber light. Most libraries had a rule of no open flames, and anyone caught with so much as a candle would be banned for life. The enchanted lamps were expensive, but they helped to preserve secrets that had been scribbled down over millennia.

Dobbin loved it here. He often thought of the life he might live when he could no longer adventure, and more often than not, he pictured himself wearing the faded blue robes of a library scholar, fetching books and dispensing knowledge to those who sought it. He'd spent almost as much gold on his private book collection as he had on gear and weapons over the years. He had tomes in vaults all across the realm, protected by the Bank of Aedrea.

He made a mental list of subjects to start with as he headed toward the master librarian's catalog. A guide on mushrooms. Something detailing the habitats and migration patterns of dragons.

Rows of shelves that stretched from floor to ceiling. Tall ladders hung at an angle, allowing scholars easy access to the volumes up high.

Behind the service kiosk, there were several books that catalogued the library's inventory. Scholars used it to keep track of items in use or those that had been checked out. There was also a separate book detailing the restricted section, which contained handwritten or primary volumes that were only allowed to be read within the building.

Dobbin stepped behind the desk, opening the catalog

for topics C-E. He flipped through the pages to the list of books referencing dragons.

"Ahem."

Dobbin jumped at the sudden sound, dropping the book to the floor and drawing his dagger.

A balding man with a wispy white beard crossed his arms, unfazed by the weapon pointed at his neck. "Dobbin." The man lifted his circular glasses, pinching the bridge of his nose. "What did I tell you about breaking into the library after hours?"

Dobbin's cheeks flushed as he lowered his weapon. "Master Corbyn. I'm sorry. I couldn't wait to get started on my research."

"I can see that." Master Corbyn removed his glasses, setting the thin frames on the desk before smiling at Dobbin. "I didn't expect you back in Eastborne so soon."

"The last quest was shorter than expected." He paused a moment before grinning beneath his fiery red beard. "Thanks to you. I was back in town less than a day before Lord Ferant had his messenger find me. Thought I might be able to enjoy the Storm Festival before he got his claws into me, but no. I still don't know how he does it, but he wants me to fetch something for the dinner cult."

"The man does have his ear to the ground." Corbyn raised a brow. "What does he want this time?"

Dobbin removed the piece of parchment from his pocket and placed it on the desk. "Some kind of rare mushroom. Dragon flame or dragon fire. I've never heard of them."

"For good reason. Dragonfire mushrooms are incredibly rare, only growing under the most specific of conditions. Truth be told, you'd have better luck finding a needle in a haystack." Corbyn motioned toward the locked door that housed the restricted section. He pulled a key from under the robe and inserted it in the keyhole. There was a soft click before the door swung inward. "Follow me."

Compared to the rest of the library, the restricted area was organized haphazardly. Some books lay sideways on the shelves, topped with rolled parchment. A long table ran along the center of the room, with half a dozen shelves to each side.

More shelves surrounded the perimeter. Due to the rarity of the items within, only academics and those with the express written consent of the council or master librarian were allowed inside. Dobbin was one of the few adventurers to attain such approval.

Master Corbyn walked with purpose, pulling a leather-bound tome from one shelf and setting it on the table. He used the ladder to pull a second book from higher up. "These will get you started. I'll pull a few more from the main room. Ring the bell if you need anything."

"Master Corbyn," Dobbin called after the librarian.

He raised a brow. "Yes, Dobbin?"

"Thank you."

The man could have kicked Dobbin out or called the city watch to have him removed, but he recognized Dobbin's thirst for knowledge. On more than one occasion, he'd helped the adventurer gather resources that had proved integral to completing a quest.

The master librarian shut the door, leaving Dobbin alone. He took a deep breath as he examined the books before him. The first was titled *Magical Mushrooms and Where to Forage Them.* The tome was heavy, with the title and an image of a mushroom stamped into the leather. It looked to be the first edition from the smudges of ink and paint upon the pages. Colorful illustrations detailed various mushrooms and their uses. Notes were scribbled in the margins, and some lines were crossed out and replaced with updated information. Dobbin slid it aside to look at the other book.

*The Final Account of Raglan the Magnificent and the Red Dragon as Told to Taryn Greenstrong.*

Like most children who grew up in Warminster, Dobbin was taught the story of Raglan's battle with the red dragon at a young age. After burning the dwarven city of Hells' Crag to the ground, the dragon set course toward the west. Raglan singlehandedly held the dragon off, forcing it to retreat into the mountains. The event was widely regarded as one of the most important battles throughout the history of Aedrea.

There was a saying among the Adventurer's Guild that if you were close enough to hear the roar of a red dragon, the only thing left to do was pray. The destruction of Hells' Crag had been so devastating that the land was still a barren wasteland five hundred years later, and the ruins were said to be haunted by specters and wraiths of the dwarves who once called it home.

The book on magical mushrooms would certainly be helpful, but perhaps he could garner some information from this one as well? Dobbin opened the book to the first page.

*It is with great sadness that I report the death of Raglan the Magnificent. While his heroics in fending off the red dragon before it could destroy another city shall survive the ages, the mana-drain has proven too much for his mortal body. Herein I leave my record of his last moments and his recount of the battle.*

Dobbin flipped through the record, reading the transcribed account of their clash. It was more detailed than anything he'd learned growing up, offering Raglan's viewpoint not only of the battle itself but of the city's destruction beforehand.

He knew what happened next. How a group of mages and adventurers set off in pursuit of the dragon and were eventually able to defeat the weakened creature. The dragon's skull still rested over the gate to Stormrest to this day. But their victory wouldn't have been possible without Raglan's sacrifice.

As Dobbin pored through the account, the door opened, and Master Corwyn returned carrying a stack of books.

He set them upon the table. "These, you are welcome to borrow. You may be able to find better resources upon the current state of Hells' Crag in Rakroft, but I assume time is of some importance."

Dobbin joined him at the end of the table, reading the titles of the books of various thicknesses.

*Dragon's Breath: A Scholarly View of the Effects of Dragons on the Environment*

*Hells and the Hauntings: The Many Spirits of Hells' Crag*

*A Geography of Ruin: How Dragonfire Turned Fertile Land to Ash*

*Echoes of the Past: A Guide to Apparitions, Wraiths, and Everything in Between*

Dobbin narrowed his eyes as he read each title in turn. "Why are so many of these focused on Hells' Crag?"

"How many places do you know that have been attacked by dragons?"

"I'm sure there is a record somewhere."

Corbyn nodded. "Indeed, there is. There is a list of outposts, farms, and small villages, but most are repaired and rebuilt in the aftermath. The soil is tilled and the ash scattered so that the land becomes fertile once again. Mushrooms require very specific conditions to germinate. Low light, humidity, decayed matter. There is nowhere else within the realm that will offer you such an opportunity for success."

Dobbin swallowed hard. "There is nowhere else in the realm that's haunted by the souls of a hundred thousand dwarves."

There were very few locations that adventurers shied away from, and Hells' Crag was at the top of the list. Rumor spoke of wraiths so powerful that their mere presence could drain a man of his will to live.

Dragons and behemoths had been responsible for many atrocities over the ages, but nothing compared to the desolation that was Hells' Crag. An entire city turned to ruin in a matter of days, and still, no one understood what had caused the dragon to attack.

But Master Corbyn was right. There was nowhere else

in the realm that provided so much land touched by dragon fire.

If he made it back before Ahtenoght, he could make sure Isabella and her son never worried for money again. A journey into Hells' Crag might be exactly what Dobbin needed to put his own ghosts to rest.

# 6. THE GUILD DISTRICT

By the time Dobbin finally left the library, the sun was peeking above the horizon. Slivers of orange and yellow reflected across the ocean, peaceful in its tranquility. There were some amazing vistas throughout Aedrea, from the mountains of Stormrest and Durendreg to the rolling hills of Honeydale and the towering forests of the wilds, but none of them offered a view like this. Whether rich or poor, this beauty could be savored by all the citizens of Eastborne.

Dobbin's eyes ached from hours of reading in the dim light, and his back throbbed from leaning over the table. While he had a great deal more information than the previous evening, this was looking like it would be one of the toughest quests he'd ever accepted. *There's no such thing as free coin* was a common saying among the guild, and it always rang true.

Not only would he have to survive in the inhospitable terrain of Hells' Crag, where the land was barren and food was scarce, he'd need to be wary of all manner of ghosts and apparitions—plus whatever else happened to be lurking nearby. This would require a very specific assortment of gear.

After a few hours of sleep, Dobbin departed for the Guild District to prepare.

Eastborne was home to many guilds, societies, orders, and clubs. Many of their offices resided in the Guild District, with a few exceptions. Some preferred to keep their business as inaccessible as possible, like the Order of Mages, which shared offices with the city council in the keep. And though they would never admit it, the Locksmith Guild had a second location in the back of the Brown Boar Tavern, where thieves and ne'er-do-wells would go to collect quests. Not to mention the Alchemist's Guild, which had been moved across the river several hundred years prior after one of their experiments leveled an entire city block.

The guild square bustled with folk coming and going during the day's business. Most of the mercantile guilds were located along Craftsmen's Row, where skilled carpenters, smiths, and other tradesmen would come to file paperwork and acquire permits. This is also where potential apprentices would submit membership applications. Each guild was easy to identify by the crest above the door—a hammer for carpenters, an anvil for smiths, so on and so forth.

Compared to smaller towns and villages, where craftsmen could mostly do as they wished, city guilds ensured a quality product and reputable service for the public, as well as fair wages and training for the workers.

Being a port city, the Merchant's Guild was a prominent fixture in Eastborne and responsible for trade oversight and the inspection of foreign cargo. Their building was more elaborate, with embellished stonework and arched windows and doors. A mighty flag depicting a ship flew above the top of the domed building.

A windowless building of brilliant white marble stood out among the crowded structures. The Aethervale Guild of Tinkerers, Runecrafters, and Magical Engineers was responsible for pretty much all runecrafted technology in Eastborne.

Dobbin had never splurged on such fanciful tech, but when he'd found his beard frozen and eyelashes frosted while passing through Mount Tor hunting for slimes, he'd wished he spent the gold on one of their portable heaters.

Dobbin lowered his gaze as he passed the Preservation Society—a group dedicated to the preservation of magical flora and fauna, no matter how dangerous—and made straight for the Adventurer's Guild.

The front of the building looked like a large tavern several stories high, but it held a wealth of resources within. Dobbin pushed open the heavy oak door and entered. The main lobby was open to the public, where people or businesses could post quests and recruit guild members for tasks. There was a large noticeboard pinned with available jobs and messages for adventurers coming and going. It had been years since Dobbin had taken a quest from the board. Nowadays, all of his offers came directly from the source.

For most missions, the guild took a percentage of the payment for negotiating the transaction and held the funds until the quest was completed. A partial payment was usually arranged up front, but if an adventurer took too many quests without completing them, their membership in the guild could be revoked.

Luckily for Dobbin, working for Lord Ferant had its privileges—they only had to pay the guild to approve the permit.

Dobbin found a man with long, salt-and-pepper hair smoking a pipe behind the lobby desk. A scar ran vertically across one eye, cutting into the gray stubble that coated his cheeks, aging his otherwise youthful face.

"There he is." Anwar stood when he noticed Dobbin. "I had a feeling I'd be seeing you soon. You finally going to join me and take a position on the guild council?"

Dobbin laughed. "I'd sooner die."

In his younger days, Anwar had been a well-respected adventurer, earning some of the best quests in the guild. Now that he was long in the tooth for an adventurer, he had taken a comfortable position on the guild council. Those who played the game as long as he had were usually rewarded with a position where they could die fat and happy.

"Oh, come on. You could help train the next generation of adventurers." He shook his head, smiling. "A cold drink and a warm bed every night is nothing to sneeze at."

"If I had to listen to you regale me with tales of your glory days every night, I'd buy up as much armor as I could carry and go for a swim."

"You'll change your tune before long." Anwar smirked. "What's it going to be for you today?"

Dobbin placed an empty duffle on the desk. "I've got

another quest for Lord Ferant. I'm going to gear up before heading out tonight."

"Already? You just got in." Anwar huffed. "What does he want this time?"

"Mushrooms."

"Mushrooms?" Anwar narrowed his eyes, taking a long drag of his pipe.

"Yeah. Mushrooms." Dobbin left it at that. The less suspicion he raised, the better.

Anwar frowned. "I already know the answer, but I'll ask you anyway. Do you want to give us the details and location of the quest so that we can send a search party if you don't return?"

The question was standard procedure for guild assignments. If an adventurer was going into especially hostile territory, they could always pay the fee for a search party. In the event they didn't return by a specified time, a group of adventurers would search them out in exchange for a percentage of any treasure or loot that might be found.

Dobbin gave Anwar a knowing look. "If I don't come back, your search party is as good as dead." He tossed the duffle bag over his shoulder and entered the guild hall, leaving Anwar standing with a confused expression and muttering about mushrooms.

The Adventurer's Guild was a trove of resources for the average adventurer. It had a training facility, kitchen, dining hall, cellar, bunkroom, small library, stockroom, meeting hall, washroom, and an armory, among many other things that one must know to ask for.

For non-magical quests, it had just about everything one might need to slay monsters, clear bandit camps, or track down a bounty. It would be fine for gathering basic equipment, but for a job like this one, Dobbin would be making his rounds before the day was over.

Compared to the guild halls in bigger cities like Tiberia or Stormrest, the Eastborne guild hall was rather empty, aside from those working or training. Occasionally, several adventuring parties would all be in the city at the same time, and the dining hall would stay full until the wee hours of the morning.

Most adventurers had learned that Dobbin worked alone, but that didn't stop him from being pestered any time they had a drink too many. This was why he preferred the taverns south of the river, where the sailors and bottom-dwellers were always gracious for his appearance, especially when he kept their cups full. They were grateful when he would tell stories, but no one begged him for more when he wanted to be left alone.

Steel clashing and wood clacking rang out as Dobbin passed by the training grounds. A young man, no more than eighteen, fought a wooden dummy with arms that rotated with each hit. He slashed hard and the dummy spun. The kid pulled a wooden dagger from his belt, blocking the second arm before it hit him. Unfortunately, the wooden mace attached to the dummy's arm kept swinging, smashing the boy in the side of the head with a thunk. The kid dropped to his knees, groaning as he rubbed the swelling knot.

Dobbin rubbed the back of his own head, remembering the many times a training dummy had gotten the better of him in his younger days.

Nearby, two men practiced with live steel in the sand-pit. Their blades rang like chimes through the guild hall, music to Dobbin's ears. He nodded to the men as he continued on his way.

In the storeroom, Dobbin filled his bag with several pounds of salt, fifty feet of rope, a handful of silver stakes, and plenty of rations for when he passed into the ruins. He would stop by towns and villages as he traveled, and hunt when needed, but it was always good to have a little something hidden away for emergencies.

Down in the cellar, he added four healing potions capable of disinfecting wounds and promoting rapid healing, two perception elixirs, preservation elixirs for keeping the mushrooms from rotting on a long journey, and an assortment of dried herbs for brewing certain salves or tonics he may need along the way. The average person had little use for a healing potion, considering clerics could mend most minor injuries and there was one located in just about every town in the realm, but for adventurers, sailors, and soldiers, a potion could be the difference between life and death.

After settling up with the clerk, he stopped by the armory to restock on arrows before heading out.

Back in the lobby, a pair of well-traveled men were returning from what looked like a troublesome adventure. The duo had the look of brothers, with dark brown hair and matching beards. They leaned against Anwar's desk, each one covered in a mixture of mud and blood. One of the men's cloaks was ripped to shreds, hanging in tattered ribbons. He also wore bandages up and down his right arm.

"You two look like you've seen better days." Dobbin joined them at the desk. "Anything worth knowing?"

They turned to face Dobbin, and he noticed the second man had his arm in a sling.

"Treewalkers are in mating season." The man grimaced. "We came upon one while clearing out a team of direhogs that had traveled down from the Arenian forest. The bastard was raging before we knew what was happening. Broke my arm, and Terry here got mauled by a direhog while he was checking on me. Lucky for us, the treewalker thought the hog was a more appealing fight."

Dobbin matched the man's grimace. "Lucky you. Not many of their kind left, but if you catch them pollinating, it's never good. They're worse than a soldier after a few drinks, ready to challenge anything that moves."

"Don't I know it." The man tapped his arm gingerly. "We're heading to a cleric next. Where you off to?"

"He's hunting for mushrooms." Anwar grinned.

Dobbin laughed, ignoring the goading for more details. "See you boys around."

The Hidden Ward was located along a quiet street just below the market. There was no sign, only foggy gray windows and a faded red door engraved with mysterious symbols making the storefront as unremarkable as those on either side. But inside, it hosted some of the most interesting items around.

Wards.

Similar to the way that gnomes were able to etch runes into objects and power them with mana, a wardmaster could enchant an object to repel certain forces. Simple wards could help farmers keep pests from infecting their crops or allow gardeners to prevent a late frost from killing their flowers. More advanced wards functioned as alarms or repellants for unwanted guests.

Dobbin had used wards in the past. A fly-repellant ward had saved his skin when he'd traveled through Greenbriar Marsh. For his next quest, Dobbin was going to need something a lot stronger.

He opened the door and was immediately assaulted by the smell of lemon and cinnamon. The combination of odors was an intense attack on his senses that made his eyes water, but he entered anyway.

Kipper was a peculiar old man, so there was no telling what he might be making. The last time Dobbin had visited, the wardmaster had been learning to pickle his own eggs, and the shop stank of vinegar and sulfur.

Once inside, a metallic taste filled Dobbin's mouth, and his ears began to ring.

An intruder ward. Not a strong one, but enough of an annoyance to keep out anyone who wasn't here on business.

He pressed forward against the repellant to the empty counter and rang the bell. His symptoms faded a moment later, and footsteps could be heard upstairs.

"Be with you in a moment," a muffled voice called from above.

Dobbin massaged his temples as he waited. The room was filled with brightly colored stones and metallic cubes that lined the shelves and display cases. A chandelier containing a rainbow of glowstones gave off a dim light, casting each corner of the room in a different hue.

The footsteps loomed closer overhead and eventually descended the stairs. Kipper was a lanky man with a wispy gray beard, and runic tattoos ran along his fingers all the way up his forearm. He smiled at Dobbin, his bright blue eyes alight with mischief.

He carried a bowl full of hard candy in shades of yellow and red, placing it on the counter. "Care for a sweet?" He unwrapped one and tossed it in his mouth. "I think I've almost perfected the lemon."

"It smells better than the eggs, but I'll pass. I'm actually here about your other offerings."

"Of course you are." The wardmaster bit down on the candy and it splintered. "What'll it be this time?"

Dobbin looked around the room at the sheer number of wards the man had created. "Do you have anything that protects against spirits?"

"Spirits?" Kipper raised both brows. "What have you gotten yourself into this time?"

"Nothing I can't handle." Dobbin winked. "So, what do you have for me?"

Kipper clicked his tongue, frowning. "Nothing that strong, unfortunately. It's not often Eastborne has need of spirit wards. They do exist, but I can't say I'd know where to begin in creating one. I simply don't have the knowledge."

Dobbin sighed. "That's no good."

Kipper unwrapped a red candy, pointing it at Dobbin as he spoke. "Tell me, what has you so worked up that you need a spirit ward?"

"I'm going to Hells' Crag."

Kipper froze, the candy inches from his lips as a long silence hung in the air. He blinked several times before finally speaking. "Are you mad?"

"It certainly seems like it." Dobbin chuckled even

though there might be some truth to the words. Venturing into Hells' Crag alone was unheard of. "So do you know anywhere I can buy a spirit ward?"

"They're a rarity. The elder elves are known for their spirit work, but even then, they just aren't that common. The dead stay dead, and when they don't, that's what we have clerics for." Kipper shook his head, pacing behind the counter. "By the gods, Dobbin. Hells' Crag, I mean, really? That's bold. Even for you. Just wait here for a minute."

He placed the candy back in the wrapper and set it on the counter before disappearing upstairs. There was the sound of heavy furniture being moved and objects tossed to the floor before he returned several minutes later carrying a white cube inlaid with gold runes.

"This is my personal essence ward. It was given to me by my master long ago." He placed the ward on the counter. "It doesn't repel spirits in the same way a spirit ward would, but it will alert you to their presence. The ward will take on a soft glow when a spirit is near."

Dobbin picked it up. It fit in his palm, slightly larger than an apple. The stone was cool to the touch and heavier than it looked. "How much?"

"For you? A hundred gold. Return with the ward, and I'll buy it back from you."

Dobbin grimaced. He knew a spirit ward wouldn't be cheap, but a hundred gold was a lot for something that couldn't even repel spirits. Awareness was half the battle sometimes.

He removed his coin pouch. "Do you take platinum?"

Kipper extended his hand with a grin, and Dobbin dropped the shiny coin into his palm. Platinum currency was rarely used outside of business transactions, but Dobbin always kept at least one on him for times like this.

"I don't know what you have planned, but take care of yourself out there. I want that back."

Dobbin placed the ward in one of his cloak's pockets. "Don't worry. Dobbin always gets the job done."

As the door shut behind him, he could hear Kipper yelling after him.

"I'm serious, Dobbin. I want that back!"

# 7. A DRINK FOR THE ROAD

The life of an adventurer meant constant travel. Dobbin hoped to settle down one day, but for now, he was content with a shack south of the river, just below the Warehouse District. Whenever he returned to Eastborne, he called it home.

He sat in the lone chair of the tiny structure reading *The Shadows of the City.* It was a gripping tale of Evangelina Shroud, a cunning rogue with a heart of gold. She worked outside the law to bring justice to those who deserved it most.

Dobbin was so engrossed in the story that he almost dismissed the patter of feet on the flimsy roof.

Almost.

The wooden stair creaked outside the front door. Dobbin pulled his sword from its resting place by the head of the bed and moved quietly toward the door, pressing his body against the wall. Whoever was stupid enough to try and rob him was in for a rude awakening. He held his breath, listening for movement, but all he could hear were the crashing waves by the dock and the music from the tavern down the street.

He loosened his grip on the weapon. Maybe it had been a bird or some other animal scurrying around the building.

Something clattered on the far side of the roof, drawing Dobbin's attention. As he turned, raising his sword, there was a flash of dark fabric through the open window, followed by cold steel pressed against his neck.

"You're getting slow." Alina kissed Dobbin on the cheek and released the pressure of the knife.

Dobbin turned around, running a finger where the blade had been moments before. All these years, and she hadn't lost a step.

He smiled at her theatrics. "What are you doing here, Alina?"

She placed her hands on her hips. "Seven years since we last saw one another, and you were just going to leave without saying good-bye?"

"I—"

"Don't care. Don't want to hear it." She poked a slender finger to his chest. "We're going out for drinks."

---

The Ogre & Anchor tavern was a favorite for sailors after a long voyage at sea. The drinks were strong, and the ale flowed like the river. Despite the late hour, the place was lively. Men gathered around a dwarf taking challengers to arm wrestle him in the far corner. Nearby, several men were growing heated over a game of darts.

Chatter and laughter enveloped Dobbin and Alina as they sat at a table, two pitchers before them.

"Cheers." Dobbin raised his mug. "I see you haven't lost your touch after all this time."

Seven years, and she was still as stealthy as ever.

Alina tapped her mug to his. "I said I was laying low. I didn't say I wasn't busy. A girl still needs to eat." She took a long swig and then leaned back against the chair. "So, where's your little lord sending you this time?"

"Far away." Dobbin took a drink in an attempt to end the subject.

"Oh, come on." She gave him a pleading look, twisting her blonde hair around a finger. "I know you work alone. We've both changed over the years. I'm just curious to know when I might see my friend again."

Dobbin grunted. What could it hurt? There was little chance of anyone willingly following him where he was going.

"Hells' Crag. I don't expect to be back before winter."

Alina gulped. It was the same reaction everyone had. "Damn."

"Yeah."

"I hope the pay's good."

"Good enough." He winked. It was a life-changing amount of coin, even for him. "What's next for you?"

"I've been offered a job." She smiled, and her gold tooth flashed in the candlelight. "Not sure if I want to take it, though. I quite like it here."

Dobbin leaned forward. Alina might have been black-listed for a while, but her skillset was undeniable. If someone wanted her for work, then it was certainly of note. "Where at?"

"Aethervale." Her grin widened.

"Gnomes?"

"Who else? It seems their ambitions have grown since the last mission I worked with them."

Dobbin reached across the table and gently squeezed her hand. "Just stay out of trouble."

"I always do."

She bit her lip, but Dobbin's eye was drawn to the sailor approaching. He was tall and stout, with muscles built from years of working a ship. He was shirtless, except for a black vest with gold buttons, and had a piece of leather tied around his head to keep his hair in place.

Dobbin could tell by the way the man staggered over that he was already drunk, his gaze lingering on Alina as he bumped into chairs and tables.

"Looks like we've got company." He nodded toward the man.

The man knelt next to Alina, wrapping an arm around her. "Hey, beautiful. How'd you like to have a drink with me?"

Alina brushed the man's arm aside. "Bugger off. Can't you see we're talking?"

"Come on, now. That's no way to talk to—"

Dobbin stood, ready to show the man the door, but he was too late. Alina elbowed the man in the stomach, and he doubled over. She was on her feet in a second, finger pointed at his chest like a dagger.

"I've had enough to drink, but if you want, we can dance?"

The man reddened, and his lip curled in a snarl. "You little…"

He swung, but Alina dodged the blow with ease,

leaving him off-balance as he stumbled toward the table. Dobbin once again prepared to intervene, but she waved him off as the tavern turned its attention toward the action.

She kicked the man in the backside, cementing his fall as he barreled into the table. "You just don't listen, do you? What's a girl got to do to get a little respect around here?"

The man grunted as he crawled to his feet. "You want respect? I'll show you respect."

He pulled a dagger from behind his back and lunged.

"I wouldn't do that if I were you," Dobbin muttered.

In that moment, it was like they were back in the old days, traveling with Henrik and Roswen. Spending their evenings drinking and fighting, and their days following wherever the coin took them.

Alina dodged the attack effortlessly, crouching and punching the man in the crotch. He fell to his knees, grimacing, and she knocked the dagger from his hand. It clattered across the grimy floor of the silent tavern. The bard had quit playing, and every eye waited to see what she would do next.

"Now that's a woman," someone whispered.

The man held both hands around his crotch, and sweat beaded down his temple.

Alina placed a finger under his chin, forcing him to look at her. "You're big and strong, I get it. There's one of you in every town and every tavern. An overgrown boy who never learned to be a man. Maybe it's time you grow up." She let the man's head fall to his chest and looked at Dobbin. "Let's get out of here."

He finished his ale in one swallow and set the mug on

the table. "You all got your coin's worth tonight, but the show's over, folks."

Outside, Alina leaned against the wall. "Just like old times, right?"

"Almost." He tried to keep the resignation from his voice, but they both knew that those days were long gone.

Without warning, she wrapped her arms around his sturdy frame and squeezed. "I think I'm going to take that job with the gnomes. But maybe one day, you and I can work together again. Nothing too crazy, you know?"

He squeezed her back. "That doesn't sound half-bad. Until then, you take care of yourself."

When they let go, there was nothing left to say. They set off in opposite directions for their next great adventures.

# 8. THE TROLL TOLL

Dobbin woke with the morning bells, eager to get on the road. Everything was packed and ready, meticulously organized and prepared the previous night, so he grabbed his gear and made for the stables.

Shadowmane would be excited to see him. There were three things Dobbin didn't mind paying good coin for—gear, books, and accommodations for his horse. Still, the horse much preferred their adventures to life in a stable, no matter how well taken care of he was within its walls.

The stables were located at the edge of the city, just below the tannery. Most people stayed away from the area because of the smell, but after years in the Warminster army, Dobbin had grown fond of the earthiness it presented. He'd smelled much worse after a long journey and found no reason to hold it against the animals.

As Dobbin approached, the stablehand recognized him, waving before disappearing into the stable. A moment later, he returned, leading Dobbin's horse.

Shadowmane was a magnificent and powerful horse,

with a chestnut coat, black mane, and matching black boots. He'd been the only adventuring partner Dobbin had had over the past seven years, and each trusted the other with their lives.

Dobbin reached into his cloak, pulling out an apple he'd bought the day before. "I brought you a present."

Shadow chomped the apple from Dobbin's hand, crushing it with a few chews before nuzzling against the man.

"I'm not sure how fond of me you'll be once you learn where we're going." Dobbin gave him a few firm pats on the neck.

The stablehand helped to saddle the horse and load the gear, and then Dobbin and Shadowmane were off. They passed by farmers entering the city to sell the day's produce, and soon there was nothing but open road before them. The road north to Arenia ran along the coast, granting beautiful vistas for much of the way. It would be an easy journey until they reached the Arenian forest.

The forest separated the human and dwarven kingdoms. While there were several main roads that ran through the forest, it presented a number of dangers as well. Wargs and direhogs were only some of the animals that the Adventurer's Guild was commissioned to hunt down. Occasionally, bandits would hide in the woods to ambush unsuspecting travelers.

Most travelers preferred to avoid the forest entirely if possible, instead choosing to sail from the halfling lands to Arenia or Eastborne and travel from there.

Traveling to Hells' Crag would likely take a month by horse, perhaps a little longer if he chose to stop in Bearmouth and resupply before heading into the ruins. He had little idea of what to expect when he arrived, so a detour to the dwarven city to gather intel might be a smart decision even if it added to the journey.

The first few days were easy traveling. They passed by small towns, even smaller villages, through rolling hills, and above seaside cliffs with panoramic views.

Dobbin camped along the beach beneath a starry sky. As he lay there, listening to the rattle of bugs in the night, his thoughts returned to Eastborne, to Isabella's shocked expression as she noticed him through the window. He regretted not staying in the city for longer, but in some ways, he was a coward. Give him a monster to fight, a task to complete, and he'd risk life or limb to see it through. But when he'd returned to Eastborne all those years ago, he was the one who should have told Isabella what had happened to her husband. He should have offered her comfort in those dark times. Instead, he had run, taking the next quest, following the next adventure until too much time had passed to set things right. That was the reason he stayed so busy, anything to take his mind off his greatest failure.

He tried to push the memories from his mind, banishing the thoughts of Isabella and her son.

It was easier said than done.

Nothing would ever bring Henrik back, but if Dobbin could pull off this quest, maybe he could finally make peace with what happened so long ago.

Closing his eyes, he focused on the crashing waves as they played their gentle lullaby.

After traveling an entire week without incident, Dobbin spent the night in a small-town inn halfway to Arenia. He went to bed after a few good ales and a warm meal and woke ready to tackle a stretch of road that was little more than farms and villages for at least a day's ride.

Just outside of the town, a bridge crossed a small river feeding into the sea. When he came upon it, a caravan of at least a dozen people stood beside their wagons. *Merrymeadow Troupe* was painted on the side of one wagon, along with several colorful masks and musical notes.

A barefoot halfling stepped out from the group, waving Dobbin and Shadowmane down. He wore a straw hat and a green tunic and had a lute strapped across his back. "The road is blocked. There's a rock troll sleeping on the bridge. It hasn't moved for several hours. There's another bridge a few miles west, you could probably make the trek on your horse, but we'd have to go all the way back to town and reroute."

"A rock troll?" Dobbin frowned as he looked down at the halfling who barely came up to his stirrups. "You haven't tried to move it?"

"We're just a troupe of performers making our way around Nelderland." He gestured toward the eclectic group of humans, halflings, and gnomes. "I can't say we've much experience fighting trolls. Though to hear some tell it, a performance might send the monster running for the hills."

Dobbin laughed at the halfling's humor. "Rock trolls are pretty docile creatures. They love to sleep and sunbathe. It's their size and strength that makes them dangerous, but only if you startle them."

He gazed across the bridge, where what looked like a massive boulder blocked almost the entirety of its width. The river looked calm to each side of the bridge, maybe even shallow enough for Shadowmane to cross, but it was too dangerous to attempt with the wagons.

Looking at the slumbering monster, there was no telling when it might move of its own accord.

The guild occasionally took quests to relocate rock trolls, but very rarely did it come to violence. The creatures had an easily exploitable weakness—a sweet tooth.

"Stay back, and I'll see if I can move the troll out of the way." Dobbin fished through his cloak and found some of the candies Kipper had given him.

"Be careful," one of the children shouted as Dobbin slowly guided Shadowmane forward.

The horse wasn't easily spooked. He'd seen a great deal during his time with Dobbin and approached the troll no differently than if they'd been going for an evening stroll.

Behind them, the halfling played a soft tune on his lute as if this was all a scene in some play. As they moved closer, the troll's size became even more apparent. It was massive, like a boulder had fallen from the sky onto the center of the bridge. The troll's gray skin was rough and knotted, darker in some areas and mossy in others. On a hillside, it would be almost indistinguishable from the terrain. As the creature slept, it had the look of a living rock expanding with each breath. It was almost impossible to tell where the troll's head and limbs were.

Dobbin dismounted and approached the remainder of the way on foot. The key was to not spook the creature.

"Easy, fella," he said, loud but calm. "I've got something you're gonna like."

The troll grunted, and the living rock shifted. Dobbin squeezed several candies together until they shattered in his palm.

"Easy, big guy." He unwrapped the candy, letting the smell of lemon and cinnamon carry through the air.

The rock shifted again, and this time, two large, mossy-green eyes opened within the gray skin. Once Dobbin identified the head, the rest of the body became evident. He held out the candy, and the troll sat up, its bones cracking with the movement.

"There we go. Easy, that's right. Here, take this." Dobbin dropped several shards of candy into the monster's open palm.

The troll licked its palm, speckling its mud-brown tongue with yellow and red. It unleashed a grunt of pleasure, immediately sitting up. After licking its palm again, the troll set its eyes on Dobbin. It mumbled unintelligibly, but the meaning was clear.

*Give me more.*

"That's right. I've got plenty more. You're just going to have to follow me." Dobbin backed toward the other end of the bridge, holding up several more pieces of candy.

Powerful arms propelled the troll as it followed, each arm long enough to touch the ground if the creature leaned forward. Drool ran down its chin and chest as it continued to grunt and groan.

Dobbin stopped, tossing another candy to the monster. It plucked the candy from the air with more finesse and grace than anything of its build had the right to, and then settled on its haunches to savor the sweet.

This was part of what Dobbin loved most about being an adventurer—the unexpected moments in every journey that could surprise and delight. Watching a monster that most feared because of its size enjoy candy like a small child brought a smile to his face.

Slowly, Dobbin led the creature off the bridge and several hundred feet away from the road before leaving it with the remainder of Kipper's candy. Dobbin whistled for Shadowmane and then rejoined the caravan.

"He's going to be upset once he realizes there's no more, so best to get moving."

"Thanks for your help." The halfling extended a hand toward Dobbin, but after realizing he couldn't reach the man on the horse, he placed his hands back in his pockets and rocked on his heels. "If you'd like to keep pace with us for a while, we can play some music as a show of gratitude."

For the next few hours, Dobbin traveled alongside the Merrymeadow Troupe. The halfling was Milo Merrymeadow, and he was the anchor that tethered the troupe together. While most halflings were content with the slow-paced life of their people, working as little as possible and enjoying the finer things in life, Milo had been born a wanderer.

He'd traveled through Tyne, and then the northern lands of the dwarves, playing taverns and inns as a bard. Over the years, he bonded with more like-minded folks until his troupe became what it was today. They played music, performed plays, and told stories to anyone who would have them. It was a grand life.

Several lutes formed a melody, tambourines jingled,

and someone kept rhythm with a small drum. The deep voice of a dwarf blended with the higher tones of the gnomes to form a chorus that was unique, yet somehow beautiful. They sang a song of a halfling relaxing on a hill smoking a pipe, and another that told of a dragon's hoard in the mountains acquired over hundreds of years.

When they came upon the next village, the caravan came to a stop. They would stay the night and hopefully put on a show for the locals. There were still several hours of good riding left, so Dobbin planned to continue on.

"It was a pleasure to keep your company for the ride." He nodded to the group. "If the gods will it, perhaps we'll meet again one day."

Milo removed his straw hat and bowed. "The pleasure was all mine. And if the gods will it, then we'll regale you with a song of the bridge and the sleeping troll."

Dobbin tugged on the reins, and Shadowmane set off. The last thing he heard was Milo humming a tune.

# 9. THE GOLDEN TANKARD

Aside from taking half a day to help a farmer locate a missing cow, Dobbin made it to Arenia in great time. Contrary to the farmer's belief, the cow had not been plucked away by bandits or the jealous neighbor down the road. A storm had knocked over a tree, allowing the cow to escape through the broken fence in pursuit of a patch of clovers, where it frolicked happily without a care in the world.

Upon arriving in Arenia, the first thing Dobbin did was restock on food and supplies, then he booked a night at The Golden Tankard Inn.

Arenia was the second largest city in Nelderland, but it lacked the expansive views and tiered streets that made Eastborne so beautiful. While Eastborne was known for its culture and temperate weather, Arenia was primarily a trade city. The forest to the north provided most of the lumber shipped along the peninsula. It also formed a natural barrier between the dwarves and halflings to the east and the human kingdom of Warminster to the north.

Dark clouds rumbled overhead, and Dobbin was glad to be sitting downstairs in the tavern when the heavens finally unleashed their fury. The building shook from the thunder, and a chandelier full of candles swayed overhead.

The barmaid delivered a steaming bowl of soup and fresh bread, along with a tankard. Dobbin let the bowl cool while he sipped on the ale. It was divine, the malty goodness easing the exhaustion of travel.

Lightning flashed through the window, followed by another resounding crack of thunder. The door flew open, and a man entered, his cloak shimmering from the rain as water trickled onto the floor.

"Do the gods wish to drown me?" He removed his cloak, hanging it on the rack by the door.

"Only with ale." The bartender grinned as he placed a mug on the counter. "Glad to see you still made it."

"It's been a long week." The man took a seat at the bar, lifting his mug and toasting the bartender before taking a drink. "I'd swim here if I had to."

More people entered over the next half-hour or so, mostly humans with the occasional dwarf or halfling. In spite of the weather and complaints of a hard week, they all seemed to be excited about something. When the barmaid stopped by to refill Dobbin's tankard, he pulled her aside.

"Quite the crowd for a storm. Is there something going on tonight?"

She looked over to the men and grinned. "Every week, we have a storytelling contest on Ahtden. Winner has their tab paid for."

He raised a brow. "They any good?"

"Some of them." She looked Dobbin up and down. "You look like you've got a story or two to tell."

Dobbin laughed. "I could fill books with my exploits."

"Is that so?" Her lip curled at the edge. "I'll add you to the list then. What's the name?"

He almost argued, but it might be fun to relive one of his past adventurers. A little practice for when he was old and gray. "Dobbin."

The worst of the storm passed, and the thunder and lightning faded to a steady downpour that pattered against the windows. The night wore on and by the time the bartender banged a tankard against the bar, there were close to two dozen people in the tavern.

"It's that time again." The bartender hit the bar one more time for good measure. "Who wants to go first?"

"I will." The man who had first entered during the storm stood up.

"Alright, Wilbur." The bartender gestured toward a small stage at the back of the tavern. "Give it your best."

Wilbur took to the stage. He set his ale on the stool and placed both arms behind his back like a child reciting lines for a tutor. He told a story about a ship ride from Barrowsturm to Narthwich, where he swore he saw a kraken peeking above the water.

Next, a younger man got partway through a tale of his escapades with the blacksmith's wife before a tankard soared across the room, clattering against the wall. The young man opened a window and dived into the street as the blacksmith chased after him yelling obscenities.

The third performer was an older man, bald except for two large tufts of hair just above his ears that looked like giant balls of cotton. He approached the stage slowly, slightly favoring one leg as he walked.

He cleared his throat, took a large swig of ale, then began. "You might not know it by looking at me, but in my younger days, I was a rather strapping lad. I apprenticed for one of the city's best carpenters, old Kristuf. I was strong as an ox and mean as a bull. I know, I know. You look at me and say, 'Franklen, you're so kind. You wouldn't harm the hair on the head of a fly.' Well, let me tell you, back in the day, I'd smash the fly to the wall just for looking at me wrong. I'd—"

"Get on with it!" someone shouted from the back of the tavern.

"Well, that's certainly uncalled for." Franklen scoffed. "Anyways, it was a hot summer here in Arenia. You know how they get. The air was so sticky and thick it seemed to cling to everything like a slime. We were working on a new build at the edge of town, right across from the drains that filtered into the sea. A storm came in, much worse than the one passing through tonight, so we stopped work and waited for it to pass."

He took another long drink, letting the anticipation build. Dobbin had to hand it to the man, he had a gift for stories.

"The storm wrecked the harbor, and more than one ship sunk to the bottom of the sea that evening. Some said that when the tide rose, creatures would climb through the drains at night and make their way into the city. Right where we were working. I never believed it much myself. Never saw much more than a rat crawling through the drains, but the day we came back to start work..." He paused again, taking a deep breath and shuddering. "I can't quite explain it, but the hairs on my arm and neck were standing on end. Like Rember himself was trying to warn me of something." He clasped his hands together and looked to the heavens. "Kristuf felt it too. There was something strange afoot. Eventually, we brushed it off as a change in the weather, and Kristuf climbed the ladder to get to work. Once he was up there, he realized he'd forgotten his hammer, so he asked me to grab it for him from the toolchest. I opened the damned thing and what do I see but a row of teeth and a tongue as long as my arm. It lashed at me with furious speed, wrapping my arm, and then the godsdamned mimic bit my hand clean off!"

Franklen rolled up his sleeve, revealing the wooden hand attached to his forearm and waving it around for the crowd to see.

There were a few gasps, but there was even more laughter.

Wilbur joined Franklen on the stage, tears in his eyes from laughing so hard. He wrapped an arm around the old man. "Now, that was good. But I know for a fact you lost your hand in a fishing accident."

"Last week, it was a mining accident," a dwarf shouted from the back.

Franklen shrugged. "Nobody said this was a truth-telling contest."

The room howled with laughter until the bartender brought order once again. "Looks like we've got a new face tonight. Goes by the name of Dobbin."

"Oy, I knew it was him!" A dwarf with a forked beard pointed his mug in Dobbin's direction. "You're one of them who found the Lost Shield of Dembry for the Queen of Warminster. Dobbin Thornhill, was it? I was visiting Stormrest when your party returned."

Dobbin stood. "That was a long time ago."

"Still, that's a story I wouldn't mind hearing."

Dobbin grunted. Henrik had always enjoyed telling that story. The improbable quest that they'd somehow managed to pull off. Finding that shield had been the first big break for their adventuring party. After that, they were able to pick and choose what quests they wanted to take. But it wasn't a tale Dobbin was ready to relive, no matter how good the story was.

"Another time." He looked the dwarf in the eye. "How about something you haven't heard?"

The dwarf raised his mug and nodded.

Dobbin stepped onto the stage even though he had the entire tavern's attention simply by standing. He was a good foot taller than anyone else in the room, but now he loomed over them with an imposing presence. The distant rumble of the passing storm only added to the effect.

There were a number of stories he could tell. Many that would be recounted for months in his wake if he chose to share them. Maybe it was the ale or the fact that he'd been reading *The Shadows of the City*, but he'd been thinking of home lately. Tonight, he would share a tale of Dobbin before he'd become an adventurer.

He took a sip of ale and cleared his throat. "Do you remember the first time you were truly amazed by something?"

The question lingered, and Dobbin waited, watching as expressions shifted. Some moved from confusion to contemplation, others stared distantly as if traveling to some faraway memory.

"I do," he continued. "I could spend the night regaling you with tales of my adventures—of the monsters I've fought and the treasures I've looted. I could tell you how I saw a dragon soar above the mountains of Drake Canyon or felt the earth rumble in the wake of a golem along the plains of Barrowsturm. I've traveled with mages who could pull lightning from the sky or conjure fire in their palms, and I've watched clerics bring men back from the brink of death."

The tavern was silent aside from the occasional slosh of ale as the crowd hung on his every word. He had them right where he wanted them.

"The first time I was ever truly amazed is nothing so grand as that. I was a young boy, not even old enough to apprentice in my father's shop. For as far back as I could remember, my father would tell me stories at night before bed. Stories of great heroes who had saved princesses, fought behemoths, and battled against terrible odds to find victory. I loved our nightly stories, loved the anticipation of what came next, and the way my father could disappear into the characters he created.

"Then one night, he told me that was the last of them, that he'd read all the stories within our little home. A wave of dread crashed over me, and I cried at the thought of no more adventures. But my father patted me on the shoulder. He looked me in the eye and told me not to worry because tomorrow, he was going to take me somewhere special. I wiped away my tears and went to sleep wondering what the next day had in store.

"Later the next day, my father let me walk by his side,

and we traveled into the inner city. I'd only been through the inner wall a handful of times in my young life, and it was always an overwhelming spectacle. The buildings were taller, guards were stationed in the streets. There were performers and minstrels in the squares. More sights and smells than I could process.

"We stopped outside of a courtyard beneath a towering statue of a man holding a sword in one hand and an open book in the other. A golden crown gleamed, and sapphire eyes sparkled beneath the midday sun. My father knelt beside me and pointed at the imposing figure. He said, 'King Lyle believed that knowledge was the power of our people and that it should be free to all who seek it.' Then he pointed beyond the statue to a large building with colorful windows. 'There are more stories and knowledge within those walls than you could ever read in a lifetime. If you are ever lost or need guidance, this is where you come. To the library.'

"Inside, there were rows upon rows of towering shelves, and the smell of vellum and aged leather welcomed us. The domed ceiling was painted with an image of the night sky. There were constellations of dragons and griffins, gods, and great warriors. The shelves stretched so high that I wasn't sure where they ended and the heavens began. My father taught me to use the catalog system, and I lost myself in the labyrinth of the library, discovering maps, biographies, and accounts of wondrous adventure."

Dobbin smiled beneath his fiery beard as he recalled what happened next. "After hours had passed, my father found me with my nose buried in a book. He knelt before me, hands behind his back, and said, 'Mighty Dobbin, great adventurer, I require your help. Will you do me the honor of completing this quest?' When I agreed, he pulled a book from behind his back. The leather cover was gilded with the image of a sword, and he held it toward me with outstretched hands. 'Please, sir, help me to return this book to its rightful home.'

"I'd received my first quest, and no sooner had I learned where the book belonged than I was ready to abandon it. My father grinned with mischief as he stood beneath the ladder of a towering shelf. At the very top, there was a gap within the volumes waiting to be made whole. My father handed me the book and I tucked it against my chest, climbing the ladder with one shaking arm and unsteady feet. My heart pounded in my chest as I ascended each rung of the ladder. Several times, my grip faltered and cold sweat erupted across my brow.

"At the top, I slid the book into its place and smiled with relief. With pride, I turned to find my father, but my sweaty palm lost its grip. Before I could react, I was falling toward the ground, toward my doom. I would go down in the histories as having completed one quest. A short but perfect record. I closed my eyes and braced for impact, but two strong arms cradled me, breaking my fall and filling my ringing ears with laughter. 'Well done, my son. Well done.' The librarian kicked us out for the noise I made, but it was the first of my many adventures within its walls over the years."

Dobbin returned to his table grinning. Whispers spread across the tavern, and bodies shifted in their seats. A few people wore confused expressions and talked to their neighbors in hushed voices.

"Booooo!" someone called out from the back. "Tell us

about the mages and dragons. No one wants to hear about a trip to the library with yer pa."

Franklen stood, wagging a finger in Dobbin's direction. "No, no, no. One story per person. That's the rules."

Dobbin laughed. The story might not have wowed the audience, but he treasured that memory like no other.

"Alright, alright." He held his hand in the air to gain everyone's attention. "How about I buy you all a round, and then I'll tell you about the time I had to defend a pruning team at the edge of the wilds against a flock of harpies?"

Franklen's frown softened as he looked down at his empty mug. "Well, I guess one more story wouldn't hurt."

Dobbin bought their drinks and told the story. And then another. And another.

Though his pockets were lighter when he left Arenia, his spirits were full as he set off for the forest.

# 10. CIRCLE OF LIFE

There was something about the forest that always put Dobbin at ease. Sure, it was full of dangerous beasts and other threats, but being miles from civilization brought a sense of peace. Out here, nature thrived in all its glory. Sometimes, it was beautiful. Other times, it was barbaric.

Compared to the wilds, where monsters lurked beneath trees so tall that they could blot out the sun, or the Ermmir Forest where the fae wandered in a constant search for mischief, the Arenian forest seemed rather tame.

The great oaks groaned as a breeze passed through their outstretched limbs. The thick branches twisted like gnarled vines, making many of the trees wider than they were tall. Birds chirped high in the canopy, and bugs rattled in the underbrush. The clop-clop of Shadowmane's hooves added to the melody as they followed the timeworn road. Occasionally, something scurried in the forest's depths. Peaceful chaos abounded in all directions as the road wound its way toward the edge of the human kingdoms.

Dobbin stopped by a stream to make camp for the evening. While Shadowmane drank his fill from the gurgling water, Dobbin started a fire. Once it crackled merrily, he tossed a line in the stream. He had plenty of rations, but the stream offered the opportunity for a fresh catch. It wasn't long before fish began to nibble at the hook. The first one he caught was rather small, but the second would make a fine meal.

He cooked both over a small fire, sprinkling them with a spice he kept within one of his many cloak pockets. Just because he was miles from civilization didn't mean he couldn't add a little flavor to the dish. Shadowmane grazed on grass and wild berries while Dobbin enjoyed his dinner.

The trees whispered and the stream babbled as he lay down for the night. Somewhere in the distance, an owl hooted. He fell asleep to the call of the wild, as wolves and coyotes howled at the moon.

---

A thunderous crash woke Dobbin from a peaceful sleep. Instincts from a lifetime as a soldier and adventurer kicked in, and he was instantly alert, scanning the area for signs of trouble. He grabbed his sword and waited. The noise sounded like lightning had split a tree in half, but it was a clear night with the moon painting the forest in a silver glow.

Shadowmane neighed and tapped his hooves in agitation. Dobbin moved to the horse, stroking his neck and ordering him to stay.

Trees rustled violently as something moved upstream. Dobbin approached with caution, his blade at the ready.

Another limb snapped, followed by a grating roar that echoed across the forest. Then more crashing, more broken branches. And finally, silence. Whatever this was, the other animals were wary of its attention.

Dobbin followed the trail of devastation across the forest floor. Broken limbs, trampled bushes, and upturned earth took away the guesswork. It was like a behemoth had traveled through, ravaging everything in its path, but that wasn't possible. Thanks to the Northern Guard, there hadn't been a behemoth this far south in hundreds of years.

He tracked the creature into a meadow, where the light of the moon painted its silhouette against the starry sky. A tree spread its branches wide and roared against the night. The massive tree split halfway down the trunk, forming two giant legs, each one as thick as a man. Two more massive limbs formed its arms. It had spindly fingers, while branches and foliage sprouted from its body around the shoulders and head. It looked as if a tree had uprooted itself from the earth and began walking.

Dobbin gulped at the sight of the treewalker and crouched behind a bush. The two brothers had been right. During mating season, the males were more aggressive than a raging bull.

He watched as it continued to stomp and beat its powerful limbs against the ground, tearing through the meadow like a plow. It was a display of dominance, raw and powerful unbridled rage. To see a treewalker was rare, but to see one rage was even more so.

The monstrous tree paused its carnage and unleashed another roar. Wood splintered and cracked. To Dobbin's surprise, there was a resounding answer. Less intense, less grating, deep and sonorous like the call of a whale.

And then she appeared. Another treewalker stepped into the meadow, her branches covered with white flowers and green sprouts. She walked proud and unflinching toward the male until they stood face-to-face.

Goosebumps prickled along Dobbin's arms. He was about to witness one of the most extraordinary displays among the animal kingdom.

For a long moment, the two treewalkers stood in silence. To a passerby, they would appear no different from the hundreds of trees surrounding the meadow.

But then their ritual began.

The male raised his limbs high overhead, his long spindly appendages whipping against the sky and his leaves whispering secrets only the female could translate. He brought them down against his trunk with a roar. Wood cracked and groaned as he repeated the gesture several times. Then, he froze.

The female raised her limbs and petals vibrated along her many branches. They seemed to pulse with energy that was separate from the moonlight. The male continued his dance, swaying his branches from one side to the other as the female's petals pulsed brighter and brighter.

There was a loud crack as the male's trunk split open. A dusty yellow fog spread around the two trees as pollen spores filled the air and the female's petals detached from her branches. They drifted like a sea of fireflies.

The surrounding trees suddenly shook, and a breeze swelled across the meadow, scattering the blossoms among the forest. Those that managed to take root would germinate and eventually become saplings. In time, they would uproot themselves and begin their life among the forest. Only a fraction would grow large enough to complete the mating dance Dobbin had just witnessed.

With their ritual completed, the two treewalkers stood like statues in the center of the meadow. Their branches touched and intertwined, but they would not move again for an entire season, indistinguishable from the forest around them.

Dobbin took a moment to savor the majesty of what had just happened—a sight so rare that he'd only read about it in books. When he made it back to Eastborne, he would tell Master Corbyn all about it. The librarian always enjoyed listening to Dobbin recount his adventures on the road.

He followed the treewalker's path of destruction back to camp, amazed at the amount of carnage unleashed by a normally peaceful creature. Treewalkers only mated once every quarter century, but when they did, they made it known.

Dobbin was passing a tree that had been ravaged and nearly uprooted when he heard a muffled squeal from the other side. He drew his sword and approached cautiously.

A direhog lay motionless, half-buried in the ground, the unfortunate victim of the treewalker's rage. Dark stripes covered her hide, and thick, prickly hair formed a mohawk down her spine. Two large tusks protruded from her mouth, curling outward. The creature was easily two to three times the size of a full-grown pig. Direhogs were ferocious creatures, capable of fending off wolves and bears.

Dobbin pulled his dagger, prepared to end her misery, when he heard the squeal again. It wasn't coming from the direhog but from beneath.

He rested a hand on the direhog's hide. It was cool to the touch. Had she died defending her den?

Dobbin grabbed her front legs and pulled, but she must have weighed several hundred pounds. There was no way he could pull her out on his own. He whistled, and a few minutes later, Shadowmane appeared. Dobbin tied a rope around the direhog and attached it to the horse's saddle.

Shadowmane slowly pulled the direhog free. Dobbin stood over the den, and dirt fell inside the wide burrow. A low snort came from within. Dobbin knelt, and a tiny snout poked out, snuffling at the air. It had no fear of Dobbin as it approached.

Dobbin stroked the small direhog behind the ear, and its tail began to wag. He searched for signs of a litter but found none. It was rare for hogs to birth only one piglet, but it wasn't unheard of.

"What am I going to do with you?" Dobbin asked himself aloud.

Leaving the piglet behind would be a death sentence, but his own journey was just beginning.

Dobbin picked up the piglet, and it nestled in the crook of his arm. "Let's go back to camp so I can think."

Even though it was young, the piglet was already bigger than a small dog and weighed a good forty pounds.

A quick examination determined it to be a female, so it would grow to a similar size like the sow they had pulled from the den. The hair along her back was sparse and the stripes along her side were only just starting to appear. It would likely be months before her tusks began to show.

Direhogs could be aggressive and territorial, but as Dobbin held the orphan pig in his arms, he was reminded of a dwarven adventurer who had tamed one under similar circumstances. The dwarf rode the animal like a horse.

They'd shared an ale at the guild hall in Silverpeak one evening between quests. The dwarf had said that direhogs had poor eyesight but an excellent sense of hearing and smell. Not to mention they were nearly as strong as horses.

Dobbin sat the piglet down when they made it back to the camp. She snorted as she rifled through Dobbin's bags that sat next to his sleeping roll.

He knelt beside her, scratching her back. "The way I see it, you've got two options. I'm not going to leave you here to die. So, I can either bring you along and find you a home in the next town or village we pass. Or you can come with me and become a proper adventurer."

She nudged her head against the bag and chirped. Dobbin laughed when he looked inside and found an apple.

"Fine, but you're going to have to share it with Shadow."

He cut the apple in two, giving half to the piglet and the other to Shadowmane. For a moment, there was nothing but the sound of crunching apple and squeaks of delight. When she finished eating, she plopped on the ground against Dobbin's leg. He rubbed her belly and she nestled even closer. One leg started to kick as he found the sweet spot just below her ribs.

"If you're traveling with us, we're gonna need to give you a name."

He quit rubbing her belly, and she snorted.

"Alright, Snort." He chuckled. When he stood, Snort jumped to her feet. "Let the adventure begin."

# 11. THE ROAD LESS TRAVELED

Over the next few days, Snort embraced her role as a member of the party. During the morning hours, she and Shadowmane chased one another playfully as Dobbin prepared for the day. When it was time to travel, the piglet was more than capable of keeping pace with the horse, and her little feet pattered as she squealed and oinked.

Whenever the young direhog grew tired, she plopped on the side of the road without warning. Dobbin would then carry her on foot or situate her in his lap while he rode Shadowmane.

She took to Dobbin easily. During the days, he told her of his adventures, and every night, he read her passages from *The Shadow of the City*. She lay beside his bedroll, snorting and chirping as Evangelina Shroud's story unfolded.

When Dobbin trained with his sword, she scurried between his legs and lowered her head, challenging him to attack.

At night, Snort foraged around the campsite for roots and wild onions, and every morning, Dobbin woke to a dirt-covered snout inches from his face.

One night, a loud screech roused him from sleep, followed by a terrified squeal. Dobbin was alert in an instant, just in time to watch Snort come barreling through the underbrush followed by a mandrake. She cowered behind Dobbin as the mandrake screamed.

Dobbin clapped his hands together, and the creature froze. The mandrake was carrot-like in appearance, only a foot tall with a purple root that split halfway up to form legs. Two additional roots formed the arms, and a crown of foliage sat atop the purple creature's head. Tiny knobs formed an angry little face that shrieked at the poor piglet.

The mandrake picked up a stick and threw it at Dobbin. He couldn't help but laugh at the little monster as it pointed its arms aggressively.

This wasn't the first time he'd encountered a mandrake. Once, he'd been hired to clear a cemetery that had been infested with them. Whenever there was a new burial, they would walk around at night wailing and shrieking, terrorizing the townspeople.

Most mandrakes lurked within the depths of the forest and spent the majority of their lives buried in the ground. Dobbin had pulled one on occasion when scavenging for wild carrots. As far as plants went, they were relatively useless. Some considered them pests. Their meat tasted horrible, and they would scream bloody murder whenever they were pulled above ground.

Dobbin leaned forward and growled at the sentient plant. It gave a final shriek before running off into the night. Snort peeked out from behind him, huffing as the creature disappeared.

---

The route Dobbin chose to take through the forest was bereft of travelers, and they would go sometimes half a day or more without passing another person. There was a trade route north that cut directly through the center of the forest, where the road had been cleared on both sides for visibility. It might be safer and more populous, but Dobbin preferred the road less traveled.

Which made it all the more surprising when he spotted a covered wagon approaching in the distance. Snort's ears perked up when she heard the carriage rattling along.

A dwarf with a bushy black beard held the reins, and a man on horseback flanked each side. If Dobbin had to guess, they were adventurers on an escort mission. Those were always the most boring quests, but they paid well enough for what they were—glorified babysitting.

The dwarf waved as the wagon slowed. "Dobbin, by the gods, is that you?" When he smiled, Dobbin recognized him by his missing front teeth. Hildir had lost them in an unfortunate accident involving too many drinks, a frying pan, and a gelatinous cube.

Dobbin grinned back at him. "Hildir, it's been ages. How are things?"

"Life's good. I've got me a missus back home." He looked down at Snort, who was investigating the spokes of the now-stopped wagon. "Is that a direhog? What have you gotten yourself into this time?"

Dobbin laughed. "Came across a treewalker during mating season a few days ago. Don't worry, they already did their dance. This one's mum wasn't so lucky, though, so she's with me now. Meet Snort."

"Snort, is it?" He chuckled. "Cute little thing now, but we'll see how you feel a year from now." Hildir gestured to his companions on each side of the wagon. "These two are brothers, Galen and Gideon, or Gideon and Galen." He frowned, shrugging. "I can never remember. They don't say much, but they could fight the horns off a devil if it came down to it."

The two men nodded at Dobbin but didn't speak.

Someone cursed in the back of the wagon. There was shuffling before a head poked through the canvas. An old man—with wispy gray hair, short stubble, and bright blue —eyes frowned.

"What in the hells are we slowing down for this time?" He jumped when he noticed Dobbin, almost hitting his head on the crossbar, and his eyes went wide as he looked from one of his guards to the other.

Hildir held up a hand. "No need to worry. This here is Dobbin Thornhill. One of the greatest adventurers I've ever had the pleasure to work with. I stopped to say hello."

The man visibly relaxed. "That's a relief. You never know who you might encounter out in the middle of nowhere."

Dobbin guided Shadowmane a little closer. "That's true. Don't see many wagons passing through these parts."

"Never been a fan of sea travel." The man grimaced. "My father said I was born without sea legs, and I like to see my cargo to its destination."

"What are you hauling?" For the man to have three escorts, it had to be something pretty important or valuable. Probably both.

He narrowed his eyes. "If I wanted the world to know, I would have taken the trade route."

"Fair enough." Dobbin grinned. "Do you mind if I borrow Hildir for a moment before you're on your way? He might be able to offer some guidance with an upcoming quest."

"Fine, but make it quick." He closed the canvas, disappearing once again into the wagon.

Dobbin dismounted, and he and Hildir walked along the side of the road, Snort following at their heels.

"He seems like a pleasant fellow." Dobbin raised a brow.

Hildir smiled, rubbing his fingers together. "He pays well enough. And he keeps to himself as long as we're moving. Half the wagon is filled with books, so I'm sure you'd have more in common than you might think."

Dobbin looked over his shoulder at the wagon. "Perhaps so."

"I'm sure you didn't ask me over for a romantic stroll, so what is it I can help you with?"

"I'm going to Hells' Crag."

Hildir stopped walking. "You're what?" He nearly shouted.

"It'll be fine. Don't worry. I'm prepared as I possibly could be. What I want to know is if there is anywhere in Bearmouth where I might pick up a spirit ward?"

Hildir grabbed Dobbin's arm and looked the man in the eye. "My people don't set foot in Hells' Crag. You know that. It's a graveyard, and whatever treasure you think you may find there, I promise you, it's not worth it. No one who goes into Hells' Crag comes out. Not even you, Dobbin."

Dobbin frowned. "Come on, Hildir. Help me out. For old time's sake."

The dwarf grunted. "You're a dead man, Dobbin. But I can see it in your eyes you're set to see this through. Stop by the Abyssal Bazaar. It's located in the back of the Trench. If there's anything that might help you, you'll find it there."

"Thank you." Dobbin grabbed the dwarf by the shoulders, grinning. "I could kiss you right now."

Hildir shrugged free. "I'm a taken man. And soon enough, you'll be a dead one. Now, let's get back to the wagon before the old man throws a fit."

He turned to leave, but Dobbin called after the dwarf. "One last thing."

Hildir sighed. "Yes?"

"What are you hauling that requires three guards?"

"Elven artifacts. A few special pieces for the Tiberian museum. You know how King Torben loves his trinkets."

"So I've heard." Dobbin had visited the royal museum in Tiberia once. It showcased the history of Aedrea unlike anything he'd ever seen. There were armor and weapons from great heroes and adventurers, relics used by mages, the crowns of fallen kings, and so much more. He nodded to the dwarf. "Take care, old friend."

Hildir shook his head. "When you meet the gods, don't say I didn't warn you."

Later that night, Dobbin woke with a sense of unease. Snort stood with two feet on Dobbin's chest, her eyes fixed on something in the direction of the road. They camped out of view, beyond a thicket of trees, but Dobbin saw it as well. A blue aura moved quickly through the forest. Shadowmane huffed and stomped.

As the aura moved closer, Dobbin noticed the trample of hooves. It sounded like a dozen horses speeding through the night. He reached for his dagger, staying low to keep from drawing attention. Snort clung to him as the hooves grew louder.

And then it passed by. A silver-haired elf upon a single black horse, the duo shrouded in ethereal energy and moving faster than any being had a right to. As quickly as they appeared, they were gone, and the forest seemed to relax as they disappeared into the night.

Dobbin shuddered as the mage vanished in the darkness, heading in the direction they'd come from. He wondered what could have the elf traveling with such urgency at this hour, and if it had anything to do with the artifacts Hildir was transporting.

He'd worked with mages on occasion, and he hoped for the dwarf's sake that the two were unrelated.

Eventually, the woods parted, revealing the rolling hills and blue skies of Darm. After a week in the forest, Dobbin basked in the warm sunlight. Wild sunflowers spread across the horizon, and swayed in the afternoon breeze. Snort's tail waggled, and she disappeared among their tall stalks.

Lush fields stretched for as far as the eye could see. The lands of the lowland dwarves were fertile, providing food and resources not only for Rakroft but for the umbral elves to the north and the halflings to the south.

There was a time when the dwarves were two separate kingdoms, the lowland dwarves of Darm and the mountain dwarves of Mount Tor. The destruction of Hells' Crag had changed that, and now they functioned as a dual monarchy under the banner of Rakroft, the ancestral name for the region, with both kingdoms working for the good of all dwarven peoples.

Dobbin always enjoyed his time among the dwarves. They took their food in large portions and their ales strong, and he'd reveled away many nights within their taverns and inns.

He was only a few days from Bearmouth, where hopefully he could find more answers about what awaited in the ruins. Until then, he would enjoy the dwarven countryside.

Snort poked her head through the sunflowers carrying a stalk she had chewed down. Her head tilted to the side as she dragged the plant beside her like a prize. She carried it for half a mile until she spotted a family of rabbits crossing the road.

She dropped the sunflower, grunting as she pawed at the earth and charged after the rabbits. They bolted into the tall grass, and Snort stood there huffing, her head raised high as she patrolled the road.

Dobbin smiled at the pig. "You're going to be a handful one day, aren't you?"

She snorted in response.

Once they intersected with the road connecting Hillside to Bearmouth, their days of isolation came to an end. Every few hours, they would come upon a trader or traveler. They passed many dwarven farms and small villages where fields of potatoes, carrots, wheat, and turnips stretched for miles.

That night, Dobbin paid for a room at the Sleeping Stag. It was a small inn by the river in a fishing village. The inn only had three rooms, but there was a roaring fire, fresh bread, and hot stew. Shadowmane and Snort shared a stall in the stable with a hearty supply of oats and an apple each.

Inside the inn, Dobbin dunked his bread in the steaming stew and shoved it in his mouth without waiting for it to cool. Even though it burned his mouth, he groaned in pleasure. The meat was wild and gamey, possibly rabbit, and the carrots and potatoes were flavorful. A hint of spice lingered on his tongue long after he'd swallowed until he washed away the burn with a swig of dark ale.

The young dwarf barmaid watched him with amusement. She had curly brown hair pulled up in a bun, freckles speckled her pale cheeks, and a thin layer of peach fuzz covered her chin. She bustled around the empty tavern clearing a bowl left by another guest and wiping down the tables. Once finished, she sat by the fire and strummed a lute. The tune was relaxing and peaceful, and she hummed along with the melody. Dobbin sat back in his chair, enjoying the music.

When she stopped playing, he clapped. "You've got some real talent."

She blushed. "I only play to pass the time."

"Still, you're quite good. I've slept in inns where the music would make your ears bleed. Where'd you learn to play like that?"

"She taught herself, believe it or not." Her father, Orlin, appeared from the storage room with a sack of potatoes over his shoulder. He let it fall on the bar with a thud. He had the same curly brown hair as the girl, with a matching beard that curled in ringlets over his chest. "Probably ten years back, a fella came in, said he didn't have any coin for a room, but he'd trade his lute for a bed and a warm meal. I told him it was too much, but he insisted. He taught Dalla a few chords. Her little fingers could barely reach the top string at the time, but she picked up the rest herself and has been playing that lute ever since."

"Do you sing as well?" Dobbin asked.

The girl's cheeks flushed even brighter. "On occasion."

"Don't let her lie to you." Orlin crossed his arms and leaned against the bar, smiling. "If you come downstairs after we've cleaned up for the night, she'll usually sing a few tunes before we turn in."

Dobbin drained the last of his ale and pushed his bowl forward. "I think I'll take you up on that."

He grabbed his cloak and stepped outside to take a walk as twilight approached. He retrieved Shadowmane and Snort from the stables, and they walked along the riverbank. Crickets chirped and frogs croaked as the sun faded, streaking the sky with pinks and purples that reflected on the calm water. The dwarven fishers were finishing up their catch for the day and loading crates of salted fish on the barge to tow downriver in the morning.

There was a chill in the evening air so far north of Eastborne. Soon, fall would arrive in all its glory, and the nights would only grow colder. Dobbin loved the temperate climate of Eastborne, but cool evenings reminded him of home. Of late nights curled under a blanket while his father read him a book.

On nights like this, he wondered if he could ever truly give it up. The traveling, the exploration, meeting new people, and experiencing the hidden treasures of Aedrea. To settle down in one place for the rest of his life trapped in a cage…

Then again, wasn't that what books were for? He could live a hundred lives and still sleep in a warm bed at night.

Once the sky was speckled with stars, he returned to the inn. The melody of the lute carried from within as he stood outside. When a beautiful voice began to sing, he cracked the door open to listen.

*"In the misty moors where ghosts do roam,*
*The thistle grows, no petals bloomed.*
*Ancient magic dwells within*
*To let the spirits rest again.*

*Oh, thistle thorns, protect us from the dead.*
*Tear through their ghastly visage.*
*In this haunted land, grant them peace and rest.*
*Oh, thistle thorns, protect us from the dead.*

*The ghosts, they come with eerie moans,*
*Haunting, their voices mournful tones.*
*But with the thistle's power, do not fear.*
*It keeps us safe, and then the ghosts do disappear.*

*Oh, thistle thorns, protect us from the dead.*
*Tear through their ghastly visage.*
*In this haunted land, grant them peace and rest."*

A chill ran up Dobbin's spine as he stepped inside, and the music stopped. Dalla sat near the fire with Orlin and several others.

Orlin stood. "There he is. Can I grab you an ale?"

Dobbin nodded. "That'd be great." He turned to Dalla,

still fixated on the lyrics. "I've never heard that song before. What was it?"

The old dwarf to Dalla's left answered. She was gray-haired with a wispy white beard and wore a shawl covering her head. A thick fur blanket was draped across her lap. "An old folk song of the lowland dwarves."

Dobbin took the ale from Orlin and joined them by the fire. "What's it about?"

The old dwarf looked at Dobbin with faded blue eyes. "The mountain dwarves have always chosen pyres or crypts to handle their dead. It used to be the tradition of some of the lowland clans to bury our dead and return them to the earth from where we came. They would plant ghost thistles over the graves to help the spirits pass on. The thistle thorns were said to tear through their apparitions before they could become incorporeal, and when they did, the flowers would bloom."

Dobbin's thoughts turned to Hells' Crag and the haunted ruins. "Is there any truth to it?"

She smiled. "There's a little truth to every story, isn't there?"

He leaned forward, setting his ale aside. "Can I ask you something?"

"You mean, something else?" She pulled her blanket a little tighter. "Go ahead."

"Can you tell me anything about Hells' Crag?"

Her smile faded and her gaze drifted to the ground. "Orlin, I think it is time for me to go to bed. Help your old ma, will you?"

An awkward silence suddenly filled the tavern. Orlin helped the old woman to her room, and the others filtered out behind them, save Dalla.

When it was only her and Dobbin, she finally spoke. "She doesn't talk about Hells' Crag."

"Why not?"

"It's easier to forget, I suppose. Our ancestors called Hells' Crag home. It was the crown jewel of the kingdom, a major trade city for both Mount Tor and Warminster. Our great-great-grandfather was a merchant. That's all I know of him. And that he was traveling to Silverpeak when the attack happened. Our family lost everything that day. Our stories, our history. When he moved south and changed his name, he never talked about what life was before, and we have no way of knowing." She sighed, staring at the door where her grandmother had left. "They say the ghosts of those who died still walk the ruins. So many lives lost. Entire bloodlines destroyed. To think of all those souls still trapped there, never to be free…"

"That's terrible." Dobbin rested a hand on her shoulder. "I'm sorry."

"We all have our sorrows." She gave him a half-smile. "But that's why we have music."

She strummed the lute and began humming.

Dobbin kept her company until she was done, wondering once again if he'd bitten off more than he could chew.

# 13. BEARMOUTH

After another week of traveling, Shadowmane crested a hill and Bearmouth came into view. The city was a testament to dwarven craftsmanship, constructed upon the highest hill in the area. Dobbin pulled on the reins, stopping for a moment to admire its beauty. A keep stood at its zenith, its copper roof tarnished green and serving as a beacon against the blue skies. Four colossal spires surrounded the keep, rising high into the heavens. The city was broken into many tiers and inner walls, giving it an appearance of a maze where streets ran in a circular pattern from the keep all the way down to the massive outer wall.

A river split around the outskirts of the city, forming a natural moat. Two massive bridges allowed entry, each one adorned with fantastic metalwork. Giant statues of dwarven heroes loomed above the city gates.

Bearmouth was a monument to what dwarven architecture could achieve no matter the environment. While the mountain dwarves carved their cities into the very rocks themselves, the lowland dwarves had built a city that seemed to sprout from the earth. It was massive and imposing, but above all, it was majestic.

As the steady stream of traffic moved toward the city gates, more details of the inner city came into view. The buildings were constructed with high arches, vaulted ceilings, and flying buttresses. Thousands of gargoyles adorned their tops, and stained glass twinkled in the afternoon light.

Dobbin passed through the city gates without issue, aside from a few confused stares at the pig in his lap. Snort's tail wagged violently as she took an interest in every person they passed.

After checking the animals into the stables, Dobbin made for the Adventurer's Guild. He would bunk there for the night and set out early in the morning.

One of the most interesting aspects of Bearmouth's architecture was that the surface level was one big facade. Numerous tunnels and chambers ran underground, reinforced by stone and forming an underbelly that was nearly as big as the surface. According to the histories, a team of dwarven earth mages had spent decades creating the interior of the city.

The entrance to the Adventurer's Guild was far more embellished than any of those in the human kingdoms. Stone pillars ran along the front, carved with intricate designs, and the twin doors were made of bronze worked into elaborate knots by the city's metalworkers.

Inside, a stone mosaic of a bear covered the center of the floor. Maps and weapons lined the walls, along with the taxidermied heads of monsters and beasts. The noticeboard overflowed with quests and missions. Two clerks tried to collect the details from a line of citizens looking to add more.

Dobbin flashed his badge and passed through a door into the guild hall. He entered a spacious room filled with long wooden tables and benches. Several tunnels led to the barracks, training rooms, and other amenities. A couple dozen adventurers of various races sat scattered about, some chatting, others working. There was a raised platform at the far end, where an umbral elf and a blonde dwarf huddled over a map. Torches and chandeliers cast the room in a warm glow.

"Looks like business is booming," Dobbin raised his voice.

The blonde dwarf looked up from the map, shaking his head as he grinned. "Well, shit. If it isn't the almighty Dobbin returning to grace us with his presence." He jumped down from the platform with surprising finesse. The clasps in his braided beard jingled like chimes as he approached. "How are ya, kid?"

Dobbin laughed as he grasped the dwarf around the forearm and squeezed. "Kid, now, is it? Good to see you, too, Guildmaster."

The guildmaster narrowed his eyes. "Save that for the new recruits."

"Good to see you, Klink." Dobbin smirked.

"That's more like it." He grinned. "And you're right, business is booming. Farmers to the east are having a rough go of it this year. There've been kobold attacks from the Ermmir Forest, and goblins coming down from Rockdale. Not to mention an uptick in bandits from here to Tyne. Every merchant in the city is trying to get an escort. Me and Torien have been looking over the reports of the attacks to see if there's a pattern to any of it."

Dobbin's eyes widened. "That'll certainly keep you busy."

Klink scoffed. "And that's not even accounting for the elder elves asking for more pruners this year. The only time we hear from them is when they're looking to keep the land clear between them and the wilds."

"Good thing there are adventurers." Dobbin grinned.

"Good thing indeed. So, what brings you about?"

"Just passing through." He tapped the bag slung over his shoulder. "Need to see if I can pick up a few things before heading north."

Klink nodded. "Well, like I said, Rockdale could use some help if you'd like to make some extra coin."

Dobbin shook his head. "Not that far north."

"Not that far north?" Klink frowned. Aside from a few towns and villages along the river, there was very little between Bearmouth and Rockdale. "Do I want to know?"

"Probably not."

"Good." He gestured around the guild hall in a sweeping motion. "I've got enough on my plate without worrying about your sorry ass."

"That's the guildmaster we know and love."

"Oh, piss off, Dobbin. If you die doing something stupid, I swear I'll come kill you myself."

"This coming from the only dwarf I know to single-handedly wrestle a direbear into submission?" Dobbin laughed. "We're adventurers. We make our living doing stupid things." He patted Klink on the back. "Gonna drop my things off and head out, but I'll be back later for dinner and some drinks."

Dobbin made his way toward the barracks and placed his items in the chest at the foot of the bed. He'd restock on supplies and rations before heading out, but for now, he wanted to stop by the Trench.

———

Being that half the city was located underground, there were plenty of secret passageways, tunnels, and alcoves hidden within Bearmouth. While the Trench wasn't exactly hidden, it was tucked away so that only those in search of its offerings were likely to stumble upon it.

One tier up from the outer wall, a cramped alleyway ran between a blacksmith's forge and a woodworking shop. The constant clamoring from the saws and anvils resounded along the corridor, and Dobbin's ears were ringing by the time he reached the end.

Beyond the shops, a narrow tunnel led underground, hidden from street view. It opened into a cavern, and the smell of coal and sawdust quickly faded, replaced by the stench of stale ale and sweat. Water dripped from the stone ceiling, forming puddles along the street.

There were several taverns where tankards clinked and raucous laughter raged within. A shirtless dwarf sat against the wall of one with a mug in his hand, and Dobbin couldn't tell if he was passed out or sleeping.

Further down, a group of dwarves stood in a circle outside of a building called The Den. Black curtains covered the windows, hiding what was inside. The dwarves took turns tossing a pair of glowing dice on the ground next to a pile of coins.

One of them approached Dobbin. He had a tattoo of a

pickaxe beneath his right eye. "Want to try your luck? First roll's free."

"I'm good." Dobbin continued onward, recognizing a swindle when he saw one.

He passed another storefront where bottles of murky liquid lined the windows and a building where a red glowlamp hung outside.

Come nightfall, the Trench would be crawling with the city's rogues and ne'er-do-wells. Certainly a fun time, but Dobbin had business to attend to.

He found the Abyssal Bazaar at the end of the tunnel. The store had no facade, but a door that seemed to lead into the mountain itself. There were no knobs or handles on the door, only a metal grille with its slat pulled shut above a collection of runes.

Dobbin knocked three times and waited. He'd spent a lot of time in Bearmouth over the years, but he'd never ventured into the Abyssal Bazaar. The Adventurer's Guild was well-stocked and had connections with most of the premium shops across the city.

After a moment, the slat slid open, and deep purple eyes stared through the grille. The eyes darted around, sizing up Dobbin and inspecting the surroundings.

"What's yer business?" A gruff voice asked.

"Hildir sent me."

The slat slid closed with a clank.

Dobbin raised his hand to knock again when the door opened and an arm reached out, pulling him hurriedly inside, where he was enveloped by a myriad of scents all vying for his attention. Cinnamon, sulfur, fish, tobacco. Dobbin's eyes watered as he tried to process everything.

A stout dwarf stood before him. She wore a corset so

tight that her bosom nearly overflowed. Her red hair was a shade darker than Dobbin's and flowed down her backside. She gripped Dobbin's cloak with one hand and held a pipe in the other. She released her hold on Dobbin and slammed the door.

The back of the door was covered with runes, some of them glowing a silvery blue.

"Hildir is a good one." The dwarf puffed on her pipe, sending smoke rings across the room. "He takes good care of my sister." She took another puff and then gestured around the room with the pipe. "Welcome to the Abyssal Bazaar. What can Frida help you with today?"

The room was filled with countless items organized with no apparent rhyme or reason. There were fluids in every color of the rainbow, some in small vials and others in large jugs. Possibly potions, poisons, or elixirs. A row of casks held only gods-knew-what. Gems and crystals lay scattered about, along with books and scrolls. One book was latched shut, and Dobbin swore the eye etched into the latch was watching him. Bones and skeletons were piled against the far corner.

A cage hung from the roof with a pixie sleeping in a small hammock. Its tiny stomach rose and fell as it snored. Nearby, a pink ooze jiggled ominously in a glass tank. Dobbin winced. He'd been attacked by one once and still remembered the scorching burn that lingered for days afterward.

Weapons were scattered around the room from mighty warhammers to sharp axes. A ruby-encrusted helm sat on a wooden dummy next to a bin of swords and spears. A lute with a single string rested against the wall between two rolled tapestries. One shelf had a row of skulls in several shapes and sizes.

If he was looking for something to help with Hells' Crag, it appeared he'd come to the right place.

"I'm looking for a spirit ward."

"Spirit ward? Hmm." Frida tapped on the end of her pipe with a finger. "Let me see." She scurried around the room, moving items aside as she searched. "Spirit ward. Spirit ward." After about a minute, she picked up a black cube covered with white runes. It was similar to the one Kipper had given Dobbin. She frowned as she turned it in her palm. "Nope, this is a spirit attractor. Very dangerous if it was activated. They're used to lure out spirits who'd rather not be found. You could visit a wardmaster and have it turned on if you wanted."

Dobbin shook his head. "No, thanks." Walking into haunted ruins with an object that attracted spirits sounded like the last thing he needed. He wanted to get in and out with as little trouble as possible. "I'm looking for something that can keep spirits away."

"That's why we have clerics." Frida gave a throaty laugh. "We might have something, though. Let me think for a minute."

She wasn't wrong. Most quests involving any type of spirit usually required the help of a cleric, with the rest of the party there to make sure they didn't die.

Dobbin crossed his arms and waited while the dwarf puffed on her pipe. As he looked around the shop, he wondered where all the items had come from. Had they been stolen, purchased, or freely given? There was a shield that was very obviously still caked in blood.

"Aha! Wait right here." Frida ran over to the sword bin

and metal clanked as she riffled through it. "Thrain said I should melt it down for the metal, but I told him that was stupid. Here we are. I knew someone would need it one day."

She pulled a sword that was nearly as tall as she was. The blade was much too thin for battle, especially to be so long. It had opalescent pearls encrusted in the pommel and ends of the crossguard. She unwrapped the fabric around the grip, revealing a line of engraved runes.

"It's made of silver," Frida continued. "Some rich asshole had it made as a showpiece, I believe. Named the sword Brightblade. Didn't seem too smart if you ask me, considering he picked a fight with the wrong crowd. It's not the same as a spirit ward, not even close, but it will dissipate lesser spirits for a time, long enough for you to escape if you come upon them. Pearls are said to provide balance." She lifted the sword to show him the hilt. "And this one is mighty big."

Frida held the sword out to Dobbin. "I can get you spirit wards, but it'll take a few weeks. I'd have to send someone to visit the elves."

Dobbin didn't have a few weeks to wait. He took the sword, feeling the weight of the weapon in his hand. It was remarkably light compared to his great sword. The blade was more for piercing than battle, even if it had been made of steel. It wouldn't do much against man or monster, but if it was all that stood between him and the dead, it would have to do. He had salt and silver stakes for making camp. Traveling would be when he was most vulnerable.

"What do the runes do?" he asked.

Frida puffed again on her pipe and shrugged. "Your guess is as good as mine."

Dobbin could ask Klink to help translate the runes when he made it back to the guild hall since they were one of the guild master's areas of expertise.

He paid for Brightblade.

Even though the runes were a mystery, Dobbin had likely bought the weapon for more than it was worth. Still, he felt better with it than without.

# 14. RUNES

Night shrouded the city by the time Dobbin returned to the Adventurer's Guild. The moon cast its silvery glow upon the buildings, creating shadows that made the gargoyles more lifelike than usual, as if they could pounce down at any moment.

The guild lobby was empty aside from a single clerk with his feet resting on the counter. He nodded to Dobbin as he entered. Inside, the guild hall was bustling. A table against the far wall boasted a savory spread of roasted meat, vegetables, and giant loaves of bread on one end. Pies, tarts, and cakes filled the opposite end. Next to the food, a handful of dwarves huddled around several kegs, filling their mugs.

"What are we drinking tonight?" asked Dobbin.

A raven-haired dwarf turned around. "We've got ale and wine. The guildmaster keeps the hard stuff in his private quarters."

Dobbin laughed. "No doubt he does. I'll have some

wine, please. Speaking of the guildmaster, have you seen him around?"

The dwarf poured a healthy mug of wine for Dobbin. "I saw him around here earlier." He scanned the room and then pointed. "There he is."

Klink sat at the head table in deep conversation with a dark-haired woman. She wore blue robes with gold embroidering. She looked familiar, but Dobbin couldn't place her.

He tapped the dwarf on the shoulder. "Who's he sitting with?"

"That's Lyra Houndstooth. Some call her the Glamour Mage. She's an illusionist."

That was why she looked so familiar. He'd seen her perform an illusion for Queen Lilion long ago in Warminster. She'd made it appear as if snow were falling from the ceiling of the royal court, and two griffins had flown over the crowd.

"She a member?"

The dwarf nodded. "One of our best. She can hold up to five illusions at a time. I heard she captured a group of twenty bandits all by herself."

Dobbin watched the woman as she talked with Klink. It wasn't often that mages joined the guild. Most took positions in the city or paraded around like they were the gods' gift to the world. A mage could turn the tide of battle, but it had been ages since any of the kingdoms were at war. Dobbin respected the power they could wield, but he'd often thought it unfair that arcane mages were free to follow their whims while blood mages were enlisted to fight behemoths in the frozen north. A few years of service might do them good.

He put his grievances aside and approached the table.

Klink waved Dobbin over when he saw him. "It's a special night when two of our best are in town. I may have to break out the good stuff. Dobbin, I don't know if you've met Lyra, yet. She joined up with us about a year ago."

"Why?" he blurted out without thinking.

Lyra's face instantly soured, and Klink gave him a puzzled expression.

Dobbin hadn't meant to say the words out loud. He cleared his throat and attempted to cover his blunder. "What I mean is, why join the Adventurer's Guild? I thought you were pretty busy with your stately performances."

Her scowl softened. "Performing for monarchs and heads of state is so tedious. It gets boring after a while. I guess you could say I was looking for a little more excitement in my life."

"And a good thing too," Klink chimed in. "She's a big part of the reason our coffers are so full."

"Coin makes the world go round." Dobbin forced a smile.

"It certainly does." Klink tapped him on the arm. "You should join us."

"Actually, I was hoping I could borrow you for a minute. I have some runes that need analyzing."

"Can't it wait until tomorrow?"

"I'm leaving first thing in the morning." Dobbin knelt beside the table. "Give me a few minutes of your time and I'll drink with you and the mage until we're all wearing buckets on our heads."

Klink stood and bowed to Lyra. "Duty calls."

Klink shut the door to his study. "Alright, what is so urgent that you pried me away from one of our greatest assets?"

Dobbin scoffed as he placed his newly acquired sword on the table.

"Don't tell me you're still holding on to that grudge?" The guildmaster crossed his arms, ignoring the sword.

Dobbin said nothing. It'd been years since he'd let his anger get the better of him, and he wasn't about to start now.

Klink sighed. "You can't blame all mages for the mistake of one."

"It wasn't a mistake." Dobbin kept his voice calm, flat. "It was stupidity. It was cowardice. It was a disregard for anyone who wasn't..." He took a deep breath. "It doesn't matter. I bought this sword today, and I don't know what the runes mean. Can you help me out?"

He removed the fabric wrapped around the hilt, revealing the four runes etched into the metal.

Klink frowned as he examined the weapon. He lifted it, feeling the weight in his hand and inspecting the hilt from all angles. "What do you have need of a silver sword for?"

"You'd rather not know, remember?" Dobbin crossed his arms. "Do you know what the runes do?"

"Do I know what they do?" Klink laughed. "If it was only that easy. The gnomes start pushing their Runetech and now everyone in Aedrea thinks that rune magic is as simple as flipping a switch. There are hundreds of runes, and it's not like an alphabet where you simply translate. A skilled reader must divine their meaning. You see this rune here?" He pointed to a rune that looked like a sun—a circle surrounded by chevrons.

"This could mean many things. Light. Warmth. Brightness. Then one has to determine what it means in relation to the others. This is why it's important to buy directly from the maker, that way you know the intention behind it. Not only that, are they active or passive runes? Have the runes been activated? Are they properly inscribed to even work?"

Klink once again lifted the sword. "Take this for example. A silver blade and pearl pommel. My first instinct would be that this was a showpiece, and the runes were likely added for artistic flavor. But when you look at the quality of the rune, what do you see? Precision. Meticulous precision, far more detailed than in the blade itself. There are matching pairs on both sides."

Dobbin leaned closer, inspecting the runes himself. "So, what does that mean?"

"It means the runes were added for a reason. The question is for what purpose? There are a few runecrafters in Bearmouth. They could tell you if the runes have been charged or not. Unfortunately, it would take me more than an evening to begin deciphering what the runes might mean beyond a guess. So, unless you're willing to wait, it's not happening before you leave."

"Dammit." Dobbin cursed his luck. "Could you at least tell me what each of the runes are? The owner named the weapon Brightblade, if that helps at all."

"Sure. I've already told you the first one. That probably explains the name. This second one that looks like a flag, it usually means wisdom. It could also have something to do with communication or understanding. The third one is similar. Knowledge, but also creativity or learning. The bottom is usually associated with intuition or mystery. Sometimes discovery." He looked at Dobbin. "There's a common theme among the bottom three runes regarding learning or understanding. They were linked together for a reason. With a name like Brightblade, maybe the blade glows when someone tells you a lie. Maybe it's a training sword that shimmers when you perform a movement incorrectly. Do you see why this is so difficult?"

"Yeah, I see." Dobbin took the sword back. Regardless of whether or not the runes did anything, the silver blade would still do its job.

"I wish I could be more help." Klink placed a hand on Dobbin's forearm. "Come on, let's go get a drink. I'm bringing out the wuiskey just for you."

<hr>

"To adventure." Klink raised his glass, toasting to Lyra and Dobbin.

"To adventure," they echoed, tapping their glasses against one another.

Wuiskey trailed down Dobbin's throat, warming his insides. His shoulders relaxed, and the smoky, spicy aftertaste lingered on his tongue.

"Gods, that is good." Dobbin set his glass on the table. "Where's it from?"

Klink turned the bottle to face Dobbin. The label had an image of a crown positioned on top of a warhammer.

"Right here in Bearmouth. This one was given to me

by King Borin Stonebeard. Some of the finest wuiskey I've ever tasted."

"I'd love a taste," called a dwarf with a braided black beard from the next table over. He wore the red tunic of a new recruit.

Klink narrowed his eyes. "If you could make it through the training yard without losing your snot to a wooden dummy, I might consider it."

The table burst into laughter, and the recruit's face soon matched his tunic.

Dobbin grinned, remembering the days when he was a green adventurer. "You've really whipped this place into shape."

"I try, but gods, is it a lot of work. It always looked a lot easier from the outside." Klink poured them each another glass of wuiskey. "How's life in Eastborne? I hear that's where you call home these days."

"It's good, peaceful even. At least when I'm there. The guild isn't nearly as busy, though. Being so far down on the peninsula, they don't get the same threats you do around here."

"Well, I guess it's a good thing your reputation precedes you." Lyra chimed in.

Dobbin fought the urge to roll his eyes. He'd avoided conversing with the mage as much as possible, but it was inevitable. She sat across from him, smiling. Her hair was dark brown with golden highlights that matched the flowers embroidered down the sleeves of her robe. She wore an emerald amulet around her neck that brought out the green in her eyes.

"I put in the work." He took a sip of the wuiskey,

looking the mage straight in the eyes. "But I'm no Glamour Mage."

She froze for a moment, and then her smile faded.

"I suppose I deserve that." She took a sip, refusing to break eye contact. "Whatever could I offer the world besides entertainment? Maybe I should have stayed in my ivory tower placating the whims of kings and queens."

Dobbin immediately felt like an asshole. "Look, I didn't mean—"

"No, I've seen your icy glares since you first entered." She scowled, and her body seemed to shimmer at the edges. "The mighty Dobbin, that's what they call you, right? Looking down on me with disgust. Wondering what right I have to sully this great hall with my reputation as a glorified performer. The Glamour Mage—" She laughed, but there was no joy in it. "—nothing more than an arcane jester. How dare I try to rewrite my narrative? How dare I try to make myself into something more?"

She slammed both fists into the table, and illusions cast out of her as if six arms pounded the table at once. Her green eyes sparkled with flakes of gold as she sat there breathing heavily.

Dobbin's own heart thundered as he searched for the words. "I'm sorry. You're right, but it's not… It's not you." He sighed. "I lost someone I cared about deeply, and seeing you here was a reminder of that, but that's my problem. Something that I need to deal with on my own. I hope you can forgive me. Everyone here speaks highly of you, and it's clear you've been a great asset to the guild."

Her scowl softened. "Grief is a powerful feeling. I won't hold it against you, but you need to deal with that shit or it will eat you alive."

"I know." Dobbin couldn't help but smile. Maybe she wasn't half-bad, after all.

Klink stood, placing the bottle of wuiskey in the middle of the table. He winked at Dobbin. "Now that that's out of the way, I've got some work to attend to. I trust that the two of you know what to do with this."

Dobbin tapped the table. "Another one."

"You think you're gonna fare better this time?" Lyra grinned at him, and her cheeks flushed.

More than half the bottle was already gone, and he still hadn't figured out how to win.

He cracked his knuckles and leaned forward. "Just pour the drink."

"Big man. So broody," she teased, tilting the bottle so that wuiskey splashed into the empty glass. "Close your eyes."

Dobbin did as he was told. When he opened them, three glasses full of wuiskey sat before him.

He squinted, searching for any clue that might help him decide. She was so good that it was impossible to tell, so he chose a glass at random and reached for it.

Dobbin's hand passed through the illusion, and Lyra burst out laughing. He reached for the glass on the left and again grasped nothing but air.

"Wow, you are so bad at this." She slid the real glass toward Dobbin. "Drink up."

He downed the shot, and his head swirled. When Lyra split into three versions, he wasn't sure if it was her illusions or the alcohol. "I really am sorry about earlier. The guild is lucky to have you."

She smiled, patting the top of his hand. "That's just the wuiskey talking."

Dobbin took her hand in his. "Maybe. Doesn't mean it's not true."

Lyra laughed, but she didn't let go. She leaned forward, her green eyes gazing intensely into his. "It's a shame you're leaving tomorrow."

The wuiskey emboldened Dobbin even further. "All the more reason to make tonight count."

"Is that so?" She bit her lip, and then poured two more shots, handing one to Dobbin. "To a night we'll never forget."

# 15. SAFE TRAVELS

Dobbin woke with a splitting headache. A pale arm draped across his chest as Lyra slept peacefully next to him, her warm breath kissing his shoulder. He ran his finger across the soft skin of her forearm. Last night had been exactly what he'd needed before heading into Hells' Crag.

Memories came to him in pieces. He and Lyra had laughed and talked and drank until the wee hours of the morning. They'd stumbled through the guildhall giggling like children as they snuck around, exploring its empty rooms. And each other.

Dobbin smiled as he watched her sleep, her chest rising and falling with each breath. She'd been nothing like he'd expected.

Klink had been right. Dobbin couldn't paint every mage with the same brush. Lyra was funny and witty, and the way she teased him reminded him of Alina. Those two would be trouble if they ever met. Dobbin found himself not wanting to leave. If he didn't keep his head on straight, he'd spend another night in the city.

He scanned the room, trying to decipher exactly where they were. Although he'd left his gear in the barracks, they were definitely in one of the private rooms. Not that he was complaining.

Lyra stirred as Dobbin slid out from under her arm.

"My head." She grimaced as she rubbed one of her temples. "Oh, gods, how much did we drink?"

"All of it." Dobbin smirked, sitting up next to her. "I've got to get going, but, uh, thanks for last night."

"Thanks for last night." Lyra laughed, mocking him. "You're funny. Will you be passing back through when you're done with your mysterious quest?"

"Maybe."

"I'd like that."

"Me too." Dobbin leaned in, pressing his lips to hers.

When they broke away, she grinned devilishly. "Too bad I'll be gone. I just wanted to hear you say it."

He tossed a pillow at her, laughing. "You devil."

"What?" She bit her lip. "Duty calls."

Dobbin's heart raced as he ran a finger across her shoulder. "You're trouble, you know that?"

She laughed. "And you're not?"

"I guess the world better watch out then." He kissed her again. "I'll see you around, Lyra."

"Only if you're lucky." She winked, spreading her arm behind her head.

Dobbin nearly walked into the doorframe on his way out.

The door to Klink's study was open when Dobbin stopped by to say his farewell. The guildmaster leaned over a stack of parchment, squinting as his finger traced over the words as he read.

When he noticed Dobbin hovering in the doorway, he leaned back against his chair, smirking. "Rumor has it that someone had a good time last night."

Dobbin fought to keep from smiling. "Is that so?"

"One of the recruits said he saw you and Lyra disappear inside the broom closet." He raised a brow. "Some late-night cleaning, perhaps?"

"Something like that." Dobbin finally let the smile consume him. "I'm heading out. I just wanted to stop by to say thanks. You were right."

"I'm very seldom wrong." He stood and flexed his fingers before walking over to Dobbin. "She's a good one. Not just a good mage, either. A good person. But I think you've gathered that." He extended his hand, and they grasped one another around the forearm. "Safe travels, Dobbin."

Dobbin stopped as he was about to leave, fiddling through his cloak for the copy of *The Shadows of the City*. He'd finished it the night before arriving in Bearmouth and had planned to read it several more times before his journey was done.

"Give this to Lyra for me." He handed Klink the book. "Tell her it's a loan."

Klink smirked. "Must have been a damn good night."

Outside, Dobbin breathed in the crisp morning air. Sunlight cast the city in a warm glow, igniting the many stained-glass windows and metal accents.

His first stop was the stables. The stablehand brought out Snort and she pounced around wagging her tail with excitement.

Dobbin knelt beside the young direhog, scratching her behind the ears. "It's good to see you, too."

Snort squealed and grunted as she buried her head in his arms.

Shadowmane was less enthusiastic to meet his owner. The horse sniffed Dobbin's neck and huffed.

"Oh, don't be jealous." He patted Shadowmane on the shoulder, and the two pressed their heads together. "That's more like it."

After loading Shadowmane with gear and supplies, they were off. Hells' Crag was at least a week's journey from Bearmouth. The city was located at the foot of a mountain range, perfectly positioned as a focal point of trade with Warminster and Mount Tor. After the dragon attack, all roads to Hells' Crag had been rerouted to Bearmouth instead.

For now, Dobbin traveled west toward Silverpeak. In a couple days, they would turn north for roads hardly used for centuries, overgrown and unpatrolled.

"Great day for a ride," a man said as his horse joined pace with Shadowmane. He had blonde hair cropped just above his shoulders and wore a burgundy cloak over a purple tunic, both items were of extremely fine quality. The gray horse was saddled with several satchels and a small crate. "Mind if I join you? Name's Eris."

Dobbin had been looking forward to the solace of his thoughts, but there would be plenty of time for contemplation soon enough. "Sure. I'm Dobbin. Where you headed, Eris?"

"Most excellent!" Eris grinned. "Stormrest, then hopefully home to Whitehaven for the winter. Yourself?"

"West for a bit. Then north."

He gave Dobbin a knowing look. "You're an adventurer, aren't you?"

Dobbin smiled. "What gave it away?"

"You just have that air about you, you know? The look of a man untethered and free. Plus, I know a quality cloak when I see one."

"Is that so? What line of business are you in?"

"I'm a trader of fine wines and spirits. I just finished a tour of Whitblossum, Hillside, and Bearmouth sampling their newest offerings. The halflings make amazing honey wine, if you can get over the fact that they mash the fruit with their feet. But I've always been partial to the dwarven reds myself." Eris tapped a satchel strapped behind his saddle. "One of the perks is that I always leave with a few samples before they ship the product. It makes the long ride home more bearable."

Dobbin laughed. "Now that sounds like a good time."

"It is, don't get me wrong, but I'm gone for half the year. I miss my family." Eris sighed. "I have two young boys, and they aren't getting any younger."

"Maybe one day, they'll be the ones doing the traveling," Dobbin offered.

"From your lips to the gods' ears." Eris kissed his finger and pointed to the sky. "You have any little ones?"

"No." Dobbin thought of Henrik and the child he'd left behind. The all-too-frequent pang of guilt twisted inside. "Adventuring isn't a life that's kind to families."

"I see." He looked down at Snort, her feet a blur as she ran ahead of the horses. "At least you've got the pig."

Dobbin discovered quickly that Eris was a talker. By the time they stopped for a rest and a bite to eat, he'd learned far more than he ever cared to know about the man. He knew the names of the Eris's children, their favorite toys, how he'd met his wife, and how Eris's grandfather had been a diplomat for King Lyle until a stately visit to Rockdale opened his eyes to the possibility of importing dwarven wines to the human kingdoms. The family had been in the trading business ever since.

"What do you say we have a little sample?" Eris grinned as he reached into his pack and pulled out a bottle of wine. The wine was the color of golden wheat and had a bouquet of flowers on the label. "If you've never had honey wine, this will be a real treat."

"This the foot wine?" Dobbin raised a brow.

"Say what you will, but the results speak for themselves." Eris uncorked the wine and handed the bottle to Dobbin.

Dobbin sniffed the wine, surprised by how floral it smelled.

"Cheers." He tilted the bottle toward Eris and took a sip. The wine had a more robust texture than he'd expected as it coated his tongue. It was good, though. Sweet, with a distinct flavor of honey and a fragrant aroma of rose petals. The sweetness lingered in his mouth long after he swallowed. He licked his lips and handed the bottle to Eris. "Not bad."

"I prefer it chilled when possible, but even like this, it's still divine."

Snort rooted around in the grass as they shared a meal of bread, cheese, and jerky. Dobbin was thankful to discover that a full mouth meant a moment of silence for

Eris. But as soon as they were on the road again, he started with a new story about the first time he'd ever met a halfling.

Dobbin tuned him out, focusing on the steady clop of horse hooves and the breeze against his face. That was until Snort stopped and plopped over on the side of the road without warning, forcing Dobbin to turn around and retrieve the direhog.

When she was resting in Dobbin's lap, Eris continued his story.

"—so I ask my father, in front of everyone, mind you, 'Why does that little boy have such hairy feet?' My father's face turned as red as a strawberry. Needless to say, we weren't able to import wine from Honeydale for over a decade after that."

Snort snored in Dobbin's lap as they trotted along. Her ears perked up at the same time that Dobbin spotted a wagon blocking the road far ahead. Two figures stood next to the wagon, waving them over.

Dobbin pulled the reins, slowing down. His instincts told him to be cautious. Hilly terrain surrounded them in all directions, making it impossible to gauge the situation.

"What's going on?" asked Eris.

"Up ahead. Might be trouble."

"Bandits?" Eris gulped. "Should we turn around?"

"I don't know. Just let me do the talking." His hand rested on the hilt of his sword, more for comfort and reassurance than anything. He'd dealt with bandits before, and they were always unpredictable, but he was a trained swordsman, a seasoned warrior, and above all, not in the mood for any bullshit.

The two men were dressed in well-worn tunics. One

was slender, with black hair cropped short. The other had long brown hair pulled into a bun and a patchy beard. Each had a sword strapped to their waist.

Dobbin stopped about fifty feet away and scanned the hills again. "Everything okay, fellas?"

"Our wagon broke down," the black-haired man answered. His voice was youthful and shook slightly, lacking confidence. "Any chance you can give us a hand?"

Dobbin shifted his gaze to the wagon. It seemed to be fine, aside from the missing horse. There were no broken spokes or wheels as far as he could see, and the bed was empty.

"What do you need a hand with?" he asked.

The second man unsheathed his sword and stepped forward more confidently than his partner. "You could start by giving us your horses."

"Godsdammit," Dobbin cursed under his breath when he heard hoofbeats approaching from behind. He glanced over his shoulder and saw a third bandit cresting the hill with a crossbow in one hand. Dobbin turned to Eris. "Stay out of the way. I'll handle this."

Eris hesitated for a moment, eyes wide, and then he whipped the reins, darting into the hills.

Dobbin dropped Snort to the ground, and she landed on all fours with a squeal. He knew from experience how hard it was to aim a crossbow on horseback, and these men were not professionals. The bandit slowed in the middle of the road, horse sideways as he aimed.

The crossbow released with a clack and the bolt whizzed by, wide to the left. The man cursed as he pulled back to reload. Dobbin took a slingshot from his cloak and loaded it with a metal ball. He fired, hitting the man's horse in the rear. The horse bucked, knocking the bandit from the saddle. The man hit the ground with a thud, and the horse galloped over the hill.

Dobbin dismounted from Shadowmane, just as the other two bandits reached him. The black-haired bandit couldn't be over twenty, probably much younger. Shadowmane joined Eris on a nearby hill, out of the action.

The young bandit swung his sword with the grace of a barbarian, grunting as the blade cut through the air. Dobbin parried the attack, spinning the blade with such force that it flew from the bandit's hand. The man stood there with wide eyes, as if uncertain of what to do next.

The sword was still spinning through the air when the second bandit attacked. Dobbin sidestepped, pirouetted, and slammed his elbow into the back of the man's head. The bandit's eyes rolled into his skull, and he collapsed to the ground.

Snort grunted as she rammed her head into the unconscious man's back.

The disarmed bandit stood frozen, so Dobbin turned his attention to the man thrown from the horse. He groaned, stumbling as he crawled to his feet. He attempted to latch the crossbow, but his hand shook as he pulled the lever.

"I wouldn't do that if I were you," Dobbin warned.

The man raised the weapon just as Shadowmane shoulder-checked him from behind at a full gallop. The bolt fired into the sky, and the man crumpled to the ground.

Dobbin turned to find that the black-haired bandit

was now holding his partner's sword. It trembled in his grip as he spoke. "Don't move."

Dobbin sighed. "I'm going to give you a choice. We can do this the easy way or the hard way."

The sword clattered to the ground.

# 16. SECOND CHANCES

"What are you going to do with them?" Eris chewed at his fingernail a safe distance from where Dobbin had subdued the bandits.

Dobbin rubbed his temple, exasperated with the turn of events. "I don't know."

The three bandits sat in the middle of the road with their hands tied behind their backs. Up close, they were much younger than he'd originally thought. Even though two of them had scraggly beards and broad shoulders, they were still just teenagers. Snort grunted as she sniffed at their boots. The trio was lucky Dobbin had recognized their ineptitude early on, or else they'd all three be lying in a ditch.

He knelt in front of the youngest of the three, the one who'd stood there frozen after being disarmed. "You're a little young to be playing bandit, aren't you?"

"Don't tell him anything!" The one who'd been on horseback snarled.

Dobbin pointed his sword at the older boy. "You tried

to shoot me with a crossbow. I'd watch your mouth if I were you."

The boy scowled, but he didn't say another word. Between the two, the boy Dobbin had knocked unconscious was still dazed, a far-off look in his eyes.

Dobbin returned his attention to the youngest. "What gives, kid? You're lucky it was me you tried to ambush. Anyone else might have killed you for pointing a sword in their face."

"Look, I'm sorry." Tears welled in his eyes. "We're just so tired of having nothing. Last year, we lost half our crops to a drought. The year before, shadow beetles ruined our corn and lettuce. And now we have to worry about bandits taking what little we do have any time we make a delivery. It's not right."

The situation suddenly made a lot more sense. There was nothing like desperation to make someone do something incredibly stupid.

"So, your plan was what? That if you can't beat them, join them?"

"It's not like that," the older boy answered.

Dobbin turned to face him. "What's it like, then?"

"We just needed some coin so that we could buy better weapons and protect ourselves."

"The weapons aren't the problem. I've seen highborn girls fight with better technique than you. Not to mention you fired a crossbow in the direction of your own men."

The boy squirmed in defiance against his constraints. "What choice did we have?"

"You always have a choice." Dobbin stood, his gaze settling on Eris for a moment before returning his attention to the oldest. "You're the older brother?"

"Cousin." The boy continued to scowl.

"What was your plan if things went south? Were you going to be the one to tell his parents he died while trying to ambush an adventurer? You think some easy coin is worth his life?"

He gulped. "I didn't…" The words trailed off.

"Gods, I don't have time for this shit." Dobbin rubbed his brow. "Luckily for you, no one got hurt." He looked down at the middle boy. "Not too bad, at least. He'll be fine in a couple of hours. I'm going to let you free. If you continue down this path, I promise you, you'll be dead before it is all said and done. You're tired of being pushed around. I get that. If you want to learn to fight back, go to the Adventurer's Guild in Bearmouth and tell them that Dobbin sent you. Klink will see that you're taken care of, and he'll give you the skills to make sure you're never in this predicament ever again."

"And what happens in the meantime?" asked the youngest.

"Sometimes, there are no easy fixes. If you want things to change, you have to put in the work." Dobbin removed his dagger and cut the bindings off each boy in turn. "The world can be a dangerous place at times. That's why we need good men to shine light in the darkness."

The oldest stood with his arms crossed. "Will the Adventurer's Guild really train us?" He stood defiant, but there was a longing in his voice.

Dobbin nodded. "If you mention my name, yes. You'll have to work to earn your keep. That will mean cleaning and kitchen duty, but you'll train with the recruits and have the chance to work your way up the ranks."

The boy uncrossed his arms. "Well, I'm sorry I almost shot you."

Dobbin laughed. "Kid, you weren't even close."

———

Dobbin and Eris stood at a crossroads where the main road branched off toward a village. Twilight was fast approaching, but Dobbin planned to get a few more hours in. The run-in with the bandits had cost him precious time, and he aimed to make it up where he could.

"You sure I can't bribe you to stay?" Eris asked. "I owe you for saving me today."

Dobbin shook his head. "There's still a few good hours of riding left, and I've already dawdled enough today."

"What do you think is going to happen?" Eris gazed back in the direction they'd come from. "With the boys, I mean."

"That's up to them." Dobbin pursed his lips as he considered. "You can lead a griffin to the mountains, but you can't make it fly. I gave them an opportunity to make a change. Becoming a member of the guild is hard work, but it can open a lot of doors. They have a chance to not only help themselves but their families as well."

"I can't speak for them, but I sure am glad to have run into you today. You really saved my bacon. No offense, Snort."

The direhog looked up at the mention of her name and then continued rooting in the tall grass by the roadside.

"Truth be told, most bandits aren't looking for a fight.

They want to take what they can and be on their way. If you turn around, most of them won't even chase you."

"Still, I'm grateful." He reached into the pack on his horse and pulled out a bottle of wine. "This is a dwarven red from Bearmouth. A mighty fine vintage. Take it as a token of my appreciation. I hope you'll think fondly of our travels when you open it."

"Thanks." Dobbin took the bottle and placed it in his own satchel. The man might talk a lot, but he wasn't half-bad. "Take care of yourself out there."

Dobbin climbed onto Shadowmane, and they trotted into the night. From waking up next to a beautiful woman to an ambush and a new acquaintance, it had been a full day of unexpected adventure. He was ready for a quiet evening under the stars.

A cool breeze carried across the hilly terrain, giving the moonlit grass the appearance of a silver sea. An owl swooped through the night, disappearing among the tall grass and darting off with its kill.

They traveled for a few more hours before making camp off the road beyond a copse of trees. After a quick dinner, Dobbin rested against a towering oak. He removed Brightblade from its scabbard and once again inspected the runes that ran along the grip. He recalled what Klink had said, that the bottom three had a similar meaning—something to do with learning or understanding. As vague as runes were, that could mean anything.

His own sword was enchanted with two runes, one for durability and another that made it feel lighter in his hand. The smith had named it Steadfast. It was a fitting name, as the blade stayed sharper for longer and had never had so much as a nick or dent. The weapon had been one of his first major purchases after completing his first big quest, and it had drained his savings mightily.

As a child, he'd often dreamed of owning an enchanted weapon like the ones he read in his stories. Swords that could burn with fire or a bow that would imbue the arrows with light as they shot across the sky. Those types of weapons were a rarity nowadays, ever since the gnomish council had placed a ban on runecrafting weapons. Gnomes were regarded as the greatest runecrafters in Aedrea, and the weapons that still existed were highly prized.

Some were still crafted in secret. Perhaps the sword he held in his hand was one.

Dobbin flicked it against the air. The blade was well-balanced, and even though it was smaller than his great sword, it fit naturally in his hand. He recalled his research at the library, the accounts of spirits walking among the ruins. Silver could temporarily dissipate a lesser spirit, and it could even damage a wraith or specter.

If Dobbin found himself close enough to trade blows with a wraith, then things had gone terribly awry. He put the sword away, hoping he wouldn't need it.

# 17. OFF THE BEATEN PATH

The path to Hells' Crag was desolate and overgrown. Grass and weeds had overtaken the packed earth where the road had been, giving the appearance of a grassy river winding through the hills. There were stretches where Snort would disappear beneath the tall growth, and the bristles on her upthrust tail would peek above the grass as the only indication of her location.

Since their journey began, Snort's endurance had increased with each passing day. She took her impromptu rests less frequently, and when Dobbin was forced to pick her up, he was certain that the direpig had put on some weight since he'd first found her. She seemed a little taller as well. It wouldn't be long before she was a massive beast in her own right.

As they traveled toward the ruined city, the rolling hills transitioned to slightly more mountainous terrain, and a low-lying fog blanketed the valleys. The blue skies took on a cloudy gray hue, and the tall grass slowly withered, revealing the well-trodden road that led to the once-great city.

Dobbin rarely got rattled, but tension radiated through his body at the prospect of what awaited. From what he'd read, the damage to Hells' Crag had been two-fold. First, there was the dragon's fiery attack. Its flames were so hot that they could melt stone and incinerate wood in seconds. Then there was the fire that had spread and the noxious smoke that continued to ravage the surrounding areas long after the dragon had moved on. One of the books detailed how the city had burned for days after the attack.

Dragon attacks were nothing new to the history books. They had often destroyed farms and villages while hunting for food. There were even records of attacks on castles after a dragon lair had been disturbed. But those were warnings and resulted in little more than scorched buildings. Full-fledged destruction and attempted annihilation were unheard of. Dragons were powerful, but they weren't cruel.

All these years and the reason behind the attack remained a mystery.

The trees grew more ragged the deeper they went until skeletal branches grasped toward the sky as if begging for sunlight that dark clouds refused to yield. The plants that survived were dark and moribund, neither dead nor growing.

Snort fell back in pace with Shadowmane as if she, too, sensed that something had changed.

Very few accounts of the ruins in the aftermath of the attack were available. The dwarves seemed to have banished the attack and the city from their collective memory. It was as if an entire people chose to mourn the loss by forgetting. That much, Dobbin could relate with.

The human kingdom of Warminster honored the sacrifice that Raglan the Magnificent had made when he chose to battle the red dragon. The city of Silverpeak had raised a statue in his memory. They knew that if not for the mage, they may have suffered a similar fate.

A few scholars had made the trek to observe the carnage from a distance, but none had dared to delve inside. According to their records, smoke had lingered around the fallen city for years afterward.

The most recent scholarly account he'd found was over a hundred years old. There were rumors of fool-hardy adventurers who had gone in search of treasure and glory, but none had returned. Everywhere, the advice was the same—do not venture into Hells' Crag.

This was a fool's errand, Dobbin knew, but the payday had been too tempting even for him. With any luck, he could find the mushrooms in the outskirts of the city and return to Eastborne without ever stepping into the crag itself.

By midday, Dobbin could see the mountains above the fog, ominous and imposing. The outskirts of Hells' Crag lay at their feet. There was an eeriness to the area that he'd never experienced during daylight. At times, it felt as if he was being watched. Even though the trees were bare, the fog made it impossible to tell what might be lurking in the shadows.

He knew he wasn't alone. There was movement out of

sight, an occasional broken branch or flutter of wings. He spotted kobold tracks caked in the mud. Shadowmane's tail flicked back and forth, and his shoulders tensed beneath the adventurer, something that rarely happened to the horse.

"Easy, boy." Dobbin patted Shadowmane on the neck. "Nothing we can't handle."

Whether or not that was true remained to be seen. From here on out, progress would be slow and deliberate.

A branch cracked like thunder, startling horse and rider. Snort squealed as she stayed close to Shadow's side. Dobbin's heart pounded, only for a loud caw to echo across the emptiness as a massive vulture took to the sky.

Dobbin laughed nervously. "Just a bird."

The day wore on, and his nerves began to ease. The road twisted and turned with the rocky terrain. When it curved alongside a steep ridge, Dobbin dismounted to try and gauge their location. The direpig snorted at him as he scaled the rockface for a better view.

Dobbin's muscles burned as he climbed, and by the time he reached the top, sweat beaded across his brow. He wiped his forehead with the back of his hand and walked to the far edge of the ridge. From where he was standing, he finally understood why they called it Hells' Crag.

A murky gray lake stretched across the valley below, its once-crystal-blue water stained by ash. Fog hovered above the still surface like clouds. In the lake's center, a gargantuan crag appeared to rise from the depths of one hell or another, sloping down toward the mountain range to the north.

The mammoth landmass was a vestige of the great city that had once claimed its surface. Melted spires and crumbled walls were all that remained of the keep over-looking the steep cliffside at its zenith. The entire city fared no better, like a sandcastle caught in a storm. Some buildings had been razed to the ground, while others were misshapen—melted or crumbled on one side. There were entire city blocks that were nothing more than rubble.

Hells' Crag bore the echo of a city, but there was nothing to jog the memory of what it had once been. Beyond the crag, the dragon's rage remained imprinted along the mountains, where miles of darkened forest ran adjacent to vibrant green lands untouched by flame.

Dobbin gazed silently into the ruins. Reading about the destruction was one thing, but it was quite another to experience the remains of a city this size. A city that had been larger than both Eastborne and Bearmouth.

After composing himself, he climbed down from the ridge. Now that he knew where the city began, he could start his search.

His research regarding dragonfire mushrooms had been extremely limited. *Magical Mushrooms and Where to Forage Them* had a wealth of knowledge on various species of fungi, but there had only been a single page dedicated to what he sought. The drawing had taken up half of the page by itself. If it was accurate, the mushroom would have a charcoal-colored cap with reddish-orange gills underneath. The stalk was the same color as the cap, making the mushroom almost impossible to spot while walking. Its camouflage would blend in perfectly with the current landscape.

Dobbin pulled out his journal. The passage had been so short that he'd copied it word for word.

. . .

### *Dragonfire Mushroom* (*Pyrofungus draconis*)

*Little is known about these mysterious fungi. As the name implies, dragonfire mushrooms only grow within soil that has been touched by dragon flame. Unlike other pyrofungus which thrive in the nutrient-rich soil after wildfires, the* pyrofungus draconis *grows where other plant life cannot. Due to the rarity of such locations, the specific circumstances which promote growth are unknown, and scholars have had limited opportunities to observe them in the wild.*

*The great gnomish scholar, Finwick Winklefuss, is said to have found a cluster of dragonfire mushrooms during an excursion into the Frozen North. Against the gnome's warnings, his party ate the mushrooms when food became scarce. Those who ingested the fungi entered a trancelike state where they claimed to experience visions. Some were transported to the past in vivid detail, others witnessed what they believed to be the future. A dwarven ranger saw the precise location of a herd of deer in his vision, which led to their ultimate survival.*

*Whether or not these mushrooms grant true divination or merely hallucinations remains to be proven.*

Dobbin closed his journal and looked down at Snort. "Charcoal-colored mushrooms in an ashen landscape. We've got our work cut out for us, little lady."

The direhog looked up from the upturned earth she'd been sniffing and grunted.

Dobbin scoured the area slowly and methodically, searching beneath rocks, logs, and within the hollows of trees. He looked anywhere that might be shady or damp, but he found nothing within the blighted soil.

If he was going to locate the mushroom, he'd need to go to where the dragon attack had been the most intense—the crag itself.

He mounted Shadowmane and continued toward the city. When an area looked particularly promising, such as an alcove along the ridge or a recess underneath an embankment, he'd pause to investigate. After a half-dozen attempts proved fruitless, he decided to make for the city without stopping.

By late afternoon, the ridge descended alongside the path, allowing a view of the crag and fog-covered lake. More than once, Dobbin caught himself staring at the ruins, imagining what it must have been like to be there when everything went to shit.

As the sun faded behind the mountains, the city took on an even more sinister tone. Streaks of light pierced the clouds at an angle, casting long shadows all around them. They would need to make camp before nightfall. Dobbin descended into the valley as the last rays of sunlight outlined the mountain peaks. They could camp in the open fields, where his protections were least likely to be disturbed.

Midway down the valley, Dobbin stopped. He rubbed his eyes and squinted, wondering if his mind was playing tricks on him. Visibility was poor in the dim light, but he swore he saw a meadow of wildflowers growing on the far side of the valley. It was extremely odd considering the state of all the other plant life in the area.

He looked over his shoulder at the fading light. If they hurried, they might make it in time.

Dobbin called for Snort, but the direhog was sniffing around the roots of a tree just off the path. She ignored him, and he called for her again, but she was enamored by something within the hollow around the roots. She pawed at the gnarled root as if there was something underneath.

Direhogs had an impeccable sense of smell, so he dismounted to see what she'd found. He knelt beside her, looking into the hollow of the tree. There was nothing but dirt and cobwebs.

He scratched her behind the ears. "What it is, girl?"

Dobbin stood, and the root beneath his boot clicked. Snort squealed and bolted as something cinched around Dobbin's foot, yanking him off the ground. His head cracked against the tree trunk as his lower body was jerked upward. Stars twinkled across his vision.

"Godsdammit." Dobbin grimaced as he touched a wet patch on the back of his head. He dangled helplessly as blood rushed to his head. His fingers blurred with streaks of crimson, and his vision blackened at the edges.

## 18. PRECAUTIONS

Dobbin swayed back and forth several feet off the ground. Thunder rumbled in his ears as blood rushed to his head, pulsing in the gash on the back of his skull. He took deep, heavy breaths, fighting against the darkness creeping in at the edge of his vision. His cloak hung upside-down, its many pockets rattling as the items shifted within.

Snort had returned, and she squealed with worry underneath.

A trap had been the last thing he expected to find on the outskirts of the ruins. The daylight was nearly gone, and if he didn't free himself soon, it would be a very long night.

Dobbin whistled and Shadowmane was by his side in an instant. The horse's head nuzzled against the adventurer's shoulder.

"Good boy." Dobbin patted Shadow on the neck and then reached for the saddle.

He grabbed the horn of the saddle with one hand and

managed to remove Brightblade with the other. Its slender blade would be much easier to wield upside-down than the heavy great sword.

Dobbin cut at the rope but it refused to give, so he took a deep breath and swung the sword hard against the rope. Tension immediately released from his leg, and he plummeted to the ground with a thud. Thanks to his grip on the saddle, his feet took the brunt of the impact.

The gash on the back of his head throbbed as blood rushed back to his extremities. The bleeding had stopped, but it was still a pretty nasty cut. There were a few health potions stuffed in his satchel, so he downed one and waited as the wound stitched itself shut. The potion was disgusting, somehow sweet and bitter at the same time, but it did the job. Dobbin never left for a quest without a few bottles. They'd saved his ass more times than he could count when there wasn't a cleric around.

Once the pounding in his head faded, he returned to inspect the trap. The rope that had caught his foot was made of several small vines braided together. They had dried out and hardened over time, which explained why the sword had trouble cutting through. The tree root had been hollowed out underneath, with the rope attached to a counterweight that activated when enough pressure was applied. By the looks of it, it was kobold or goblin made. The bastards were ingenious at finding ways to capture their targets without having to fight head-on.

Dobbin looked over his shoulder, wondering if the trap was a remnant of the past or if the creatures might be lurking in the shadows even now.

Either way, Dobbin wanted to get moving. He picked

up Snort and sat her across his lap as they continued into the valley. "You could have warned me, you know?"

Snort grunted and nestled against his stomach.

At the edge of the valley, Dobbin found a clearing to make camp. He wanted to travel further, but there was little time to get his protections in place for the night.

After unloading his satchel, Dobbin found Kipper's essence ward. The wardmaster said it would take on a soft glow if spirits were near. Right now, it looked the same as it always had—a white cube with gold runes. He set it on his bedroll as he continued his preparations.

He removed a bag of salt, a handful of silver spikes, and a roll of silver wire from his gear. There were three bags of salt, enough to last a week, but the wire and spikes would be reusable. They wouldn't keep out kobolds, goblins, or other creatures, but anything ghastly wouldn't be able to cross the barrier unless it was broken.

Dobbin drove the spikes into the ground in a circle big enough for all three of them. Then he took the silver wire, wrapping it around each spike and forming a barrier.

Using the salt, he poured a circle around his bedroll. As much as he would have preferred to make the circle big enough for Shadowmane, there simply wasn't enough to last more than a few days. The second circle might not have been necessary, but it was better to be safe than sorry when spirits were involved. Riches weren't built on the backs of hopes and dreams. They were built through research, preparation, and dedication.

Dobbin pointed to Snort, who was plopped on her side within the salt circle. "You do not go past this until morning. Understand?"

She didn't so much as move in acknowledgment.

Shadowmane had enough space to pace and lay down within the silver wire. If he needed to leave for any reason, the horse could easily step over the barrier.

Dobbin lay on his bedroll, resting his head on his satchel while Snort snored nearby. His dinner consisted of hard bread, cheese, jerky, and an apple.

After he finished eating, Dobbin lay there, listening to the sounds of the night. There was an eerie quietness that was rare in nature. No bugs or critters rattling and calling into the night. Even the stars were concealed by the omnipresent clouds.

The sooner he was in familiar lands, the better. Tomorrow, they would go into the city and begin the search anew. Stopping in Bearmouth had added to the journey, but he still had several weeks to locate the mushrooms and head back if he wanted to secure the bonus.

The screech of an owl pierced the darkness from somewhere across the valley. Dobbin rolled onto his side, frowning as he gazed into the darkness. If there was an owl, that meant there was something for it to hunt. Maybe it was an actual meadow he'd seen earlier.

Out of the corner of his eye, Dobbin noticed a silvery blue glow from within the ruins. He couldn't make out any details from so far away, but he recognized the ethereal glow of apparitions. Some areas glowed more fervently than others.

Everything he'd read was true. Dobbin swallowed hard as he glanced at the ward. Even though his heart threatened to pound through his chest, the essence ward remained dark.

His gaze drifted up the remains of the city to where

the keep had once stood. Energy strobed within the vestiges of the ruined castle. He watched, entranced as it flared and pulsed.

Dobbin's hair stood on end as if lightning brewed all around him. Then, the light faded within the keep and a dull thrum filled the silence.

# 19. DREAMS AND SHADOWS

Sleep didn't come easy for Dobbin. Camping in the open without knowing what was happening in the crag had his nerves fluttering. Fighting monsters was easy. They all had weaknesses. Weaknesses that Dobbin could exploit. Ghosts, though…

A ring of salt and some wire were all that stood between him and whatever lurked beyond.

His gaze kept drifting toward the essence cube as if he expected it to burst into a beacon of light at any moment, but eventually, sleep claimed Dobbin's tired muscles and weary mind.

He slept with the essence ward in one hand and Brightblade in the other.

Dobbin dreamt of Hells' Crag. In the dream, he ran through the burning city without weapons or armor as shadows engulfed the world and angry spirits warned him to turn back. Toxic green flames licked at his heels while voices shrieked in all directions.

Above the chaos, Snort oinked loudly. Dobbin

searched for her as he ran, but she eluded him. Shadow-mane neighed from the shadows, and a phantom pressure rammed against Dobbin's side, almost knocking him to the ground. Something tugged at his arm, and then another blow hit his ribs as the direhog's snorts grew more frantic.

Dobbin opened his eyes to Snort's panicked squeals just in time to notice a pair of small, cold hands attempting to pry his fingers away from Brighblade. Snort rammed her head into Dobbin again, bringing him back to reality.

The blade of the sword flared with energy. He clenched the hilt, and the bright blue eyes of the shadow fairy widened in alarm. It released its hold, hissing and snarling at Dobbin as it took to the air. Its forked tongue whipped between sharp, ravenous teeth.

The creature had translucent blue wings, bone-white horns that wrapped around its skull, and dark iridescent skin that shimmered in the light of the sword. It hovered in the air, and Dobbin spotted two more fairies several yards back. Their long, spindly fingers were tipped with obsidian claws, and they grasped greedily as the fairy inched closer, its eyes fixated on the blade.

Dobbin raised the sword, and the fairy hissed again. Only then did he notice the three pearls in the pommel glowing like miniature moons.

Snort lowered her head and kicked at the ground as if readying to charge.

Dobbin crawled to his feet, never lowering the sword. The shadow fairies continued to hiss like angry cats, but they kept their distance.

This wasn't Dobbin's first run-in with the creatures.

Long ago, he'd encountered them deep within the Vaglir Forest. Despite their appearance, the creatures weren't usually violent unless provoked. They were mischievous, and notorious thieves with an affinity for magical items. Some adventurers would seek out fairy hollows in search of the treasures they hoarded.

"Bugger off!" Dobbin waved the sword in their direction. "Go on! Get out of here!"

The fairies curled their lips, revealing their pointed teeth before hissing again. Even though there were only three of them, they sounded like a den of snakes. The closest one turned to the others, speaking in some ancient language before they darted away.

Dobbin lowered his sword. The blade no longer glowed. He questioned if it truly had glowed or if it had been the reflection of the moon. The fact that the fairies were here meant that there was something special about the weapon, though.

But what? It had glowed in their presence, but there were too many variables to know why. Perhaps it glowed in the presence of fairies, or around certain types of magic. Maybe there was something else entirely that Dobbin had missed.

He sheathed the sword, and a silver powder fell from the front of his cloak.

Dobbin wiped it away, and the fine particles glittered as they fell. *Shadow dust.* This explained the terrible dream.

All fairies could create fairy dust, and many types were prized by alchemists and potionmakers. Some dusts could help one sleep or provide a sense of relaxation or calmness. Shadow fairy dust altered dreams and brought about nightmares.

Dobbin knelt next to Snort, rubbing her behind the ears. "Good job." He turned to Shadowmane and patted the horse on the shoulder. "Both of you. If not for you, they'd have the sword and whatever else the little bastards wanted to take."

Shadowmane huffed as he nuzzled against Dobbin.

To the east, the first rays of sunlight were already peeking above the mountains. Dobbin rolled his shoulders and stretched. Dull pain pulsed in his lower back, and he massaged it away. There was no way he was going back to sleep after this.

"Might as well get a move on." He rolled his bed and then pulled some rations from his satchel, breaking a carrot in half for the animals.

Snort and Shadowmane crunched blissfully as Dobbin removed the silver wire and pulled the stakes from the ground. He'd have to figure out a way to deal with the shadow fairies should they set their eyes on his sword again, but for now, he wanted to get into the city with as much daylight as possible.

His skin prickled at the memory of the aura around the ruins and the pulsing energy within the keep. The last thing he wanted was to be inside the city walls when darkness fell over the crag. At least until he knew what he was dealing with.

The plan was simple—travel to the city, explore for a few hours, and make camp outside before nightfall. With a little luck, he'd find the mushroom and be back on the road the next day.

With everything packed away, they set off toward the crag. Mist hung across the valley in the early morning as if it had rolled down from the mountains. There was a brief moment before the sun disappeared above the clouds where the rays shone through at an angle, igniting the fog with beams that stretched for miles. Even in such a bleak environment, there was beauty to be found. Anywhere else, there would have been chirping birds and insects rattling, but here, there was nothing but an unsettling quiet.

Cool air kissed Dobbin's cheeks as he guided Shadowmane toward the city. They were still a few hours from the gates, but the crag looked down upon them with its imposing presence.

The city may have perished in the attack, but the crag still stood tall and unbreakable.

Dobbin began to understand why the Dwarves no longer spoke of this place. It wasn't the death, but what the destruction of their homeland represented. Whether from mountains or hills, the dwarves were a people defined by where they lived. Legend said that the gods formed the dwarves from the earth itself. To witness their city destroyed but the crag remaining was a fate even the poets could not portend.

To the east, the clouds suddenly parted, pulling Dobbin from his thoughts as a beam of sunlight shone on the far side of the valley. A streak of light pierced the dreariness like a sword, shining on a copse of trees in the distance with divine radiance.

Dobbin frowned as he took in the scenery. Compared to the skeletal trees everywhere else, those within the light were a vivid green and appeared to have new growth. He squinted harder. For the second time, he was sure that there were wildflowers on the other side of the valley.

Curiosity got the better of him and he changed course. It would likely only add an hour or two to his trek, and if plants were thriving in this desolate landscape, he wanted to know why. It would be an opportunity for the animals to graze, but more importantly, there might be a clue to help him on the quest.

The sun only lasted for a moment before the clouds closed again, and the vibrant trees took on the drabness of the surroundings.

Dobbin's jaw dropped when he came upon the small wooded area. Somehow, an oasis had blossomed among the devastation that had lingered for centuries.

A mighty oak towered in the center surrounded by slender pines. Fruit trees grew around the edges, speckled with lemons, apples, and peaches. Birds chirped within their branches. Wildflowers spread for nearly a mile in the direction of the eastern mountains, as if a river of life was flowing into the valley. There were a myriad of bushes, trees, flowers, and vines, many of which Dobbin knew were not native to the area. He rubbed his eyes, wondering if this might be a lasting effect of the shadow dust.

Snort sniffed the air and took off running.

"Wait!" Dobbin shouted as he urged Shadowmane to follow. "Godsdammit, Snort! Let me make sure it's safe."

As he chased after the direpig, the smell of flowers

washed over him. He'd been in the ruins for so long that the scent of fresh air hit him like a charm. Even Shadowmane's muscles relaxed beneath him.

Snort looked back at Dobbin before disappearing within the tall grass and flowers.

"That pig is going to be the death of me." Dobbin sighed.

He halted at the edge, taking in the beauty of the wildlife. Nature was thriving on this particular piece of land. But why? There was a clear boundary between where the meadow ended and the ruinous soil began. Bees buzzed as they flitted from one flower to another, and grasshoppers rattled beneath the leaves, but none of the animals left the safety of the oasis.

Dobbin grabbed a low-hanging apple from a nearby tree and dismounted Shadowmane. He sliced off a piece of apple with his knife. Juices ran down the blade and a fruity, ripe aroma filled the air.

Tart sweetness exploded in his mouth when he took a bite, and the taste of honey lingered on his tongue. Dobbin closed his eyes, savoring one of the most delicious apples he'd ever eaten.

"Wait until you try this." He handed the rest of the apple to Shadowmane.

Dobbin stepped further into the meadow, wondering how any of this was possible.

"Snort!" he called as he searched for the direhog's tail above the flowers. "Where are you?"

A grunt answered, but it was more guttural than the pig's normal greetings.

Dobbin's hand went to his sword out of instinct. "Snort? Is that you?"

Leaves rustled, and a lizard-like head peeked out from behind a bush. A kobold. The creature was several feet tall, with long ears that jutted upward and several horns that ran along a ridge from its head to its neck. It stood on two legs with lilac-colored scales that spiked around its shoulders and arms. A flower dangled in its hand as it licked at the air.

The kobold growled as it stepped out from behind the bush, revealing its lighter-scaled underbelly and dangerous claws. Its eyes focused on Dobbin, and it grunted again.

Dobbin quickly scanned the area for more kobolds. The lizardfolk were as tricky as goblins. While a single one might pose little threat, they were extremely clever and used numbers to their advantage. They had a fondness for traps and tough scales that made them hard to kill.

Dobbin unsheathed Steadfast and pointed his weapon at the creature. "Where's the pig?"

Leaves rustled around the adventurer like a thousand snakes hissing, and vines shot up from the ground, wrapping around Dobbin's arms with lightning speed. More vines encircled his legs, squeezing tight until Dobbin couldn't move.

A soft whistle came from behind the kobold, and a moment later, a dwarf joined its side. She stroked her golden beard as her gaze fell upon Dobbin.

The dwarf was bigger than the kobold by a couple of feet, but she was barely taller than Dobbin's waist. She wore her blonde hair in a messy bun, and flowers and vines clung to her dirt-stained clothing. A brown cloak draped from her shoulders beneath a set of antlers covered in flora, and a string of flowers circled her neck. One hand gripped a gnarled staff, while the other glowed with a blue aura, outstretched in his direction.

She frowned at Dobbin. "That will be enough of that."

# 20. DRUIDS AND DRAGONS

Dobbin's heart raced as vines cinched harder around his extremities. He cursed his luck for the second time in as many days as his fingers went numb and the sword toppled to the ground.

The dwarf narrowed her emerald eyes. "Are you in the habit of drawing your sword on everyone who tries to say hello?"

The kobold cowered behind the dwarf, peeking its head around her side to lick at the air.

Dobbin struggled against the vines holding him in place, but every movement only made them grow tighter as they continued to constrict around him.

He struggled to speak as pressure mounted against his chest. "Just…looking…for…pig."

"I bet you are." She rolled her eyes. "You adventurers are all the same. Willing to stab anything that moves."

"No. Not…food…pet."

The pressure released slightly, and Dobbin gasped for

air. Nearby, Shadowmane grazed on wildflowers without a care in the world. There was no way the horse would allow something to happen to Dobbin. The dwarf had to be doing something to keep him calm.

"Is that so?" She moved closer and the kobold followed, its shoulders hunched forward. "Then why did you pull your sword on Gru?"

"Are you serious?" Dobbin did little to hide his irritation even though he was at her mercy. "It's a kobold."

Kobolds were as mischievous as goblins. Not only did they use traps and rudimentary weapons, they also had dangerous talons, sharp teeth, and powerful jaws. Dobbin once witnessed a gnome lose a hand while trying to wrangle one of the monsters.

The dwarf wagged a glowing blue finger at him. "Gru wouldn't hurt a fly."

Dobbin was about to argue when Snort's familiar grunts came from behind the bush. A moment later, she appeared next to the dwarf and kobold. She sniffed at them both but showed no fear of the monster.

The kobold held its flower toward Snort, and she chomped off the flower head, leaving the kobold holding a stem. It growled at Snort, but there didn't seem to be any malice behind it.

The dwarf gave Dobbin a knowing look. "See?"

"Okay, I get it. It's not dangerous."

The dwarf laughed. "Oh, Gru's plenty dangerous. He's just not violent." She took several more steps until she was standing only a few feet in front of Dobbin. "What I want to know is what you're doing in Hells' Crag?"

"I could ask you the same thing." He nodded toward the trees. "This all your doing?"

She stared at Dobbin but didn't respond. Behind her, Gru picked a handful of flowers and was feeding them to Snort one by one.

After a long silence, Dobbin answered. "I'm here on a quest. I'm trying to find a special mushroom that only grows where a dragon has attacked."

"I see." Her gaze shifted toward the crag. "Many say that only fools venture into Hells' Crag. Are you a fool?"

Dobbin fought the urge to say he could ask her the same thing. He had a feeling that she wasn't going to hurt him, but he didn't want to press his luck.

He tried to shrug, but the vines restricted the movement. "It certainly seems that way at the moment."

To his surprise, she smiled. The vines unwound, retracting into the ground.

She held out her hand. It was no longer glowing. "Name's Myrtle."

"Dobbin." He flexed his fingers a few times to restore the circulation, then he shook her hand. Her grip was firm.

Myrtle pointed to the kobold with her thumb. "This is Gru. It's short for Grunt since that's how he communicates. His clan kicked him out when he was a hatchling because he's nonverbal. He's a sweet soul, though. Brilliant in his own way."

Dobbin laughed at the coincidence.

Myrtle placed a hand on her hip. "Something funny?"

He chuckled as he pointed at the direpig. "I call her Snort because of the noises she makes. And this one is Shadowmane." Dobbin narrowed his eyes at the horse. "I thought he was my partner, but I'll be reevaluating that soon enough."

"You should be thanking him. He's the reason I released you, after all. Despite your appearance, Shadowmane seems to think that you're decent enough." Myrtle gave Dobbin a side-eye. "I always trust a horse's intuition, and he has a good one. He didn't help you because he knew there was nothing to fear."

Dobbin rubbed his wrists. "You sure about that?"

"We don't get a lot of visitors around here. When we do, they're usually up to no good, so I hope you can understand my caution when I see someone waving a sword around." Myrtle knelt and Snort approached, sniffing at the flowers around her neck. "If I wanted to hurt you, you'd know it." She scratched the direpig under the chin, and Snort grunted with pleasure. "Who's a good little piggy? You are. Yes, you are."

"You seem to have a way with animals. I'm guessing you're a druid." Dobbin had assumed as much when the vines wrapped around him, but there were other branches of arcane capable of such magic. Druidic powers, however, went beyond summoning. They were attuned to the natural world in a way others were not. If she could communicate with Shadowmane, then she had to be one.

"Astute observation, Adventurer." Myrtle stood, staring at Dobbin with a look that reminded him of his mother. She was small but projected an undeniable authority. "If you're willing to risk life and limb for a mushroom, it must be a pretty good payout."

Dobbin nodded. "If I can make it back before Ahtenoght, it'll be enough to set many things right."

"Ahtenoght. The Festival of Fortune." She smiled. "How fitting."

"I'm beginning to think fortune isn't on my side. I saw flashes of light in the crag last night." He turned toward the ruins, remembering the energy pulsing within the darkness. "Do you know anything about that?"

"Do I know anything about that?" She laughed. "Do I look blind?"

Dobbin was so surprised by Myrtle's sarcasm that his cheeks reddened. If she was the one responsible for all this growth, then of course she knew about the crag.

"Fair point. Do you know what it is?"

"Truth be told, I've been rather busy out here. It's not easy cleansing blighted soil, and I've been working my way in for over two years now."

Dobbin's mouth dropped. "You did all of this by yourself?"

"I did. Inch by precious inch. But Bearmouth wasn't built in a day, so I press ever onward." She met Dobbin's gaze. "I ventured into the crag once, and I'll warn you, it's not for the faint of heart."

"I've read the stories," Dobbin said solemnly. He took a moment to appreciate how much work must have gone into reviving the land he was standing on. It couldn't have been easy. "Why is no one helping you?"

There was a flutter of wings as an owl descended from the sky, landing on one of the antlers attached to Myrtle's cloak. The owl held a mouse in its beak. Gru ran over, his arms outstretched toward the bird.

The owl released the mouse, and Gru grabbed it out of the air, devouring it in seconds.

"This is Tawny, the third member of our little party. She's my eyes in the sky." Myrtle stroked the owl under the neck, and its beak clicked. "I was just about to break for a bite to eat before you showed up. If you'd like to join, I can tell you what I know about the crag, and why you should go ahead and turn back."

# 21. HONOR THE DEAD

Myrtle was a nomad in every sense of the word. Her camp consisted of a wagon full of supplies and a firepit. She slept in a hammock that hung between two apple trees, and Gru had a smaller one that connected to one of the apple trees at an angle. The simple setup allowed them to move around the valley depending on where Myrtle was working at any given time.

They had the bare necessities but with such lush vegetation, they didn't need much. The work Myrtle had put in provided for all their needs. Animals roamed among the land she'd raised, providing ample food for both Gru and Tawny.

Dobbin sat near a fire as skewers of vegetables roasted over the open flame. Snort and Gru played in the tall grass, making a cacophony of noises while Shadowmane wandered around grazing.

Myrtle stood by the wagon filling her flask from a large cask. She lifted it in the air, sloshing the liquid around. "Thirsty?"

Dobbin grabbed his flask. "Sure, what are we having?"

She laughed. "None of the good stuff, I'm afraid. Just water."

"I was wondering about that." He joined her by the wagon. "The water in the crag looked about as rough as the rest of the ruins."

"There's a stream that filters down from the mountain about a mile away. I made a dam to keep the pure water separate from the tainted. I go and top off the water every month or so."

"I still can't believe you've been doing this all by yourself for two years?" Dobbin wore a look of wonder as he gazed upon the sprawling green that stretched toward the mountain. "You've made so much progress."

"And yet it's still just a drop in the bucket." Myrtle filled Dobbin's flask and then returned to rotate the skewers. "It was me, Tawny, and Nightwalker for the longest time. The horse loves to roam the valley, but she still shows up whenever I need to move the wagon or fetch water. About a year ago, I found Gru." She pointed toward the western mountains. "There's a clan of kobolds that live beyond the ruins. There was a nasty thunderstorm, and Tawny spotted Gru while she was out hunting. I found the poor thing whimpering beneath a bush, shivering from the cold. He's been with me ever since."

"You speak of the animals like you can really understand them."

"That's because I can." Myrtle turned to Dobbin, one eye narrowed. "Let me ask you, do you talk to your horse? Do you talk to the pig?"

Dobbin wasn't sure where she was going with this, but he answered, "I do."

"They can understand some of your words, right? And when they're hungry, or tired, or frustrated, you're able to intuit that, yes?"

Dobbin nodded. "Most of the time."

Myrtle pulled one of the skewers and handed it to Dobbin. Steam wafted from their charred edges. "Being a druid is not that different. I can sense what they are feeling. And in turn, I can project my thoughts to them."

"That's fascinating." Dobbin finally took a bite of the skewer. The char to the outside was crisp and flavorful. A tomato burst as he bit into it, exploding juices down his beard. "Wow, this is delicious."

Myrtle smiled. "You'd be surprised what plants can do when you give them a little love."

"Is that why you're here? It's impressive work, bringing all of this back to life, but I have to think the kingdom could really use someone with your talents."

"What I'm doing here is important." She took on a more serious tone. "When you venture into the crag, you'll understand why."

Dobbin finished the last of the skewer and tossed the stick into the fire. "What does that mean?"

"You asked me if I saw the glow around the crag at night." Myrtle sighed. "How could I not? It's haunting. The glow comes from the spirits that still reside within the ruins. Thousands of them. They continue with their lives, reliving the same routine night after night." Myrtle stood, clenching her fists as if anger was bubbling just beneath the service. "Everyone forgot about them. Our entire people pushed the city from their memories as if it had never existed in the first place. We're a people bound by our community, or at least we used to be. In dwarven culture, we honor the dead, but somehow when it comes to Hells' Crag, everyone would rather pretend that the attack never happened. I, for one, want to set the spirits to rest."

Dobbin wanted to offer comfort, but he didn't know where to begin. For too long, he'd been haunted by his memories of Henrik, a ghost he'd never been able to put to rest. Since that night long ago, there was always another quest or another bounty, as if enough coin could clear his conscience and make things right.

He looked up, aware of Myrtle's lingering gaze. "How do you plan to do that?"

"By bringing life back to the crag." She pointed to the ruins that towered in the distance. "If I can cleanse the blighted soil and nurture the flora and fauna to return, the fog will recede and the clouds will open once again. Spirits linger because they are still tethered to the past, but they have guarded the ruins long enough."

In all his years, he'd never heard of druids being dispatched to deal with ghosts or angry spirits. It was always clerics. But given what Myrtle had done already, Dobbin wasn't going to write her off just yet.

He frowned. "Wouldn't it be easier to just go into the crag itself and start the cleansing?"

"Shall I start instructing you on the best way to swing a sword or ride a horse?" Myrtle laughed. "Follow me."

She led Dobbin to the edge of the meadow where they'd first met. The ripe plant life formed a stark barrier against the tainted soil.

Myrtle stepped beyond her sanctuary into the thick fog, walking a ways before turning around. "The gods have blessed me with many gifts."

Her hand took on a white aura, and the fog began to glow from within, slowly dissipating around a patch of land to reveal the blighted soil. It sizzled as dark gray smoke rose from the earth, changing the soil from an ashen gray to deep brown. Myrtle grimaced as sweat beaded down her face. The ground continued to smoke, and pieces of decrepit grass shriveled away until there was nothing but a patch of fertile soil.

She wiped sweat from her forehead with the back of her hand. "I can cleanse disease and negative effects from plants and animals, water, and soil. I can tend to their injuries and mend imperfections. Anywhere else, I could cleanse rotted soil with a wave of my hand, but dragon flame is toxic and lingers long after the fire is gone. I've never had to work so hard for so little."

Myrtle reached into a pouch around her waist and scattered a handful of seeds over the area. Then she uncorked a small cask hanging from her back and doused the soil with water. A yellow aura surrounded her hand as she reached for the sky, and a moment later, sunlight pierced through the clouds, just like Dobbin had witnessed earlier. The light pushed the fog back even further as it bathed the area in light.

"I can call upon the power of the sun to help promote growth, but even that is troublesome here."

The seeds split open and began to sprout. Shoots and roots spread out as the saplings took to the soil. Leaves unfurled and after a few minutes, a layer of fresh green growth coated the area. The plants were small, but they grew where nothing would moments ago.

Sweat glistened on Myrtle's forehead once again. "Growing full plants from seedlings takes a toll. I could spend more time nurturing this piece of land until it was the same size and strength as the rest, or I could work smarter."

She returned to the meadow, repeating the same process to cleanse an area of soil that bordered the thriving prairie. Once the soil was ready, Myrtle knelt, placing her palm on the ground. A vibrant green aura surrounded her as the plant life shuddered in unison. Fruit fell from the nearby trees, and then roots spread outward from the meadow as the plants began to spread and propagate. Soon, it too was covered in new growth.

Myrtle stood, and sweat droplets shimmered within her beard. "To answer your question, it's easier to encourage strong plants to spread outward than it is to raise them from seeds on blighted soil. When I'm surrounded by nature, my magic thrives. The effects of the dragon's flames are most potent in the crag. A flower cannot sustain itself without roots, and if I were to try and push back the darkness from the center, I would surely fail."

"So you're working your way from the outside in."

She tapped the side of her temple. "Precisely."

Dobbin turned to face the crag. Although Myrtle had made a great deal of progress, the goal was still so far away. "You've got your work cut out for you, I'll give you that."

"If it were easy, I wouldn't be the only one doing it. I'm guessing the same thing could be said for you."

"Truer words have never been spoken." Dobbin laughed. "Speaking of which, I should probably get moving. I'm sorry we got off on the wrong foot, but I wish you the best. You're doing good work out here, Myrtle."

Myrtle frowned as she gauged the sun's position in the sky. "You've lost a good piece of the day learning how I do things, and I doubt you'll make it to the crag before night-fall. I'll come with you, at least to the gate, and show you what you're up against. I have a few tricks to keep you safe at night."

Dobbin sighed. "Don't take this the wrong way, but I work alone."

"I'm not asking to be your partner." Myrtle rolled her eyes. "But if you think you know these lands better than me, then by all means, go get yourself killed."

Dobbin cursed under his breath. She was right. More adventurers than he could count had ventured into the ruins to never return, while Myrtle had survived for over two years. For every job and every quest, Dobbin put in hours of meticulous research, and yet here he was about to turn down a primary source.

"Fine," he grumbled.

"What's that?" Myrtle wore a mischievous smile.

"I said, 'Fine.'" Dobbin gestured toward the crag. "Show me the way."

# 22. HELLS' CRAG

Dobbin and Myrtle returned to camp and gathered the animals before heading to the crag. They arrived to the growls and squeals of Snort and Gru as the duo wrestled in the tall grass. They had managed to flatten a large patch of wildflowers by rolling around and chasing one another.

Snort looked up when she heard Dobbin, giving him her attention for a moment before ramming her head into Gru. The kobold unleashed a menacing growl as he pounced on the direpig, playfully biting at the mane of tough hair on the back of her neck. Snort spun around, slamming her backside into the kobold and knocking him to the ground. Their scuffle continued for several minutes while Myrtle packed a satchel for the journey.

When she was finished, Myrtle put her fingers to her lips and whistled. The sound cut through the air, garnering the animals' attention. "We're moving out."

Both creatures stopped fighting and gathered by her side.

"Now that is impressive." Dobbin grinned.

Myrtle winked. "Oh, you sweet adventurer. You haven't seen anything yet."

Dobbin raised a brow. "Somehow, I don't think that's as comforting as you intended it to be."

"Darling, it wasn't meant to be comforting." Myrtle smiled as she tapped Dobbin on the arm. "You chose this path. Now, let's get moving."

Dobbin chuckled to himself as he climbed onto Shadowmane. He patted the horse on the neck and whispered, "What have I gotten myself into, old friend?"

Shadowmane flicked his tail and set off.

With Myrtle traveling on foot, the pace was slower than Dobbin would have liked. He offered her a seat on Shadowmane, but she refused, saying she was a "one-horse dwarf." Her horse, Nightwalker, was roaming free somewhere in the valley. Dobbin wished Myrtle would've called for the horse to speed the journey along, but at least he was finally heading toward the crag.

Fog clouded the ruins in the distance, where stone walls and crumbled structures rose above the mist like islands. Dobbin's skin prickled every time he looked upon them, wondering what might be waiting.

Tawny perched on Myrtle's shoulder as she walked. The owl bobbed her head with each step while Snort and Gru punctuated the silence with their snorts and grunts. The pig and kobold had become great friends rather quickly, and Dobbin hated to think of breaking them apart.

That would be a problem for tomorrow.

As they moved closer to the crag, Dobbin sensed a change in Myrtle. Her playful and sarcastic nature was replaced by something more somber. No doubt she was feeling the same sense of dread that he was.

"So, where'd you live before you came here?" asked Dobbin. As much as he hated small talk, he did his best to take her mind off the journey.

"Bearmouth." Myrtle kept her gaze on the ruins.

Dobbin rubbed the bridge of his nose. Apparently, he was going to have to pry the words out of her. "I was actually just there. I'd hoped to find a little more information about this place."

Myrtle glanced in his direction. "How'd that work out for you?"

"About as well as you'd expect." Dobbin sighed. "Nobody wants to talk about Hells' Crag. Every person I've spoken to has told me to turn back."

"That's how it goes." Myrtle gave him a sympathetic expression.

"Do you ever think you'll go back?" he asked.

She shrugged. "Maybe one day. Bearmouth is a wonderful city, but I prefer the solace of nature."

"I understand that. There's nothing like the cool night air under a blanket of stars. But don't you ever miss being around other people? I love being on the road as much as anyone, but after a long journey, there's something special about sharing a drink and a story with likeminded folk."

Myrtle laughed. "That is something I miss from time to time. It's been ages since I last had a good ale. But the work makes up for it."

Dobbin recalled the bottle of wine Eris had given him.

"If we make it out of this, I've got something that might brighten your spirits."

Myrtle waggled her brows. "Well, aren't you the man of mystery?"

Dobbin smirked. "I've been told it's an attractive quality."

Myrtle stopped in her tracks and cackled. "I'm sure for some it is. Personally, I prefer someone who isn't afraid to put it all on the table."

Dobbin matched her grin. "I don't think you're going to find that hiding away here."

"This won't be ruins forever." Myrtle waved her hand through the air as if banishing the idea. "One day, I'll wake up to the sun shining overhead and my lady's beard resting against my shoulder. That's when I'll know that everything was worth it."

"That's a nice sentiment." Dobbin's thoughts drifted briefly to Lyra. Would he ever see her again, or had their night together been a shooting star, never to return? He pushed the thoughts away and returned his attention to the conversation. "What'd your folks think about you leaving? Are there other druids in your family?"

Myrtle wagged a finger at Dobbin. "Once you get going, you don't stop, do you? And here I was thinking you were the silent, brooding type."

Dobbin held in his laughter and shrugged. "What can I say? You're an interesting person."

"Don't I know it." She grinned. "My folks told me I was wasting my time coming here. They said that nothing would ever grow here again. I'm proving them wrong one day at a time."

"Spite can be one hell of a motivator."

"It's not spite." She shook her head. "At least not entirely. I want to leave behind something that I can be proud of. There have been other druids in the family, and they've all done great things. My grandmother was a servant of the people. When there was a famine a couple of centuries back, she went from farm to farm across the countryside to nourish the crops. What should have been death was one of the most bountiful harvests the kingdom has ever seen. Her grandmother attended the royal gardens in Bearmouth and was said to have caught the eye of Prince Bordin. There's a legacy among the druids in my family. The gift seems to skip a generation and only runs on the maternal side."

"Look at what you've done already. It won't be long before you have your own legacy."

Myrtle looked over her shoulder, where the meadows she'd blossomed were hidden beyond a wall of fog. "If the gods will it."

A coolness pressed down upon the valley, growing colder the closer they moved toward the ruins. Conversations died and they traveled in silence. Even Snort and Gru walked closer together, their noises few and far between. Tawny let out a soft hoot, and Shadowmane tensed beneath Dobbin as the daylight turned to dusk.

Something moved in the foggy depths, and Dobbin's hand went to his sword out of instinct. He raised the pommel of Brightblade slightly, and its blade glowed faintly within the sheath.

He swallowed hard, gripping the reins tighter. Dobbin still didn't know what caused the weapon to glow, but this was the second time it had activated.

Myrtle held up a hand for them to stop. "This is the

road that leads up the crag and into the city. Be careful. It gets a bit treacherous now."

A moment later, Shadowmane's hooves clopped against ancient stone that had once been the road. The stones were melted and misshapen in places. In some areas, it was as if they'd erupted from the earth.

Dobbin dismounted, leading Shadowmane the rest of the way on foot.

Myrtle turned to face them. "I'll take you to the gate, and then we can go back down and camp for the night. You'll want to save your adventuring for daylight."

Dobbin nodded. He held the reins in one hand and rested the other on the hilt of his sword.

The terrain sloped gently upward, and the slosh of water nearby reminded him that the lake was close, even though it was obscured by the fog. Up the way, remnants of a tall wall stretched from one side of the crag to the other, ending at the cliffside above the lake. The stone was melted in places and crumbled in others. Some sections were half their original height, while others were destroyed entirely.

Snort pressed close to Dobbin's legs as they approached the gate. To his left, Gru clutched Myrtle's cloak between his scaly fingers.

They stopped about fifty yards from the gate, taking it all in. One of the guard towers had been obliterated. Another had a door-sized hole in the side. The metal that had once been the portcullis lay deformed across the battered street. There was a stench to the air that Dobbin couldn't place, unpleasant and toxic.

Behind them, the sun dipped beyond the mountains, taking the last rays of light with it. They'd made it just in time, and now the moon lingered beyond the overcast sky, bathing the clouds in a silver radiance.

"What's that?" Myrtle pointed at Dobbin's cloak where the essence ward glowed beneath the fabric. Tiny pricks of light illuminated the pocket it was concealed in.

Dobbin removed the ward from his pocket. It shone with the intensity of a glowstone.

"This is an essence ward." He held it up for her to see. "It detects when spirits are close."

"You've got to be shitting me." She rolled her eyes and turned to Gru. "He brings an essence ward to haunted ruins. How useful."

Dobbin frowned. "I didn't know what I was going to—"

Something clanked beyond the gate, making Snort squeal. The hair on Dobbin's neck stood on end, and a moment later, more noises emerged from beyond the wall. If Dobbin didn't know any better, he'd have sworn there was a bustling city on the other side.

A blue aura appeared beyond the gate, wispy at first, but then it began to take shape. Ethereal bodies formed from the energy, walking through the ruined city with purpose. A trio of dwarven guards marched in perfect sync past the gate, their pikes standing high above their heads.

Dobbin felt a chill as the ghost of a farmer appeared from the fog behind them, his cart loaded with produce. The wheels rattled against the stone, passing through the debris as if it weren't there. A guard in the watch tower waved him through. Somewhere beyond the wall, the forge of a blacksmith clanked rhythmically.

Myrtle's eyes glistened as she watched the farmer

disappear into the city. "This happens every night. I've watched that farmer enter the gates a dozen times."

Dobbin gulped. There were so many of them. He'd read the stories, but words on a page didn't do this justice. There were some things one had to experience to truly understand them. This was one of them.

Myrtle tapped him on the arm. "Let's go."

They made it back into the valley just as the wailing began.

"That would be the specters. They scream and howl all night." Myrtle gazed toward the crag, and there was an overwhelming sadness about her. "I'm sure you saw the flashes of light within the keep? I believe there is a wraith in there as well, but I've never seen it."

Dobbin frowned. He'd read about the different types of spirits at the library. Ghosts and apparitions were mostly harmless. While a ghost had enough cognizance to interact with the world around it, apparitions existed in a cycle. Like the farmer and the guards, they would replay scenes from their death day in perpetuity. Specters were dangerous beings created when someone died a tragic death. The cries told Dobbin that there were more than a handful beyond the wall.

And then there were wraiths, the untethered spirits composed of anger and hate. They were the most danger-ous, capable of destroying entire villages, and extremely difficult to defeat. Their presence alone provided an anchor for lesser spirits to congregate. If there was a wraith, it explained why there were so many apparitions.

Dobbin wasn't sure what led to one type of spirit forming over another. As tragic as the attack on Hells' Crag had been, he wouldn't have been surprised if there were thousands of specters in the ruins. But it seemed that the apparitions were the most prominent, at least from their viewpoint beyond the gate.

If there was a wraith in the keep, Dobbin wanted to stay as far away from there as possible.

He kept watch while Myrtle began making camp. Tawny circled overhead, a second pair of watchful eyes. Myrtle cleared an area of land big enough for all of them to sleep, pushing back the fog and cleansing the soil. Her face was covered in sweat by the time she finished.

"I've got salt and silver wire to wrap around the camp," Dobbin offered.

"That won't be necessary. I have my own means of protection."

Myrtle took a pouch of seeds from her cloak and started humming as she spread them around the edge of the clearing. The tune sounded familiar, and Dobbin tried to recall where he'd heard it before.

Myrtle covered the seeds with her foot while she sang softly, "*Oh, thistle thorns, protect us from the dead.*"

Dobbin recognized the words. It was the same song Dalla had sung at the inn near Hillside.

"*Tear through their ghastly visage.*" Myrtle continued to sing as she covered more seeds with the cleansed soil. As she moved around the perimeter, her hand glowed green and stalks shot up from the earth. "*In this haunted land, grant them peace and rest. Oh, thistle thorns, protect us from the dead.*"

Being in the crag, the words had a heavier weight to them than at the inn.

"I've heard that song before. What is it you're planting?" Dobbin asked.

The plants grew more rapidly than they ever would on their own. Leaves sprouted along the stem, and a prickly ball formed at the top.

"They're called ghost thistles. In ancient times, the lowland dwarves planted them on the graves of the dead. They're meant to prevent ghosts from forming. If a spirit passes by the thistle, its thorns will tear through the visage, granting them the peace to move onward. Once the thistles have served their purpose, the bracts will open, revealing beautiful blue flowers to let the loved ones know they've passed on."

Dobbin nodded. The old dwarf at the inn had told a similar story. In the right situation, it might be a comforting notion. Out here, it only reminded Dobbin of the danger they were in.

"They can really protect us from what's in there?" Dobbin raised a brow as he pointed toward the ruins that glowed an intense blue.

"We don't have much to fear down here but yes, ghost thistles can disapparate ghosts and apparitions. They can even temporarily dissipate specters. As long as the animals don't eat them. They love the taste for some reason. I've been planting them across the valley, but the deer keep eating them."

"And wraiths?"

"I'm not sure." Myrtle stroked her beard. "The thistles are intended to grant peace before a spirit ever reaches that level of anguish."

Dobbin drew Brightblade from its sheath. The silver blade glowed a light blue, not quite as intense as the previous day. Silver could disapparate the lesser three spirits as well, but they would all reform with time. The fact that a plant could actually send ghosts to the next life was wondrous.

He raised the blade for Myrtle to see. "I bought this in Bearmouth. I got it because the blade is forged of pure silver, but it has these runes along the hilt. They cause the blade to glow under certain conditions. It happened yesterday when shadow fairies tried to steal the sword, and again now that we're near the keep. It doesn't work the same as the essence ward, and I still don't have the faintest idea as to what it actually does."

Myrtle shrugged. "Runes are not my area of expertise, unfortunately." She frowned. "Though shadow fairies and spirits often lurk in similar areas, maybe there's something to that."

"Maybe." He put the sword away and retrieved his satchel from Shadowmane. "Don't take it personally, but I'm going to stake the perimeter and run silver wire just to be safe."

Myrtle shook her head, grinning. "Of course you are."

After he finished running the wire, they all sat around a small fire. Snort and Gru cuddled together at Myrtle's feet, unusually quiet even when Dobbin gathered his rations.

"They can sense it," Myrtle said as she handed out apples from her satchel.

Dobbin felt a sense of unease as well. It practically radiated from the crag. "What does it feel like to them?"

Myrtle caressed Gru along the back of his skull. "Despair."

They ate their dinner in silence, listening to the sounds of the crag. The wailing specters became less intense, but they flared occasionally. With no wildlife for miles in either direction, the sounds from within the ruins carried far, amplified by the lake's surface. It was as if Dobbin was in his shack back in Eastborne, listening to the city through his windows. Occasionally, the wail of a specter reminded him just how false that notion was.

"There is a beauty to it." Myrtle patted him on the leg. "As tragic as it is, to know that so many people once lived and loved within those walls is special."

Dobbin wasn't sure if he saw it that way. "I hope that one day, you can grant them peace." He stood, watching the eerie glow of the ruins. "Do you want first watch or should I?"

"First watch?" Myrtle raised a brow. "What do you plan on doing when you're on your own?"

He shrugged. "I'll cross that bridge when I get to it."

"Get some rest." Myrtle smiled. "Tawny will keep watch. She has better eyes than both of us, I assure you."

Dobbin hesitated. He'd trusted Shadowmane to watch after him when they were on the road, but sleeping without someone on guard this close to the keep went against every instinct he had. Myrtle had survived out here far longer than he had, though.

Reluctantly, Dobbin took his bedroll and laid it on the ground. "See you in the morning."

# 23. INTO THE UNKNOWN

When Dobbin woke, Snort was nestled in the crook of his arm. Gru sat on his haunches next to them, watching Dobbin intently. The kobold's tongue drooped out of the side of his mouth.

"Morning, Gru."

Gru growled, which Dobbin assumed was a similar sentiment.

Myrtle was already up. She held a steaming mug in her hand and smiled at Dobbin. "He's been awake for hours waiting for Snort."

"That's considerate of him." Dobbin reached out and scratched Gru underneath his chin. The kobold tilted his head back and grunted.

"I told you he's a good boy." She lifted her mug slightly. "Tea?"

"That would be great." Dobbin sat up without disturbing the direhog. "I guess you'll be on your way this morning?"

"Actually, I've changed my mind." Myrtle took a sip

from her mug and grinned. "We'll go with you. You might need someone to keep watch at night."

Dobbin had the feeling she was mocking him, but he didn't argue.

As much as he wanted to work alone, with specters and a possible wraith within the keep, it would be foolish to turn her away.

Snort finally woke and the first thing she did was pounce on Gru. The two tumbled around, rolling through the ash of the dead fire and flattening one of the ghost thistles.

While Myrtle poured Dobbin a mug of tea, he examined the ring of plants surrounding their camp, noticing that none of them had bloomed overnight.

"I told you," Myrtle said as if reading his mind. She handed Dobbin the mug.

He wasn't much of a tea drinker, but it would help fight the morning chill. He raised the mug and sniffed before taking a sip. The tea had a beautiful floral aroma, and the taste was slightly sweet and fruity. The warmth trailed down his throat and into his belly.

"This is pretty good. You make it yourself?"

Myrtle raised a brow. "No, I get a delivery every fortnight. Shall I put in a request for you?"

"Funny," Dobbin said dryly.

"You make it too easy." Myrtle smirked.

Dobbin finished his tea and began preparing for the day. He pulled Brightblade from the sheath before attaching it around his waist. The blade still had a dull glow to it, even in the morning light. The essence ward, however, was completely dark. Dobbin frowned at his lack of understanding before putting the ward back in his cloak pocket.

Myrtle handed out apples to Shadowmane and Snort and then tossed one to Dobbin. For Gru, she pulled an egg from within her cloak. The kobold swallowed it in one bite.

After removing the silver wire and stakes from around the camp, Dobbin saddled Shadowmane. Myrtle pulled a knife from her belt and began cutting the thistle heads from the top of the plants, tossing them in an empty sack.

"What are you doing?" asked Dobbin.

She held up one of the prickly flower heads. "If you have to ask that question, you really do need my help."

Dobbin narrowed his eyes but chose not to respond. The only other person who antagonized him this much was Alina. His size and demeanor were enough to intimidate most folk, but somehow, those two found enjoyment in goading him. For a moment, he imagined the two of them in a room together. The thought of them both taking their shots was enough for him to squash the image immediately.

In the early morning light, the gate into the city was less ominous than it had been at night. Though it still had an eerie atmosphere from the thick fog that spread across the ruins, there was an air of mystery to their surroundings. Ghosts and apparitions didn't usually appear during daylight, especially out in the open, but Dobbin wasn't sure if the fog might alter that. Clouds concealed the sun, leaving them in a state of perpetual gloom. Even so, specters could appear during the day, though their power was said to be mitigated. They could also blend into the ether, making them impossible to notice before it was too late. And the wraiths… Dobbin preferred not to think about them.

He led Shadowmane on foot as they passed underneath the gate and entered the city. Even with the fog, widespread destruction stretched in every direction. There wasn't a building in sight that hadn't been affected by the dragon attack to some degree.

Scorch marks abounded. There were city blocks that had been completely leveled. One building had the stone melted to the ground on one side but was untouched on the other. For most of the structures, it was impossible for Dobbin to imagine what they'd once been.

According to the records, Hells' Crag had been an imposing city in its prime. Dobbin had seen sketches and paintings of what it had looked like before the attack. The crag grew taller the further it went into the lake, and the buildings grew more magnificent as well. The keep had been the tallest structure around. Its towering spires were the pinnacle of dwarven architecture.

As Dobbin looked around, he realized they could spend days searching the ruins for signs of mushrooms.

"Where should we start?" asked Dobbin. Since Myrtle was the only one who'd been here before, it made sense to follow her lead.

She looked around as if sizing the city up. "Mushrooms like to grow in damp and dark places. There's plenty of opportunity for that here. There's a constant source of moisture from the fog, but that doesn't mean a whole lot. I'd start by searching for areas where buildings form natural shadows along the sun's path.

"How about over here?" Dobbin pointed toward a building that had once been a temple. A corner of the building had collapsed, but he recognized the crest of Pidros, the God of Mining, that was a common sight in dwarven cities. The door it adorned was warped along the edges.

"That's as good a spot as any." She nodded. "What is it we're looking for exactly?"

Dobbin pulled the sketch from within his cloak and handed it to her. The paper depicted a mushroom with a charcoal-colored cap with reddish-orange gills underneath. "They call it the dragonfire mushroom."

"I've heard of it. Never seen one, though." Myrtle rubbed the bridge of her nose when she saw the sketch. "This is going to be like searching for a needle in a haystack. The damned thing's the same color as the rubble."

"I didn't expect it to be easy." Dobbin shrugged. "Can't you, I don't know, try to talk to the plants or something?"

Myrtle cackled. "Is it a sentient mushroom?"

Dobbin's cheeks burned, and he focused on moving some of the rubble around. "I don't believe so."

Myrtle grinned mischievously. "Why don't you ask that rock if it knows where the mushroom is?"

Dobbin focused on a particularly uninteresting rock to avoid her gaze. "Point taken."

They rummaged among the rubble, moving stones and charred wood. Some of the pieces were so heavy that Dobbin had to attach a rope to Shadowmane in order to move them, but nothing grew even in the darkest corners they uncovered.

Myrtle stopped to catch her breath, wiping sweat from her brow. "What's so special about this mushroom that they'd send you halfway across the realm to find it?"

Dobbin lifted a plank of wood and tossed it aside. "They believe it has the power to grant visions."

Myrtle stroked her beard. "Is that so?"

"For what they're paying, I certainly hope so."

"People will spend their coin on anything these days." She shook her head. "If they wanted to hallucinate, I've got some special tea leaves they can buy."

Dobbin laughed. "You don't believe a mushroom could grant visions?"

"I don't know one way or another. But in my experience, true divination is a gift to those who work for it."

Snort's ears perked up and she stared into the fog. Next to her, Gru let out a menacing growl. Even Shadowmane huffed his agitation.

"What is it?" Dobbin scanned the area but saw nothing.

Myrtle narrowed her eyes. "They heard something. I'll have Tawny do a fly-by to check it out."

They continued searching for signs of the mushrooms while the owl investigated the area. After several minutes, Tawny returned carrying something in her mouth. She dropped a broken shell the size of Dobbin's fist on the ground in front of Myrtle.

Myrtle picked it up. "This is odd."

Gru stood in front of Myrtle, grasping for the shell and sniffing at the air. The shell belonged to a massive cave snail, and there were remnants of its slimy flesh still within.

Dobbin frowned as he examined it. "I thought nothing could live here?"

"So did I."

He extended a hand. "May I?"

Myrtle handed him the shell and he crouched next to Snort, holding the dead snail for her to smell. A direhog's sense of smell was one of the best in Aedrea, allowing them to track down roots and tubers buried underground. Snails and mushrooms often inhabited similar climates, so if there was somewhere a snail could survive within the crag, then a mushroom likely could as well.

"Can you find this?" he asked Snort.

She pressed her snout to the shell and sniffed. Then she stared at Dobbin.

"Here, let me help." Myrtle knelt, closing her eyes and cradling Snort's head in her palm.

The normally energetic direpig calmed, closing her eyes as well. When she opened them, Snort sniffed at the air and set off deeper into the crag.

"We best tread carefully," Myrtle warned. "Something cracked that shell open, and I have a feeling we're going to find out exactly what it was."

Dobbin's mind went to the trap that caught him on his way into the valley. Maybe it hadn't been that old after all. He raised Brightblade an inch from its sheath. The blade was glowing stronger than it had been outside the gate. Whatever was activating it was close.

They abandoned the search for the mushroom and followed Snort. She worked like a hound, zigging and zagging as she followed the scent. A moment later, she stopped, her nose pressed against the dried carapace of a crustacean. There were definitely creatures living some-where within the ruins.

Tawny circled overhead, but the fog was thick enough that she likely couldn't see anything too close to the ground. Dobbin had assumed the tunnels that ran beneath the city were destroyed or filled with rubble, but there was a possibility that some had endured the attack. The crag had been designed similarly to Bearmouth, with a maze of underground tunnels and structures. Some had been documented, but many that ran underneath the keep were kept from official records.

Was it possible that something had moved into the ruins?

If there was, it was venturing to the surface as well.

They passed more shells and carapaces the deeper into the city they traveled. Some were long-dried, but others still had flecks of meat attached.

Snort stopped in front of a stairwell that led under-ground. A neighboring building had collapsed, and rubble nearly concealed the entrance. There was a narrow passage along one side, barely big enough for Myrtle to fit. The way the dirt was disturbed on the steps told Dobbin it had been used recently.

Myrtle looked him in the eye. "This isn't ominous at all."

Before he could reply, a gong sounded, and feet scur-ried within the fog. Dobbin drew his sword, which blazed with light. A high-pitched, guttural language could just barely be heard as the gong continued to ripple.

A small green humanoid appeared from the fog pointing a spear in their direction. The goblin had large green ears, and one drooped across its massive forehead.

Yellow eyes flared, and it snarled, revealing a mouth full of sharp teeth. The creature was slender and wore pieces of leather stitched together. Thick yellow nails covered its fingertips as it held a crude spear in one hand. The stone tip of the spearhead passed through a thistle several inches from the end. The goblin shouted in a high-pitched tone, thrusting the spear forward and speaking a language Dobbin couldn't understand.

Snort took a protective stance, and Gru bared his teeth. For the first time, Dobbin understood the difference between the kobold's playfulness and anger. Shadowmane neighed, shifting his hooves as if ready for a fight. Next to them, Myrtle's hands glowed a vibrant orange.

The goblin stepped forward, thrusting the spear in their direction again. It spoke, and more voices answered from within the fog. They were surrounded on all sides. Dozens of goblins had appeared from within. Some pointed arrows from the top of ruined buildings. Others held spears or primitive axes and hammers. They all wore necklaces of thistle bracts. Many had attached the flowers to their weapons as well.

The goblins quieted, and footsteps—soft like raindrops on a still lake—echoed from within the tunnel. Pebbles rattled as they descended the stairwell into the underground depths.

Brightblade flared with light as a pair of green ears tipped with gray fuzz appeared from within the tunnel. An elder goblin emerged, her skin wrinkled and the same dull gray as unformed clay. Her eyes were a piercing blue as they moved from the goblin holding a spear at Dobbin and then over the rest of their party.

The elder goblin held a crustacean in one hand, slurping at its insides as she sized them up. She tossed it aside, and her hand flashed with a blue aura. Dobbin gripped his sword tighter, and Myrtle gasped as the fog disappeared in a wide circle, revealing nearly two dozen goblins, as an orb of water formed and hovered in front of the mage. The elder goblin manipulated the water, drinking from it as it floated in the air.

Dobbin swallowed hard. An arcane goblin living among the ruins. What had they gotten themselves into?

# 24. STRUGGLES

After drinking her fill, the goblin mage released her hold on the floating orb and it splashed against the blighted soil. Her orange eyes gave nothing away as she stared down Myrtle and Dobbin.

Every instinct told Dobbin to attack, but he hesitated, not wanting to put Myrtle or the others in danger. The goblins hadn't attacked yet, so perhaps there was a way out of this without a fight. And if not, an opportunity would present itself if he kept his head about him.

Brightblade shone brighter than ever as he pointed it at the goblin. Compared to his great sword, its light weight was barely noticeable as he held the weapon at arm's end.

There were legends of kobolds and goblins possessing arcane magic, but he'd never believed them. In the tales, the creatures wreaked havoc on par with behemoths and wyverns, causing incalculable destruction because they had little regard for the rules of society. The Narrow River was said to have been born when a kobold possessing earth magic had burrowed from Barrowsturm to the sea.

Right now, they were all in immense danger. If Dobbin killed the mage quickly, they could fight off the rest. But one false move and the elder goblin could end them all. Dobbin's free hand slid to the great sword at his waist, resting on the hilt.

Myrtle held a hand in front of him as if sensing his thoughts.

"Wait," she whispered, not taking her eyes off the elder.

The goblins surrounding them snarled and growled, all except the elder. Dobbin didn't care how many of them there were, the mage was the threat. If they took her out, the rest would be manageable.

"They don't want to hurt us." Myrtle kept her arm raised, as if dropping it would unleash a tidal wave of destruction.

Dobbin held his blade steady as he scanned the area. Dozens of goblins stood with weapons pointed in their direction, their catlike eyes hungry for violence. "You could have fooled me."

"We intruded on their land." Myrtle's voice was calm and steady.

He raised a questioning brow. "How do you know this?"

"I can sense it. In the same way I can communicate with Gru. Goblins are connected to the animal world as much as kobolds."

"You're willing to risk all of our lives on this?"

"I am." Her voice was resolute.

Dobbin felt the aged leather on the grip of his great

sword. It was soiled with the blood, sweat, and tears of battle, a weapon that had saved his life countless times over the years. As steadfast as its name. He gave it a squeeze and then his hand dropped to his side. He lowered the brilliant blade of the enchanted sword as well. It glowed vibrantly, and Dobbin thought he might finally understand what caused it to activate. Both the shadow fairies and the elder goblin were creatures capable of using magic. While arcane monsters were rare, the person who'd forged his weapon might have been a collector who needed an easy way to identify them—especially considering where the weapon had ended up.

Though Dobbin lowered his sword, the goblins still stood aggressively, all except for the elder. She watched Myrtle with a curious expression. It was as if the two of them were having a conversation without the need for words.

Myrtle stepped back, and there was chatter among the goblins. A word from the elder quieted them.

Dobbin's hands twitched restlessly, but he didn't move. He'd chosen to trust Myrtle's instincts for now. Even so, standing idle while surrounded by threats went against his very nature.

A white aura surrounded the druid's hand and she began to cleanse a small area of soil beneath the rubble. Smoke rose from the ground as her abilities took effect, and sweat blossomed on her brow. The goblins watched in silence. After several minutes, the gray soil was a healthy brown.

Myrtle reached into a pouch at her waist and pulled out a seed, tossing it on the ground. She looked to the elder goblin expectantly.

The elder spoke in her guttural tongue, and then her hand took on a blue aura once again as the fog cleared even further. Another orb of water formed from the mist, and the goblin released it over the seed, darkening the soil.

Myrtle smiled as she knelt, using her powers to grow the seed. Roots took and a sapling sprouted from the earth, growing leaves and bark as the plant flourished under her touch.

There were mumbles among the goblins and some even lowered their weapons as they moved closer to watch.

The tree continued to grow, and Myrtle strained as she worked. Her brow furrowed and her breaths grew ragged. She'd spoken of how much harder it was to promote growth on new land, yet she continued to push harder.

But why? What was she trying to prove to the goblins? If it was difficult for her to cultivate adult plants in the valley, he couldn't imagine the toll it must be taking on her now.

Soon, the tree was Dobbin's height, and Myrtle grimaced as she pressed onward. The trunk thickened, and the bark hardened as limbs shot off in several directions. Then the tree blossomed, and whitish-pink flowers erupted along the branches.

She'd grown a mature fruit tree. Many of the goblins shared the same shocked expression. Where nothing had been only minutes before, there was now a flowering tree with its leaves rustling in the breeze.

Myrtle trembled from the effort, but she wasn't done yet. Dobbin knelt beside her, holding her steady. She closed her eyes, leaning into him as she made the final push. The flowers fell from the branches like fresh snow, replaced by tiny green apples. The apples expanded, growing nearly the size of Dobbin's fist as they changed from green to pink.

The aura around Myrtle faded, and she collapsed into Dobbin's arms from exhaustion. She'd exerted herself too much. Hopefully, whatever she'd tried to prove was worth it.

The elder goblin spoke to one of the other goblins, and it set its weapon aside to climb the apple tree. Its slender arms and legs scaled the tree with ease, and it plucked an apple from one of the branches, tossing the fruit to the elder.

Goblins gathered closer as the elder inspected the apple. She examined it from all angles, admiring the fruit before sinking her sharp teeth into its flesh. Juice burst from the apple, trickling down her dull gray chin. She closed her eyes as if savoring the taste. When she finally spoke, several goblins rushed up the tree, picking apples and dropping them below.

For the moment, it was as if Dobbin and the others didn't exist. The goblins devoured the apples, eating the seeds and core. Dobbin's eyes widened as he watched. He'd always viewed the creatures as killers that only ate meat, but they were clearly omnivores.

Gru walked underneath the tree and reached his arms overhead, grunting for attention. One of the goblins noticed and dropped the kobold an apple. Gru gave the apple to Snort and then asked for another. Next to Dobbin, Shadowmane stuck his tongue out, but he didn't move. Dobbin took pride that the horse's disposition toward goblins was as distrusting as his, regardless of how many treats the creatures bore.

While most of the goblins ate, one disappeared into the stairwell. Dobbin kept his eye on the entrance, and after a few minutes, the goblin returned with a woven basket. It was quickly filled with apples until the tree was barren of fruit.

The elder goblin spoke and then shuffled toward the stairwell. At the entrance, she turned back in their direction.

"Moss Ears wants us to follow," said Myrtle.

"Moss Ears?" Dobbin furrowed his brow. He'd never considered that goblins might have names for one another. The gray hair that coated the goblin's ears did have the look of dried moss.

Myrtle grinned. "They're a literal race."

"Are you okay to walk?" Dobbin still held Myrtle by the arm. "You really pushed yourself there."

"Oh, I'll be fine." She grimaced as she straightened. "These old bones have been through worse."

Myrtle had a youthful face, but dwarves didn't age the same as men. Dobbin wondered just how old she was.

He turned to Shadowmane and pressed his head to the horse's while patting him on the neck. "You wait here until we get back."

Shadowmane huffed in response. He was as uncertain of their situation as his rider.

Tawny perched on the horse's saddle, and Dobbin stroked her wing. If something happened while they were gone, the owl should be able to alert Myrtle.

Dobbin took the lead as they followed the goblins underground. If this was a trap, then he wanted to be the first in line. His boiled leather armor would hold up against the crudely made spears of the goblins.

The passage was narrow, not only because of Dobbin's height and broad shoulders but from the amount of rubble that littered the stairwell. The tunnel was dim, but Dobbin unsheathed Brightblade to light the way. Menacing shadows jumped along the walls and ceiling. They passed several dark corridors, each in an equal state of disrepair. Dwarven bones were scattered everywhere, and Dobbin wondered if they'd all died from the dragon attack. The underground tunnels must have been like a furnace while the city burned above.

The air cooled as they descended deeper underground, and somewhere below, water trickled. Snort kept close to Myrtle while Gru and the goblins grumbled and grunted down the tunnel.

A piercing shriek made the goblins stop abruptly. Dobbin ran into the back of one and nearly knocked it down the stairs. Further ahead, several goblins were stopped in front of a dark corridor with spears pointed toward the darkness.

Another shriek echoed from below.

Dobbin pushed his way between goblins until he was standing near the front of the corridor. A ghastly being hovered ahead of the line. It had the appearance of a dwarf, but something about it was distorted. Tendrils of wispy energy lashed out from the apparition and when it wailed, the dwarven visage stretched and tore, leaving gashes of darkness within.

Part of him felt sorry for the dwarf it had once been, but there was nothing but hurt and anger trapped within it now.

He stepped toward the specter. Brightblade would be enough to momentarily disperse the monster so they could continue.

A slender hand tugged on his cloak, and Dobbin turned to see a small goblin shaking its head. The creature pointed in front of Dobbin, where two goblins were already entering the corridor. One had a spear tipped with a thistle. The other held several thistle bracts in its hand. Both goblins moved with caution.

When the specter noticed their presence, it unleashed another ear-splitting shriek. The second goblin threw one of the thistles, and it sailed down the corridor. It hit the specter, tearing pieces of ethereal flesh as it passed through.

The specter howled, and Dobbin's hair stood on end. Tendrils of energy flared around the spirit as it darted forward with unnatural speed. The goblin tossed another thistle, ripping a large hole where the ghost's shoulder would have been.

The second goblin charged with its spear raised, meeting the specter head-on and stabbing the thistle-covered spear through the monster's core. There was a flash of light, and the specter's cries cut off as it dissipated.

Where the spiny bracts of the thistle had covered the spear, there were now several sky-blue blossoms. More littered the floor from where they'd been tossed.

"Shit," Dobbin muttered. The way the plant had torn through the specter was unlike anything he'd ever seen.

He was still staring at where the specter had vanished when Myrtle grabbed him by the arm.

"Pretty amazing, huh?" She smiled.

"I had no idea this was possible."

"Nature provides. But we best get a move on." She pointed down the stairwell to where the goblins had already continued onward.

Not long after, the stairwell emptied into an underground cavern that seemed untouched by the devastation above.

Stalactites hung from the ceiling like a giant maw, and water trickled from their tips into a pool below. The water took on a lilac glow from the algae within. A crustacean stirred the algae, and the water sparkled as the creature darted into an underwater tunnel chased by a cavefish.

Rugged terrain surrounded the pool, and spiders, snails, and cave crickets lurked upon the cavern walls and ceiling. Patches of green moss covered the rocky ground, and long ferns grew from within the crevices.

"This is beautiful," Myrtle whispered. Her mouth hung open as she looked around.

Fish bones and cracked shells lay scattered around the edge of the pool. In one corner, dwarven bones had been piled like a catacomb with rows of dwarven skulls stacked upon one another. Had the goblins moved them there out of respect?

Dobbin's heart leapt when he spotted a mushroom growing from a crack in the foundation. Snort followed him as he went to investigate. She sniffed at the fungi as Dobbin knelt to inspect it.

"What do you think, girl?"

The mushroom had a gray cap with brown spots. Dobbin pressed his ear to the ground to peer underneath the cap. The flesh was bone white, not the vibrant red he was searching for.

Still, it was a good sign that mushrooms were growing in this climate.

Moss Ears climbed onto a rock formation overlooking the pool. It stood taller than the others and gave the elder the appearance of someone about to address a crowded room. Goblins gathered around her.

As she spoke, her gaze fixed on Myrtle. The guttural language sounded hostile, but the druid gave a sympathetic smile to the Moss Ears as she spoke, nodding along as if she understood.

When the elder finished speaking, she gestured toward the pool. Her hand took on a familiar blue aura, and an orb of water rose into the air. A crustacean swam within the sphere as it hovered above the glowing pool.

With a wave of her hand, the orb floated across the cavern and stopped in front of Myrtle. She reached into the water and grabbed the creature. Gru sniffed at the air by her side, reaching for the crustacean that squirmed in Myrtle's hand.

She dipped her head slowly. "Thank you."

Dobbin joined Myrtle. "What's going on?"

"It's an offering. Her tribe is grateful for the apple tree. She says we are honored guests here anytime."

"Did you ask her about the dragonfire mushroom?"

"Not yet. I don't want to be rude. She just told me how her tribe ended up within the ruins."

Dobbin raised an eyebrow. "How's that?"

Myrtle turned to the elder. They exchanged a look, and then Moss Ears took a seat among the ferns. Her tribe surrounded her.

"She will help us as much as she can." Myrtle glanced at the goblins with sadness in her eyes before returning her attention to Dobbin. "Things haven't been easy for them, and I believe it's important that you understand them before you accept their help. They live among the wild and abide by the rules of nature. Your kind, you see them as monsters, as vile creatures standing between you and your goals. They can be monstrous, but so can man and dwarf and elf."

Dobbin nodded.

She continued, "Goblins are well-known as scavengers. They take what others leave behind and make homes where others no longer reside. This tribe once lived high in the mountains of Mount Tor before a raging frost giant destroyed their home and killed half their people. During the attack, the giant caused an avalanche. While the goblins were searching for survivors amongst the chaos, a pack of giant snow spiders descended on the bodies, forcing the tribe to leave or suffer more losses. So, they moved south, where they were constantly hunted by dwarves and men as they tried to forge a new life. And when they finally believed they'd made a home in the nearby mountains, they were attacked by a clan of kobolds."

Dobbin wasn't sure if he felt sorry for them, but he recognized their struggle. They had endured a lot.

Myrtle cast a sympathetic look at Moss Ears. "She's tired of fighting, and the haunted ruins have been the only place they've been safe, even with its many dangers. She led her tribe here knowing that the ruins would keep others out. Even kobolds fear the supernatural. There's not much for them to survive on, but an underground spring runs into this cavern, bypassing the blighted soil above, allowing them to drink and fish. They want to live, the same as you and me, but right now, it feels like they can only survive. The tree that I grew, she sees it as a symbol of hope and a chance at a new future."

Dobbin stood in silence, pondering on the goblins' story. "You learned all of that just by her thoughts?"

Myrtle smiled. "Sometimes, words aren't necessary to understand another's struggles."

"So, what now?"

"Now, we ask for help."

Dobbin crossed his arms. He'd already allowed Myrtle to join him on this quest, and now he was about to ask for help from the very creatures he'd been hired to hunt before. Entrusting the fate of his quest to monsters he couldn't communicate with seemed like he was begging for trouble.

Considering the state of things, he didn't have much of a choice.

## 25. FOLLOW THE LEADER

Dobbin watched Gru and Snort play with the goblins while Myrtle sat near Moss Ears on one of the rock formations.

Not even a day ago, he would've expected kobolds and goblins to try and kill the direpig for dinner. Yet here they were, sharing apples and snails like they were old friends. He wasn't sure what to make of this new revelation. He'd experienced attacks and ambushes from goblins firsthand on several quests, but this was proof that they could coexist together under the right circumstances. The current circumstance being their ultimate survival among the haunted ruins with a druid bridging the communication gap between species.

After slurping a snail from its shell, Gru dove into the pool, chasing after a fish that darted among the luminous algae. He swam deep underwater, but the fish was too agile. When the kobold resurfaced, his scales shimmered in the dull light of the cavern, covered in the glowing algae.

Myrtle tapped Dobbin on the leg. "Can I see the sketch of the dragonfire mushroom?"

Dobbin took the folded parchment from his cloak pocket and handed it to her. The sketch depicted the mushroom from several angles, showcasing the charcoal-colored cap and reddish-orange gills underneath.

Moss Ears held the parchment in wrinkled hands, her orange eyes narrowing as she looked it over. After a long moment, she called another goblin over and pointed at the picture. The two conversed in their native tongue before the goblin returned to the others.

Dobbin tapped his foot restlessly. Time was a pressing issue now that they were beyond the city walls, and every second they were here was a second they weren't searching for the mushroom. He hoped that Myrtle's instincts were right and this all came to something in the end.

"She's going to help us." Myrtle grinned at Dobbin.

Goblins scurried around the cavern as the elder barked orders in their guttural tongue.

Dobbin arched one brow. "And what does that entail exactly?"

"She's sending her tribe on a search mission. They'll scour every nook and cranny far faster than we can. She's instructed them to bring back any mushrooms they find, and in the meantime, she wants to show us something."

Dobbin couldn't imagine what an arcane goblin would want to show them in the haunted ruins of Hells' Crag, but he was sure that it couldn't be good.

He gestured toward the stairs. "Lead the way."

Back on the surface, goblins dispersed into the fog in all directions. Two stayed with Moss Ears, each carrying a spear and armed to the teeth with thistles.

Dobbin was quite impressed with how obediently they listened to the elder. In his experience, there was always a leader among goblinkind. They respected power, no matter who wielded it. In the tales of old, there were many stories of goblins living among giants or dragons and doing their bidding.

He'd even heard the legend of the Goblin King, a fire mage who'd led a party of goblins to Greenbriar Marsh and attempted to claim it as his kingdom. But that tale was more of a warning of what happened when you fucked around with the halfling people. They might seem relaxed and lazy to a fault, but they bowed to no one. They rose up, and his kingdom crumbled as quickly as it began.

Moss Ears waved a glowing hand and the fog parted, revealing a path leading further up the crag.

"That's convenient," Dobbin muttered as he guided Shadowmane by the reins. "Any idea where she's taking us?"

Myrtle shook her head. "No, but I have theories."

The elder led the way, flanked on each side by her two minions.

"Can't you just dig around in her mind and find out?" He tapped on the side of his head.

Myrtle burst out laughing.

"What?" Dobbin frowned, knowing she was about to give him a good ribbing.

"Can you put words into the mouth of another when

you speak?" She tilted her head, waiting for a response that wouldn't come. "I'm not an oracle, nor do I practice divination. I can only intuit what is freely given. She wants this kept a secret until we arrive."

As they journeyed up the crag, an apparition would occasionally flicker within the fog as if it were trapped between worlds. Dobbin's skin prickled every time the ethereal outline of a dwarf would appear, mumble or groan, and then vanish among the fog.

Gru clung to Myrtle's cloak like a small child holding his mother's dress while Snort walked between the druid and the adventurer, choosing security over exploration.

The sun had moved from overhead, and the countdown to twilight had begun. Goblins had exceptionally good dark vision, so they didn't need torches except in pitch-black areas like the tunnels. Dobbin kept his blade drawn as they walked. As long as Moss Ears was present, Brightblade would provide enough light for them to walk by. They still had four or five hours before nightfall, but Hells' Crag was a large city. It might take that long to travel from the gate to the upper tier on foot.

Snort squealed and turned her attention to the fog. Chaotic energy flared as pale tendrils lashed out from a spectral dwarf. A scream tore from its misshapen mouth, and Shadowmane neighed in response.

Dobbin released his hold on the reins and slashed Brightblade across the specter. It flashed a brilliant white as it tore through the phantasma, and the ghastly form momentarily dissipated back into the fog.

Moss Ears swiped her hand in a quick motion, and the fog receded. A few dozen small water orbs hovered, and both of her guards rushed to the front, their thistle-covered spears raised to where the specter had just been.

The air shifted and crackled as energy pulsed and the specter reformed. Only this time, the goblins were ready. The specter shrieked, and one of the goblins stabbed its spear through the spirit's core. The scream cut off abruptly as the thistle bloomed and the specter vanished into thin air.

Over the next few hours, they went through so many thistles that Dobbin began to wonder if they would have enough for the return trip. As unsettling as the spirits were, Myrtle seemed to take solace that they were being released.

Dobbin watched the sun with unease as it moved beyond the clouds. Eventually, they arrived at what had once been the city's upper district. His stomach sank when he realized where the goblins were taking them.

Up ahead, the remnants of what had been the inner bailey loomed above the fog. The memory of his first night in the crag flashed across his mind, where light had flashed from within the keep.

Dobbin turned to Myrtle. "Why is she leading us to the keep?"

The druid shrugged. "I guess we're about to find out."

At least someone was relaxed.

They passed through the crumbled walls that had once surrounded the keep. Dobbin recalled the painting of Hells' Crag from before the attack. Colossal spires had framed the castle's four corners, piercing high into the sky. The city had gleamed, a beacon at the foot of the mountains. On a clear night, the lights of the city were said to reflect off the lake like a mirror, adding to its imposing beauty.

Three of the spires had been completely destroyed, one of which lay on its side, shattered by the impact of toppling from its full height. The fourth spire stood only a few stories tall, melted down like a candle at midnight. The keep itself had borne the brunt of the attack, and rubble piled high at the far edge of the inner bailey, where the keep had once overlooked the lake below. Melted stone lay strewn about, and what remained seemed to drip off the edge of the crag's steep face.

Dobbin felt the eyes of the elder goblin on him, and Moss Ears spoke in her guttural tongue.

Myrtle tapped Dobbin on the arm. "This way." She pointed toward where the leftmost spire had once stood, the one that had collapsed across the courtyard.

They traversed the ruined courtyard, where fountains and magnificent statues were nothing more than rubble. A bronze bust of a dwarf holding a hammer nearly as big as his body lay buried in the debris, the lower half melted like chocolate in the sun. Apparitions flickered in and out of the fog as phantom guards marched by and servants carried on with their tasks in perpetuity.

As they approached the spire, Dobbin felt a change in the air. Gru and Snort both stopped walking, and Shadowmane huffed, flicking his tail in agitation. The hair on Dobbin's arms stood on end, the way it did before the summer storms rolled through Eastborne.

"You feel that?" he asked Myrtle.

She nodded. Strands of her hair floated from her head like tendrils.

Moss Ears spoke again and pointed toward where the base of the spire had been.

"She says not to worry." Myrtle translated. "The danger is at night."

"Right." Dobbin couldn't help noticing the sun creeping toward the mountains.

Up close, the massive stone slabs of the collapsed spire were even larger than Dobbin had imagined. Deep gashes ran along several pieces where the dragon had likely toppled the structure with its strength instead of its flame. The gouges were deep enough that Dobbin could bury his arm up to his elbow in the stone. Talons that sharp could rip a man clean in two. Once again, he was reminded of just how destructive a red dragon could be.

But why had it attacked Hells' Crag? That was the part that remained a mystery. A pissed-off dragon might burn a farm to the ground or set a section of forest ablaze, but this had been a sustained attack over several days. Dragons weren't mindless creatures. By all accounts, they were better tacticians than even the brightest minds across Aedrea. Whatever caused this, it had to have been personal.

They gathered around where the spire had once stood. Debris littered the area, and there were cracks in the foundation from the collapse, but the stairwell that ran underneath was still intact.

Dobbin could scarcely imagine the force it took to snap the spire at the base like a dried twig. Dwarves were renowned for their stoneworking, and many of their castles had survived for millennia. They were some of the oldest structures in the realm.

The two goblin guards peeked over the edge of the

stairwell. For the first time on their journey, they seemed hesitant. Moss Ears pulled a vial of purplish liquid from within a pocket of the tattered rags she wore and removed the cork, summoning the liquid into an orb that hovered in front of her.

She nodded to the guards, and they descended into the stairwell. A moment later, she followed. As the sunlight faded down the tunnel, the water took on a purple glow as the luminescent algae provided dim light.

Dobbin applauded her ingenuity. Goblins were known hoarders. The surprising part was that she'd managed to find a vial that wasn't broken among all the rubble. Considering the maze of tunnels that ran underground, who knew what other treasures might be hidden within.

Gru whimpered as he watched the goblins disappear into the dark. Myrtle gave him a reassuring squeeze on the shoulder.

Dobbin watched as the glow around the goblins disappeared, then he turned to Myrtle. "You sure about this?"

She stared into the underground abyss. Stray hairs fluttered around her as if she was underwater. "I feel like whatever is down there is important." She returned her gaze to Dobbin and smiled. "Besides, we've come this far."

Dobbin ordered Shadowmane to wait above ground with Tawny. He hated leaving the horse behind, but there was no way he would fit in the stairwell, especially with all the rubble. The hair of Shadowmane's mane and tail drifted through the air by some unseen force as if they were in the midst of a lightning storm. The sky was the same cloudy gray it had been since they'd arrived, and there was nothing to indicate an approaching storm.

He knelt next to Snort and caressed the direpig behind the ears. "Are you going to be a brave girl for me?"

She oinked in response and her tail stuck straight up.

"Good girl."

Dobbin held Brightblade in front, using the glow to light the way as he descended into the cavernous stairwell.

# 26. ECHOES OF THE PAST

The warm glow of Brightblade illuminated the dark tunnel. Cobwebs were draped across the ceiling and walls. Dobbin used the sword to cut away the silver webbing before it could cling to his face and beard. The others' short stature left them oblivious to the impediments that came with such a massive frame.

Further down the stairwell, Moss Ears's orb of luminescent algae bathed the ancient stone with purple light. Whatever unseen presence she was leading them toward shifted the very air around them, causing Dobbin's arm hair to stand on end and his beard to fluff like a startled cat. Myrtle's messy bun fluttered like seaweed in rough waters.

Dobbin rested his free hand on the hilt of his great sword. For some, comfort was a soft bed and a warm fire. For him, the familiar weight of forged steel helped set his mind at ease.

He had an idea of what they were walking into, but he

pushed those thoughts away, hoping for once that his instincts were wrong.

Behind Dobbin, Gru grunted as he clung to Myrtle's cloak, and Snort kept close at hand.

The purple light grew denser as they caught up to the goblins. The trio had stopped, and one of the guards spoke hurriedly to the elder. A chittering sound filled the stairwell. The noise was soft at first but grew louder, morphing into a sharp rattle. Snort whimpered and stepped between Dobbin's legs.

Then the chittering stopped, leaving them in silence.

Just beyond the goblins, a dark corridor merged with the stairwell. Dobbin tightened his grip on his weapon. Moss Ears spoke to one of her guards, and it cautiously moved forward with its spear raised.

The goblin stepped onto the landing and its eyes went wide as a stream of silver thread shot from the darkness, pinning the goblin to the wall with its spear across its chest.

Moss Ears and the other guard rushed to their kin.

"Godsdammit!" Dobbin reached forward, grabbing Moss Ears by the back of her tattered tunic and pulling a moment before a second jet of silver exploded from the darkness. The substance caught the second goblin on the arm as it tried to free the first, fastening his spear and forearm to the wall. Next to him, the first goblin squirmed against the sticky fibers, but the webbing refused to give.

Moss Ears was shouting in her guttural tongue, but Dobbin ignored her. He pulled a dagger from his belt and extended it across the tunnel, using its polished blade as a mirror. Eight green eyes glittered in the reflection before another strand of silk webbing shot by, further pinning the goblins in place.

A shiver passed through Dobbin's body involuntarily.

"Spider," he whispered, confirming his suspicions.

Of all the creatures across Aedrea, giant spiders were one of the most unsettling. They could immobilize a man with one bite, leaving them petrified as their bodies were mummified and slowly drained of ichor over days and weeks.

He'd once been sent to clear a spider nest terrorizing a village near the outskirts of the Vaglir Forest. After the spiders were slain, his party had found one of the missing townsfolk inside a massive cocoon, shriveled and gaunt but still alive.

The spider chittered from within the tunnel.

"Try to hold it off." Myrtle flashed her dagger. "I'll cut the others free."

"This is why I work alone," Dobbin muttered as he stepped in front of the tunnel. Of all the scenarios he'd imagined risking life and limb for, defending two goblins from a giant spider wasn't even on the list.

The spider's saliva-coated fangs shimmered in Brightblade's light. They clacked together beneath its mandible as it chittered, and the unsettling noise echoed down the tunnel. Dobbin stepped forward, waving his sword.

The spider hissed in defiance.

While Myrtle cut through the silk threads trapping the goblins, Dobbin stared the spider down, hoping it would turn and run.

He might have hoped for a nice steak and a cold ale for all the good it did.

The spider leapt to the ceiling, twisting unnaturally

mid-jump. The light of the sword revealed the barbed iridescent body in all its grotesque glory as the arachnid screeched. Dobbin's eyes watered as toxic spittle spewed from the spider's open maw. A rotten, acidic stench filled the narrow corridor and made him gag.

Dobbin spared a glance over his shoulder, where Myrtle had nearly freed one of the goblins. Next to her, Gru tore at the webbing with his claws. Snort paced across the landing while Moss Ears muttered to herself. A blue aura surrounded her hands, but there was no water nearby for her magic to power aside from the small orb of algae.

The spider clicked its fangs and tapped its legs against the walls. Dobbin stabbed at the spider, though it was just out of reach. The silver blade burned like a beacon in the reflection of its monstrous eyes. The spider hissed in response, swiping at Dobbin with a barbed claw and missing the adventurer by inches.

Dobbin's heart thundered in his chest as he pressed the attack into the tunnel in an attempt to force the arachnid to retreat. He brought the sword down hard against one of the beast's many legs, but Brightblade didn't carry the force of his great sword. It was made for piercing, not slashing, and it slid off the hardened exoskeleton with a clack. The spider seized the advantage, kicking Dobbin in the midsection. Sharp pain radiated through his side as he was launched against the wall mere inches from crushing one of the trapped goblins.

Snort rushed to Dobbin's side, pressing her cold nose against his hand as he leaned against the wall. Dobbin groaned as he crawled to his feet, pain shooting down his right side.

"You okay?" Myrtle asked as she continued to cut at the webbing.

Dobbin pressed a hand to his side and felt wetness.

"Never better." He grimaced as he squared off with the spider again.

It was nearly in the stairwell now, eyes set on its prey as vibrant green saliva oozed down its pincers.

Dobbin swung the sword and the spider moved back a few feet.

"Any day now," he called to Myrtle.

"To hells with it." Myrtle abandoned her efforts on the goblins, reaching into one of her pouches and tossing a handful of seeds on the floor. "Stand back!"

Moss Ears acted in concert with the druid, splitting her orb in half and splashing water on the seeds. The orb dimmed slightly, and Myrtle screamed as her hands flashed with blue energy. The seeds sprouted rapidly, and vines sprung across the tunnel to form a barricade that trapped the spider within the tunnel.

It clawed at the vines, tearing through them with sharp barbs. Myrtle's anguish echoed through the tunnel as she strained, forcing the vines to weave together again and again.

"I can't hold it for long." Her voice was weak and face pale in the light of the sword.

Dobbin stabbed Brightblade between the vines, piercing one of the spider's eyes. Green fluid sprayed from the wound, and its shriek drowned out Myrtle's cries. Dobbin released the sword and its light faded as he used both hands to wield his great sword. In the purple glow of the algae, Dobbin slammed Steadfast through the vines, piercing another eye.

The spider unleashed a high-pitched howl, and Dobbin twisted the weapon until something cracked. Tension released from the blade, and the monster scurried down the tunnel, leaving a streak of green in its wake.

Dobbin dropped to a knee, where Myrtle was already heaving against the stone floor. Snort nuzzled against him, licking the ichor from his clothes.

The gash in Dobbin's shirt was caked with crimson. He removed a potion from his cloak and downed it in a single gulp, grimacing at the sickly-sweet taste.

"Thank the gods." He sighed in relief as the pain immediately ebbed and the wound began to stitch itself together. He patted Myrtle on the back. "You need one?"

She shook her head and lurched like she was about to vomit. "There's nothing to remedy. Just exhaustion."

He helped her to her feet and then used a dagger to free the two goblins still trapped in the spider's webbing.

Moss Ears scowled down the tunnel and muttered.

Dobbin turned to Myrtle. "I get the feeling that she didn't bring us down here for that."

The druid and elder goblin shared a moment, and he knew there was some unseen communication.

"She says she didn't expect the spider. It wasn't here the last time she came. She says that it moves through the tunnels and has captured more than one of her tribe." Myrtle snapped her fingers. "Gru, put that down!"

Gru had both arms stretched through the wall of vines, grasping at something. He carefully pulled one of the spider's pincers through the opening, part of the mandible still attached. Apparently, it had snapped off when Dobbin twisted the sword. The young kobold tilted the fang, and green ichor poured into his mouth. He licked at the hollowed chitin until Myrtle forced him to stop.

"That is disgusting." Dobbin scrunched his nose as he watched Snort licking at the puddle that seeped beneath the vine wall. "And you're no better."

As they continued their descent down the stairwell, the two goblin guards were noticeably more hesitant. Gru accidentally kicked a rock, and one of them nearly jumped through the ceiling. It turned, snarling at Gru, no doubt shouting goblin obscenities at the kobold.

Dobbin felt the unease himself, constantly checking over his shoulder, wary of the spider returning.

They passed several more corridors without issue. The air grew more electric the deeper they went, and Dobbin swore he heard a voice coming from below. When they came upon a blue light that flickered and flashed up the stairwell, Moss Ears held up a hand for them to stop.

"We're here," said Myrtle.

"How are you feeling?" asked Dobbin.

"Drained." Myrtle forced a smile. "But she assures me that there is no danger as long as we don't enter the room."

Dobbin chuckled. "I've heard that one before."

The goblins stepped aside, and Moss Ears gestured for Dobbin and Myrtle to pass.

Dobbin ordered Snort to stay with the goblins, and Myrtle did the same to Gru. The situation was already tense, and Dobbin didn't care what the elder goblin said. He didn't trust that what waited below was truly safe.

As they made their way down, a soft buzzing filled the air. Occasionally, a crackle or pop would ring out from below, like an ember bursting within a roaring fire. Dobbin was certain now that someone was speaking, and the voice began to take form.

"...so much power." The words echoed up the stairwell.

There was a loud crackle, and the voice cut off. Light pulsed in the dim corridor, and the light from Brightblade grew less intense the further they traveled from Moss Ears.

Another pop and the speaking resumed. "With even a fraction of a dragon's power, I can help turn the tide of this war. Not even an invite to their council," the man's voice grumbled. "Soon enough, I'll be one of the most revered mages in all Aedrea. For all the acclaim Raglan the Magnificent has, he is little more than a servant. He could shift the realm to his whims if he chose. Instead, I'll be the one to guide Aedrea into a new age. Kings across the realm will whisper my name, and when it all finally comes to fruition, Hells' Crag will be..."

The light flared, its ethereal glow painting the arch of the stairwell exit like a portal.

Dobbin was well-versed in the tale of Raglan the Magnificent. The mage had been referenced several times during Dobbin's research. He'd fought the red dragon alone, giving it such grievous wounds that it had fled high into the mountains. There had been no mention of other mages in the accounts. Those in Hells' Crag had already perished by the time Raglan arrived, and those in neighboring cities had not been able to make it in time, so who was this?

Dobbin knew a power grab when he heard one, and the ghost on the other side of the arch might hold the answer to the question that had plagued scholars for centuries. Why had the red dragon attacked?

He crept forward slowly, inching his head around the last curve of the stairwell. On the other side, an apparition of a dwarf paced around the room. Most apparitions consisted of the being and the items they were attached to at the time of death. This one manifested an entire study rendered in luminous energy. Underneath the glow, the current state of the room was shattered columns and broken furniture. A large fissure ran up the far wall, revealing the eastern mountains and the far side of the valley. Debris and rubble littered the room. Whatever power was responsible for the apparition had recreated the entire scene of this dwarf's death.

The dwarf wore a long robe with several amulets draped across his chest. His beard was shorter than most dwarves, forked and braided to reveal the jewelry around his neck. Tendrils of energy randomly flared from his being, while at other times, sparks crackled within his ghost-like body like exploding embers.

Whatever this was, it was no ordinary apparition.

The dwarf leaned over a table, flipping through the pages of a large tome and reading to himself. "To bond the dragon, there must be a token of flesh and blood." The dwarf held up a diamond-shaped scale nearly the size of his head. Even in its spectral form, the scale gleamed. "Thanks to you, Archibald Proudhammer, and your battle with the dragon some two hundred years ago, I have just the thing." He grinned as he dropped the scale into a bubbling cauldron. "Next, we need a connection to the dragon's element. For a red dragon, this fire elemental should suffice."

He lifted a jar. Inside, a small flame burned without a source. After tapping the glass and smiling at the creature, the dwarf opened the jar and dumped the elemental into the cauldron. He rubbed his hands together greedily and returned to the book.

"A precious stone that embodies the power you seek." The dwarf chuckled. "A ruby seems fitting enough. It is a stone that represents power and strength, and both shall soon be mine." He dropped the stone into the cauldron and turned back to the desk. A change came over the dwarf as he picked up a gold coin. He stared intently, reciting the next line from memory. "To siphon the power of a dragon, one must obtain something it values above all else." He admired the coin as he tested the metal against a tooth. "A stolen coin from the dragon's hoard." He grinned as he flicked the coin into the cauldron. "And finally, to bind the spell, a sacrifice of flesh and blood from one who would usurp such power."

He grimaced as he took the dagger in his hand and sliced his open palm over the cauldron. Blood poured inside as he made a fist, and the cauldron bubbled to life. Steam wafted from within.

Energy suddenly burst from the apparition, casting the entire room in blinding light. Dobbin closed his eyes, and for a moment, he couldn't move. An overwhelming sense of dread consumed him. The essence ward shattered within his robe, and Dobbin was frozen as power enveloped him. It was so intense he couldn't tell if he was hot or cold.

The presence faded, and Dobbin was left shivering in its wake. He opened his eyes to darkness, the form of the apparition barely more than a wisp.

Dobbin gulped. The passage he'd committed to memory from *Echoes of the Past: A Guide to Apparitions, Wraiths, and Everything in Between* was as clear as day in his mind.

*There are times, usually during daylight, when wraiths lose their spectral integrity and return to a lesser form such as a ghost or apparition. Do not let this phase fool you into thinking the wraith is gone. Though their rage may remain dormant, specific events or memories may trigger a surge in power. While a wraith may seem vulnerable in this form, they can only be dispersed temporarily. Their core is not present and therefore they may not be truly vanquished.*

That was part of the reason wraiths were so deadly—because they could only be killed while in their most dangerous form. A form that could drain the energy from those who simply stood within their presence.

A hand gripped Dobbin on the shoulder, startling him. For that brief amount of time, he'd forgotten Myrtle was there at all.

Her eyes were wide, and she swallowed hard. "We need to go."

# 27. FORGOTTEN WAYS

"She wants us to deal with a wraith?" Dobbin shook his head. "No, thanks. I'll find my own mushrooms."

Myrtle grabbed him by the arm. "Dobbin, wait. Please."

The urgency in her voice made him pause.

"Look, we need to get out of the crag now." Dobbin pointed toward the mountains, where the last rays of sunlight cast an orange outline over the mountain peaks to the west. "It's almost nightfall, and you know as well as I what is about to happen."

What they'd witnessed below was merely a precursor of what awaited. He'd seen the flashes of light within the keep when they first arrived in Hells' Crag. Soon, the wraith would take its true form, and while it may be bound to the room beneath the keep, they needed to be far enough away that it didn't sense them. Some wraiths were said to cast their influence over lesser spirits within their domain, and Dobbin didn't want to discover how true that might be.

Shadowmane tugged against the reins as if telling Dobbin it was time to go.

The goblins hadn't stopped to wait while he and Myrtle argued. They had the wherewithal to keep moving and were now a good way ahead. Fog was already closing the path that Moss Ears had created with her magic.

Dobbin sighed. "Talk while we walk."

Myrtle nodded. "I always had my fears of what could have caused the attack. It's worse than I imagined. To try and steal the power of a sacred being..." Her gaze dropped as she shook her head. "No matter his reasons, he should have known better. Especially someone in such a position of power."

Dobbin's eyes widened. "You know who that mage was?"

She fixed her gaze on the ground. "I believe so."

"Who?" he asked. According to Master Corbyn, no one knew the true cause of the attack.

"I told you that there have been druids in my family for generations and that one of my ancestors tended the royal gardens in Bearmouth. She also had a brother who was an earth mage. While she curried favor with Prince Bordin, he was sent as a ward to Hells' Crag. Growing up, no one ever talked about him much. We speak precious little of the history of this city, and even less of the attack itself."

She kicked a rock and it tumbled into the darkening fog. All around, apparitions began to flicker in the fading light. A guard passed by and shouted at an unseen figure. A moment later, a dwarf shuffled through with a basket of bread. Behind her, a child grasped the back of her robe the same way Gru held onto Myrtle's.

"Over the years, I pieced together fragments of his life here and there. He was a studious dwarf with ambition of holding a seat on the king's council one day. He wasn't a particularly powerful mage, but he had a knack for locating precious jewels within the surrounding mountains. He served on lesser councils and over the years worked into a position of respect within the city, becoming one of Hells' Crag's top advisors." She took a deep breath, and her voice quivered when she spoke. "I guess he wanted more."

That explained a lot. For Myrtle to come here with the goal of making the crag inhabitable once again only to find out one of her ancestors was likely responsible... Dobbin couldn't even imagine the burden she must be feeling.

He placed a hand on her shoulder. "You are not your family's mistakes."

"I know that." Myrtle held Dobbin's gaze. "But it doesn't mean that I can't set things right. If we can destroy the wraith, then it will help push back the veil that still lingers in the crag. Without its presence, the other spirits will finally be free."

"Even if I wanted to help you, what can we do against a wraith? They say it takes a dozen clerics to put one down, and even then, it's not guaranteed." Dobbin stopped, gesturing at Myrtle from head to toe. "Besides, look at you. You've already pushed yourself too hard."

"Don't worry about me. There are other ways." She tapped a thistle that hung from her waist. "Forgotten ways."

Dobbin frowned. The idea of fighting a wraith was ludicrous. The presence of the thing had shattered the essence ward like it was made of the finest crystal. What would it do to them if they provoked it?

He grunted. Unsure why he was even considering the notion after what had just happened. "We can talk about it later."

A pile of mushrooms as tall as Dobbin's waist sat in the center of the cavern. They came in numerous shapes and sizes, from cones of deep indigo to flat circles of tan speckled with blue. Some were convex, others bell-shaped or knobbed, all in a variety of shades and colors.

He held one with a white cap that had thick droplets of red that resembling blood seeping from a wound.

Dobbin had to give the goblins credit. They were thorough. The overcast, foggy atmosphere provided the perfect conditions for fungi to thrive, which only made finding the dragonfire mushroom even more difficult. Sifting through the blues, yellows, and browns would be easy enough, but the darker ones would take some time. They were all vaguely similar in the dim light.

Snort ran over to the mound of fungi, taking one in her mouth and scurrying away.

"Dammit, Snort. Bring that back!" Dobbin chased after the direpig. "I need to check it first."

Myrtle cackled as she rested near the pond. The algae within provided the cavern with a dull purple glow.

Dobbin grabbed Snort around the waist and pulled the mushroom from her mouth. The cap was dark gray with flecks of black. His heart raced at the prospect of finding the dragonfire mushroom but the underside flesh was off-white, not the fiery red he was searching for. Dobbin released Snort and she grunted happily as she sat in a corner and ate.

He made eye contact with the druid. "We need to make camp. I'll have to go through these in the morning."

Myrtle kicked her feet in the luminescent water. "Moss Ears says we can stay here tonight."

Dobbin narrowed his eyes. "Here?"

"It's safe." Myrtle pointed toward the stairwell. "There's only one entrance, and they guard it at night."

"And what about Shadowmane?"

"We can place protections around the tree. I'm sure she'll station a goblin with him if we ask."

"I don't like it." Dobbin frowned as he examined another mushroom and tossed it aside. The flesh underneath had been the correct shade of red, but the cap was brown. Snort took it in her mouth and returned to her corner.

"Please." Myrtle's green eyes bored into his own. "We will find your mushroom. But you know as well as I that there is more at stake here than the whims of your patrons."

Dobbin sighed. She didn't understand that this was more than just completing a quest for him. If he found the dragonfire mushroom, he'd ensure that Isabella and her son were taken care of for good. Dobbin could leave Eastborne if he wanted. He could finally settle down without worrying that the boy would follow in his father's footsteps. Dobbin's debt to Henrik would finally be paid.

Knowing all that, Myrtle was still right. They had an opportunity to do something truly good for the realm. An opportunity not many adventurers found—to leave a legacy that would endure longer than a completed quest and a mound of coin. A legacy like the heroes he'd once read about as a child.

Dobbin wasn't sure he was the man for the task. He'd made a reputation as the man who always completed the job, but they were talking about a wraith, for gods' sakes. His skillset was in his preparation, and his research regarding Hells' Crag was about how to avoid the very thing Myrtle wanted to destroy.

He returned aboveground as he ruminated, where apparitions were about the city in full force. An eerie glow came from the fog, and dwarves would emerge from the within, carrying about their business as they had in life. Dobbin found it interesting how apparitions repeated moments from their daily lives while wraiths and specters were born from the moments surrounding their death.

Shadowmane flicked his tail and huffed.

"You're going to stay up here tonight, boy." Dobbin pressed his head to the horse's. "But I'm going to make sure everything is okay."

Shadowmane was no stranger to staying alone on adventures. There had been several instances when Dobbin had traveled belowground to explore caverns or abandoned mines. Other times, he'd climbed mountainous areas where the horse couldn't traverse. In those cases, Shadow would wait, stalwart as ever, until Dobbin returned. None of those locations had been infested with spirits, of course, but if the goblins could live among the ghosts, then Shadowmane could at least survive a night.

Dobbin hammered silver spikes into the ground around the apple tree. Once they were in place, he ran the wire in an octagonal shape, giving Shadowmane enough room to move about beneath the branches. Then he circled the wire barrier with a protective layer of salt.

"If anything happens, you take off running." Dobbin patted Shadowmane on the neck, and the horse nuzzled his shoulder. "Get outside of the crag, and I'll find you."

Footsteps approached from the stairwell, and Dobbin turned to see Myrtle. She was followed by two goblins wielding thistle-tipped spears. One of the goblins stood on its tiptoes as it offered a mushroom to Shadowmane.

"Wait—" Dobbin reached for the fungus.

"Don't worry. I already checked it." Myrtle grinned. "Brown Toes and Sharptooth are going to keep him company tonight."

Shadowmane took the offering, and the two goblins carefully stepped over the wire and climbed the tree. Myrtle reached into her pouch and pulled out a handful of thistle seeds, spreading them around the inside of the barrier.

"Haven't you pushed yourself enough today?" asked Dobbin. She'd been barely able to stand after their fight with the spider.

"I've already cleansed this area. This won't be as difficult. Besides, I can sleep when I'm done."

Myrtle knelt beside the wire and her hand took on a green aura. The seeds sprouted and a minute later, thistles encircled Shadowmane's enclosure. Tawny returned from scouting and perched upon the topmost limb of the apple tree.

"Shadowmane will have plenty of company." Myrtle tapped Dobbin on the arm. "If anything happens, I'll know."

Dobbin sorted through more mushrooms while goblins tended a fire against the far wall. They used flint against a steel rod they'd found among the rubble to ignite a pile of dried moss. Within a few minutes, a fire crackled.

Moss Ears used her magic to capture fish from the pond, trapping them in orbs of water until the others skewered them with spears.

Soon, several fish roasted over the fire. Gru sat nearby, drool dripping onto his ragged tunic as he waited patiently. The smell had wafted in Dobbin's direction, and his stomach growled. Snort was content to munch on mushrooms as Dobbin discarded one after another.

There were more varieties of fungi than Dobbin knew existed. He had a strong knowledge of the more common edible mushrooms across the realm, but occasionally, Snort would sniff at one and leave it alone. He made a mental note that these were likely poisonous.

So far, he'd sorted through half the pile and hadn't found anything special.

He hadn't expected the job to be easy, but the ruins had proven to be more challenging than he'd anticipated. Somehow, his list of responsibilities kept growing.

Moss Ears sat atop the tallest rock formation, watching her tribe. She'd led them here, and they'd built a life among the ruins. It was a dangerous life, but they endured. Dobbin couldn't imagine what it must have taken for her to ask for help from him and Myrtle.

A young goblin he hadn't noticed before clung to its mother as she sorted through a batch of thistles, fastening them to spears. The goblin's large eyes followed its mother's hands as she took the barbed thistle and tied it to the tip of the spear. The child reached for the weapon, and the mother gently patted its hand away.

What was it about babies that could make even the most monstrous creatures seem adorable?

Two other goblins, slightly older, played with a frog, chasing it as it hopped around the cavern. It didn't matter if they were goblin, direhog, or a human child, they were all full of curiosity in their youth.

Dobbin took a deep breath. For a man who claimed to work alone, the cavern was awfully full of those who had placed their faith in him. He had respect for Myrtle and all that she had accomplished, and he knew that even if he didn't help, she was going to try and root out the wraith one way or another.

He called to her as she sat by the pond with her feet dangling over the edge. "Want to help me sort through these?" Dobbin held up a mushroom before tossing it into the pile.

They were inspecting the mushrooms when Moss Ears approached, followed by another goblin who carried a piece of slate topped with several roasted fish. Moss Ears spoke as she offered a fish to each of them. The grating sound of her native tongue contradicted the generous gesture. She could be professing her love and it would still sound threatening.

Dobbin took the fish and nodded. "Thank you."

Myrtle took one as well. "She wants to thank us for saving them from the spider."

Dobbin nodded again and took a bite of the fish. He'd expected it to be bland and mushy from living beneath the ruins, but the fish was actually quite delicious. The goblins didn't use spices when they cooked, but the meat had a nice smoky flavor that was amplified by the fire.

Snort abandoned her mushroom and propped her forelegs on Dobbin's knee. He ripped off the fish head and tossed it to her. She squealed with delight as she devoured it, bones and all. Though they often rooted for underground vegetables, direhogs had stomachs that could handle anything. Their powerful jaws could tear through bone with ease. He'd witnessed a group scavenging an abandoned carcass on more than one occasion.

Grunts and slurping filled the cavern as everyone ate their fill. Dobbin wondered just how large the underground pond actually was to provide so much food. He thought back to Bearmouth and the maze of tunnels beneath the city. There was no telling how much of Hells' Crag was hidden beneath the ruins.

After eating, Dobbin returned to the pile of mushrooms. Myrtle joined him.

He turned to her. "Alright, tell me about this plan of yours."

Myrtle smiled. "I knew you'd come around."

# 28. PREPARATIONS

Dobbin woke to pain radiating down his right side from sleeping on the hard surface. Just one of the many reminders that he was no longer a spring griffin. Goblin snores rattled like the giant saws used to clear the towering trees of the wilds during pruning season.

Snort curled against Dobbin's chest as he lay by the cavern entrance. Her legs kicked as she embarked on an unknown adventure in her dreams.

Despite being surrounded by a cavern full of goblins, Dobbin had slept without fear of being stabbed or robbed. For now, at least, they were on the same side. Their enemy was the dead, and they attacked the living with no regard to species, race, or creed.

He massaged his back and leaned against the cavern wall. Life was catching up with Dobbin, and every ache and pain reminded him of a life well-lived. For all the good the clerics did across the realm, they couldn't heal the effects of time.

The gentle slosh of the pond was peaceful, and they

were far enough underground that the thick stone blocked out the sounds of specters howling into the night. Dobbin worried about Shadowmane, but Myrtle had made a trip to the surface before laying down. She insisted that she'd calmed the horse's nerves and he was as placid as could be.

After everything Dobbin had witnessed from the diminutive druid over the past few days, he trusted her word.

There was movement nearby as one of the young goblins woke. It sat up, groggy-eyed, and looked around. The creature grumbled, using its fists to wipe the sleep from its eyes. Dobbin grinned as it stood, grumpy-faced, and toddled across the cave in his direction.

The goblin approached without fear, like a newborn deer who had not yet learned to be wary of hunters. It stood a few feet from Dobbin and stared, large orange eyes full of curiosity. Observing the creature, Dobbin wondered how much of the animosity between their two species was learned versus ingrained in their very nature. It took a few more unsteady steps before extending a slender green arm and grasping for Dobbin's beard.

"You want to touch it?" Dobbin whispered.

He held out his arms, and the goblin climbed into his lap. It ran its fingers through the coarse hair of Dobbin's beard and babbled. Dobbin had held precious few babies in his life, and the goblin couldn't weigh more than a small cat, yet there was a power in its grip as it curled wiry fingers around his own.

"You're not so scary, are you?" Dobbin gently ran his hand down the goblin's back, and it cooed in response.

He wasn't sure if he'd ever look at the creatures the

same way again. Even so, he knew that letting his guard down anywhere else could result in serious injury, or worse. Just another one of life's many complexities. For now, at least, he enjoyed the moment.

Eventually, the little goblin fell asleep in Dobbin's arms, one hand grasping a handful of beard and the other curled around the man's finger. Dobbin's legs prickled from sitting in one place for so long, but the creature was so adorable as it slept that he didn't want to disturb it. He leaned against the cavern wall, resting until the others woke.

Once the goblins woke, the little one returned to its mother. They made a breakfast that consisted of snails and fish. Dobbin declined the offer of a snail the size of his fist, instead opting to share his bread and cheese with Myrtle.

He'd been forced to eat snails on a mission once, and while he wasn't a picky eater, the memory still turned his stomach. In some areas of the realm, snails were treated as a delicacy, but Dobbin never understood the appeal. To him, they tasted like chewy, slime-covered dirt. As bad as the taste had been, the texture was worse.

After they finished eating, it was time to begin preparations for the wraith. A line of goblins followed Dobbin and Myrtle through the crag. Half of the tribe would continue to search for mushrooms while the rest assisted Myrtle and Dobbin. The druid's plan was pure chaos, but she assured Dobbin that it would work.

"Dwarves have defended themselves from wraiths for ages. Goblins have, too. Long before the Order of Clerics established themselves across the realm." She huffed as they walked toward the gate. "But just like with anything, once a more convenient option comes along, the old ways are often forgotten."

Dobbin couldn't argue with her logic. There were gnomish inventions every year designed to make life easier and quicker. What the gnomes had achieved through runecrafting was fascinating. Glowstones made candles unnecessary for the homes that could afford them. Chillers had transformed how long food could be stored. Runetech, they called it. Alina had mentioned that the mainland inventions were nothing compared to what the gnomes had in Aethervale. She'd witnessed a balloon capable of transporting gnomes from one mountain peak to another.

As nice as new amenities could be, Dobbin sometimes wondered if the obsession with progress meant that people were moving toward their graves without having ever really lived.

Myrtle stopped and turned to face Dobbin. "I finally discovered why my thistles have been disappearing. I thought that they were being eaten by the deer and mountain goats as they returned to the valley. They love them for some reason. They'll pick the flowers right off the stem, and their tongues are so tough that the spines don't seem to bother them." She pointed to the right. "It all makes sense now, though. Look what Tawny found."

The owl sat perched among the remains of what had once been a massive courtyard. Many of the tiles were broken or melted, and most of the raised platforms for gardens had been destroyed. The large statues and columns that had once adorned the area lay in a thousand pieces among the rubble. Dobbin kicked a piece to the side, and it rolled over to reveal a stone hand with chipped fingers wrapped around a broken scroll.

Myrtle gestured toward one of the flowerbeds that remained. It had been cleared of debris, and there were a few dozen thistle heads half-buried into the ground.

"Bless their little goblin hearts. They tried to plant them." She placed a hand over her chest. "It might have worked, too, if not for the barren ground."

Dobbin had to give them credit. The goblins were doing everything within their power to survive.

---

Half of the day was spent traveling back to the thriving meadow where Dobbin first found Myrtle and Gru. When they arrived, the goblins frolicked among the tall grass, climbing trees and plucking fruit from the branches while Myrtle got to work. Snort and Gru loitered underneath the tree, taking the occasional offering.

Simply returning to the meadow did wonders for Myrtle's spirit. She seemed more cheerful and vigorous in the presence of nature. Plants leaned toward her as she passed, as if she was the sun.

Her hands glowed, and sunlight pierced through the clouds. There was a whisper among the meadow as thistles blossomed and their thorny bracts swayed in the breeze. Dozens of them dotted the tall grass.

"Time to put that blade of yours to use." She grinned. "I want you to cut the thistles. The goblins will gather them in bunches and tie them off with lengths of vine, then we can saddle them onto Shadowmane for the trek back. I'd use the wagon, but there's no way it's making it all the way to the keep."

Dobbin removed his dagger and got to work, cutting thistles and tossing them to the ground. The goblins followed behind him, gathering the thistles and bundling them into neat little bouquets. The system was simple, and they moved around the meadow like a well-trained unit. He imagined how productive society could be if there was a Myrtle in every sector, providing detailed instructions telepathically to workers.

He laughed. One Myrtle was more than enough.

"What's so funny?" Myrtle raised a brow as vines slithered across the ground. The goblins cut them into strips to tie more thistles.

"Just imagining a world with more of you in it."

"Can't get enough of me, eh?" She waggled her brows.

Dobbin smiled. "Something like that."

They continued harvesting thistles and by nightfall, Shadowmane looked like a sheep in need of a shearing with the many bundles draped across his body.

The hour was late, so they made camp in the meadow. Tomorrow, everything would come to a head.

As Dobbin drifted off to sleep, light flared from the top of the crag.

## 29. MEMORIES

Dobbin had never seen so many thistles in his life. They hung from Shadowmane in bunches like he was a pack mule gearing up for a long journey. Each goblin carried several bundles in their arms as well. There had to be thousands of the spiny flowerheads, each one like a miniature mace before it blossomed. Considering their purpose, it wasn't too far from the truth.

"You think we have enough?" Dobbin teased, but underneath the joke, he wondered if they truly did. If they pulled this off, the story would be worthy of a tavern with a strong drink and a roaring fire. If they didn't, there would be no one left to tell the tale.

Myrtle bit her lip as she looked over the mass of thistles. "By the gods, I hope so."

After traveling for most of the day, the sun dipped across the sky as they passed through the gate, once again entering the crag. A heavy tension settled on the group. Even Snort and Gru could sense it. They walked calmly, abandoning their usual antics as they marched toward the goblin cave.

Dobbin was risking everything by agreeing to help, but after the past few days, there was no way he could just turn away—with or without the dragonfire mushroom. If he failed to find it, there would be other quests, but this was a chance to really make a difference in the world.

Moss Ears was waiting for them at the stairwell when they arrived. She spoke to Myrtle and after a moment of silence where the two communicated, they turned toward the keep. If things went according to plan, they would arrive before nightfall with a few hours to put everything in place.

To have a chance at defeating the wraith, they would have to face it at night. Although a vestige of the wraith remained during daylight hours, it was theorized that its core sheltered somewhere between planes. During the day, the wraith was weaker, but it couldn't be killed. At night, its core became vulnerable, but that was also when it was at its most powerful.

Dobbin's skin prickled just thinking about it. What they'd witnessed in the stairwell was only a minor display of what awaited.

The elder goblin cleared a path through the fog as they ascended the crag. Occasionally, a specter appeared, and the goblins dealt with it swiftly. They'd sent dozens to the next life since Dobbin had arrived. Hells' Crag had been a large city in its prime, and there was no telling how many of the spirits still roamed through the fog and lurked within the shadows of ruined structures. He held the silver sword at the ready all the same, its blade shining even in the afternoon light.

By the time they arrived at the keep, the sun kissed the peaks of the mountains. Within an hour, it would be night.

"Let's get to work," Myrtle ordered as she untied a bundle of thistles from Shadowmane. "Dobbin, would you do the honors of accompanying me into the tower? We need to make sure it's clear of spiders and that there are no specters lurking."

Dobbin nodded. He considered pointing out that it was no longer a tower since the structure had been toppled but thought better of it. If anything, it was more like a dungeon they were walking into.

He walked toward the stairwell, the glow of Bright-blade lighting the way. Behind him, Myrtle carried a bouquet of thistles. The way she held them reminded Dobbin of Isabella on the day she and Henrik married. They'd wed in the ruins of an ancient fortress a year before everything went to shit. Henrik and Dobbin had cleared out a hill giant living there a few weeks earlier. Apparently, Henrik's description of the structure convinced Isabella that the place was romantic and full of history.

Dobbin shook his head to clear the thought. *Now is not the time.*

"Everything okay?" asked Myrtle.

"Yeah, I'm fine." He forced a half-smile. "You just reminded me of someone for a second."

They descended the stairwell, bypassing the landing where they'd fought the spider. The vines remained, blocking off a corridor caked in green ichor.

Dobbin and Myrtle locked eyes. He took a deep breath, letting the stale air fill his lungs. He'd spent his life preparing for the unexpected with every quest he took. Never would he have imagined the situation he found himself in now, deferring to a druid and an arcane goblin on the most effective way to kill a wraith.

Myrtle grabbed his forearm, and her green eyes bored into him. "This will work."

Dobbin grunted. Despite his uncertainties of the situation, there was nothing but conviction in her words. He wanted to believe her, but he'd seen things go south before.

They continued downward, and light occasionally flashed from below. It was almost night. Incomprehensible words intermingled with violent screams as they descended until the ethereal light from the mage's chambers basked the arched entrance in a brilliant blue.

The words became coherent as the dwarven mage spoke to himself, once again preparing the cauldron in an attempt to siphon the dragon's power.

Dobbin already knew how this story ended.

He turned to Myrtle, who wore a look of fierce determination. The tunnel was clear. It was time for the goblins to do their work.

Dobbin waited aboveground as the last of the goblins exited the stairwell. Once they were out, he stepped over a pile of thistles and entered the tunnel one last time. For their plan to work, they needed to start at the opportune time.

Thistles ran along the stairs from top to bottom, thousands of them. They crunched beneath Dobbin's boots as he and Myrtle made the final descent.

Snort squealed from the top of the stairs, begging to join them.

"I'll be back before you know it," Dobbin assured her. He hoped it was true.

Myrtle followed closely. She had been unnaturally quiet since their return, no doubt at war with herself over her ancestor's role in all of this. How fitting it was that she might be the one to set things right.

In silence, they went down until they came upon the entrance to the mage's chambers. Blue light flared from within.

"No, no, no!" The dwarf raged on the other side.

Glass shattered, and Dobbin peeked around the edge to see the now-familiar scene. The dwarf leaned over the bubbling cauldron, and the room shook. The dragon had arrived in the crag and begun its reign of terror.

The mage steadied himself on the rim of the cauldron as its contents sloshed over the edge. Bottles tumbled from the table, and another shattered against the floor.

There was a grating sound from the outside, like claws raking against stone. The dwarf stared at the window that revealed the fog-covered waters of the lake far below.

"Damn me, what have I done?" The dwarf buried his face in his hands, sobbing for a moment. Then he stood straight, taking a deep breath before returning to the text. "I don't understand. I did everything right!" His fingers trailed across the tome as the room rumbled again. "A token of flesh and blood. A connection to the dragon's element. A precious stone that embodies the power you seek. Something it values above all else." He held up a hand, where a dark blue gash ran along his palm. "A sacrifice of flesh and blood from one who would usurp such power."

A dragon roared, and pieces of ethereal stone crumbled from the wall overlooking the lake.

"Oh, gods!" the dwarf screamed as blue flame poured through the fissure in the wall.

Tendrils of energy flared from the mage as he burned beneath the dragon's fire, and then blinding light exploded from his core.

Myrtle tugged on Dobbin's cloak. "It's time."

Demented screams echoed through the stairwell as they raced toward the exit. Dobbin took the stairs two at a time until light flashed around them, and he stopped as an icy dread settled within his core. He suddenly had the insatiable urge to turn around, to join the chaos below. The wraith called to him, offering relief from the burdens of life and an end to his anguish and torment.

Myrtle grabbed him by the hand and pulled.

Dobbin couldn't move. He fought the desire to run back to the mage's chambers with his entire being. If he lifted his boot, it would lead him to his end.

Myrtle reached into a pouch around her waist and grabbed a handful of greenish-purple powder. She blew it into Dobbin's face, and he was enveloped in the aroma of mint and lavender.

"Come," she ordered and tugged his arm again.

Dobbin blinked several times as the pull of the wraith lessened, and he fought against a desire he knew was not his own, a yearning to embrace the doom. With determination, he put one foot in front of the other and they climbed the stairwell together. Through it all, Myrtle never released her grip on his hand.

Aboveground, Moss Ears stood with hands in front of her as if she were cradling an invisible ball from the sides. A blue aura enveloped her, giving her green skin a soft glow against the night. Goblins surrounded her, wielding thistle-covered spears as specters approached from the lower districts. They, too, felt the call of the wraith.

As soon as Dobbin and Myrtle exited the stairwell, the arcane goblin twisted her hands with a flourish. Her face strained as the aura around her flared. She moved her hands down and stepped backward as she brought them overhead.

The normally tranquil water below roared and a moment later, a torrent rushed over the edge of the crag, guided by the elder's power. It snaked across the ruined keep like a godly elemental as she navigated the raging river toward the stairwell. It crashed through the entrance like a waterfall, carrying thousands of thistles toward the mage's chambers.

"Gods," Dobbin whispered, but the rushing water drowned his words.

Water continued to flow as Moss Ears siphoned the lake into the stairwell in an attempt to cleanse the keep once and for all.

Suddenly, the specters were in a fervor, attacking the goblins with tendrils of rage and unleashing ear-splitting shrieks that carried above the surging water.

"Protect Moss Ears!" Myrtle shouted above the thunderous water as she grabbed one of the spears. "Without her, this is all for nothing."

Dobbin unsheathed Brightblade, and its blade glowed

like a beacon as he slashed and hacked, dissipating specters long enough for the goblins to position themselves. When a specter would reappear, a thistle-tipped spear blossomed from its core.

Dobbin lost track of time as he fought. For every specter they killed, two more emerged from the fog to take its place as the wraith drew them closer. Thunder rumbled overhead, and even the ghosts that floated outside the keep turned their eyes toward the living. Howls filled the night.

The living continued to fight, even as lightning crashed among the ruins, sending debris exploding across the keep. Dobbin hacked a specter in half, tearing through its ghastly visage. A goblin joined him, jabbing a spear through the specter as it reappeared.

More and more swarmed, and then, without warning, the spirits began to retreat, returning to the fog. The thunder faded, and the clouds parted overhead. For the first time since entering Hells' Crag, Dobbin saw the moon and starry sky.

Moss Ears released her control on the water and it lost its form, falling to the earth and sloshing about their feet. Fog receded across the lake, and the reflection of the night sky was one of the most beautiful scenes Dobbin had ever witnessed.

Snort ran over, and Dobbin knelt, scratching her behind the ears. She grunted with pleasure. Shadowmane drank from a puddle of water that had gathered in the aftermath.

"Did it work?" Dobbin asked Myrtle.

The druid leaned over Moss Ears. The elder's breath was ragged, and the tribe surrounded her, dozens of eyes radiating concern for their leader. Gru patted her gently on the shoulder.

"She'll be okay. I can't heal the effects of mana drain, even on a goblin." Myrtle caressed Moss Ears's arm. "She pushed herself hard, but she's tough. A few days rest and she'll be back to normal."

"That's good." The elder goblin had wielded more power than many mages he'd met. His gaze drifted toward the stairwell. "Do you think it worked?" he asked again.

Something had definitely changed—even the air felt different. Whether they'd killed or wounded the wraith remained to be seen.

Myrtle stood. "I guess we should probably find out."

The stairwell was almost unrecognizable as they entered. Centuries of dirt and debris had been washed away, revealing smooth stone. All traces of the thistles were gone. There were still pieces of rubble here and there, but they glistened in the light of Dobbin's sword.

Snort's hooves clacked as they descended. They passed the corridor where they'd fought the spider. The green ichor was gone, but Myrtle's vines had survived the raging water.

When they made it to the mage's chambers, the ethereal aura that had coated the arch was gone, replaced by a gentle white.

Dobbin gripped his sword tighter, but when he stepped into the room, it was only the light of the moon shining through the fissure in the wall. Everything within the chamber had been washed into the lake.

The wraith was no more.

Gru walked over to the massive chasm in the wall, peering over the edge and grumbling his assessment of the situation. Snort sniffed around the edges of the room.

Dobbin laughed.

"What's so funny?" Myrtle asked, but she was grinning too.

"It worked." He closed his eyes and breathed in until the tension of the past few days began to ease. "I can't believe it worked."

"You've got to be shitting me," Myrtle whispered.

Dobbin opened his eyes, and the dread returned. Had a part of the wraith survived?

Myrtle was staring at the ceiling, her mouth agape as she pointed at the crack where the dragon had burned through the wall.

Dobbin's eyes ran up the fissure. At the very top, gray mushrooms sprouted from the cracks, their underbelly a fiery orange.

# 30. VISIONS

Dobbin and Myrtle sat on the ledge of the mage's empty chamber, their feet dangling over the edge. With the wraith gone, the cloudy sky and dense fog had retreated. Not all of it was gone, but enough to show the effect that the wraith's presence had on the area. The fissure where the dragon had attacked provided an expansive vista of the eastern mountains, moonlight casting their peaks in a pale outline. Far below, water sloshed gently against the crag, and a streak of silver ran across the lake.

The goblins had all returned to their cave hours ago, but Dobbin and Myrtle remained. They were finally going to share the bottle of wine Dobbin had promised before they'd ever entered the city. *If we make it out of this*, he'd said at the time. Somehow, they had.

Even though it had only been a few days ago, it felt like ages had passed.

Gru growled as he and Snort wrestled in the empty chamber.

Dobbin took a long swig of wine before passing the

bottle to Myrtle. Eris had been right. It was a mighty fine vintage. Dark fruit and spice lingered on Dobbin's tongue as the wine settled in his stomach. There was nothing like a relaxing buzz after a hard-fought battle, just one of the many simple things that made this life worth living.

He held onto the dragonfire mushroom between his fingers. While he might be content with a strong drink and a good book, there were always those who desired more. The charcoal-colored cap had blended in perfectly with the stone walls. If not for the orange underbelly, they might have never spotted it. How crazy it was to think that something so commonplace as a mushroom could fetch such a high price.

But this was no ordinary mushroom. It could grant visions. And yet, Dobbin could crush it to pulp with a squeeze of his hand. Would it grant a glimpse of the future or a look into the past? Perhaps it would offer something more. Or maybe it had been a fool's errand.

There'd been a handful of the mushrooms growing within the crevice, so high that they'd managed to survive the torrent of water flooding the room. He'd taken them all, placing them in a vial with a preservation elixir.

"Wow, this is good." Myrtle tipped the bottle in Dobbin's direction and sipped again. "Nobody does red wine like the dwarves."

He took the bottle and drank. "What now?"

Dobbin knew what awaited him. In the morning, he'd begin the long journey back to Eastborne to collect his fee from Lord Ferant. Then, he'd settle his debts once and for all.

"Now, the real work begins." Myrtle leaned back on her arms. "Do you think you'll ever come back this way?"

"Do you think I'd miss Hells' Crag's return to glory?" Dobbin smiled. "Besides, Snort might gore me in my sleep if I don't."

"I'll hold you to that." She sat up and tapped Dobbin on the leg. "You're not half-bad for an adventurer. I'm gonna miss having you around."

"Yeah?" He passed the bottle. "I'm gonna miss having you around, too."

Dobbin meant it. He wasn't sure what it was about Myrtle, but he knew he could count on her. He'd worked alone for so long because he never wanted to put that kind of faith in another person, not again, but the druid was genuine to her core. She'd pushed herself to her limits and still found the strength to be kind and compassionate to those around her.

He chuckled as he thought about their situation. "We defeated a wraith. I still can't fucking believe it."

"Impossible is a mindset." She tilted the bottle, draining the last of the wine. "We could move mountains if we put our minds to it."

Dobbin took the vial from his cloak and prepared to put the mushroom with the others.

"No." Myrtle shook her head. "You should eat one."

Dobbin raised a brow. "Why would I do that? This thing is worth a small fortune."

"Why?" Myrtle frowned. "Money isn't everything. You risked life and limb so that someone else could enjoy the spoils. If you'd only found one mushroom, I'd understand, but you have five. Dragonfire mushrooms are legendary for a reason, and you're going to give them all to someone who's probably never fought for anything in their life? You may never have another opportunity."

Maybe it was the wine, but Myrtle was making some awfully good points.

He held the mushroom to the moonlight, admiring it one last time before he tossed it in his mouth. It tasted unlike any mushroom he'd ever eaten. There was a familiar earthiness, but there was also a smokiness and a hint of spice, and another flavor he couldn't place.

Dobbin swallowed. A moment later, his head began to spin. He laid back against the cool stone. "Would you do me a favor?"

"What's that?"

He closed his eyes. "Don't let me fall in the lake."

The world blurred, and then Dobbin found himself standing in an empty corridor. The bodics of several gremlins lay scattered around the hallway. One was charred like meat that had roasted over a fire for too long. An arrow protruded from another's neck. He paused when he saw one with a hack mark running from its shoulder to midsection.

That one had been his handiwork.

Dobbin turned to leave. This was the last place in Aedrea he wanted to return to, in reality or through a vision. He'd sit on the steps of the keep and wait for it to pass.

Suddenly, Henrik stood before him, a finger pointed at Dobbin's chest. "I didn't take you for a coward."

Dobbin froze. It'd been seven years since he'd seen that face. Seven years since he heard the melodic voice that sounded calm in even the tensest situations.

He stared at his friend for a long moment. His slender frame and curly brown hair that ended just above his eyes. Dobbin had forgotten how handsome Henrik had been with his chiseled jawline, high cheekbones, and perfectly symmetrical features. While Dobbin had size, Henrik had beauty. He had grace. His brown eyes were always alert, even now as they stared at Dobbin with disdain. Probably part of the reason he'd been such a good ranger.

"I'm not a coward." Dobbin sighed. "I just know how this ends."

Henrik scoffed. Further down the hall, someone yelled, followed by a growl. "Is this what you've become?"

Dobbin tried to walk through Henrik, but the man's finger held firm against all his weight as if he was really there.

Henrik's eyes softened. "It wasn't your fault, you know."

"Don't you say that." Dobbin swatted Henrik's hand away, grabbing his friend by the tunic. He wanted to shake him. Shake him until he understood. "Don't you dare say that."

Henrik smiled even as Dobbin threatened to unravel. "Come and see, old friend."

"I don't need to..." Dobbin let the words fade. He wanted to argue, wanted to run, but more than anything, he wanted more time with his friend. He'd relived this moment a thousand times in a thousand nightmares. What was one more?

They walked down the corridor littered with destruction.

"We should have never taken this job." Dobbin sighed.

"It was a good job. Would have set us up nicely. Just unlucky is all." Henrik said it with the same casualness as he did everything, as if this hadn't been the job that cost him his life.

"Unlucky is losing a finger. This was a disaster."

Henrik shrugged. "If we'd wanted an easy life, we wouldn't have joined the guild. There are a lot safer ways to earn a living. This was always a risk."

Dobbin recalled the moment when they'd taken the quest. Owyn the Turbulent had recently passed. He was a distrusting mage, and rumors spread across Aedrea that he'd scattered his worldly possessions among his various dwellings throughout the realm. No one knew if there was any truth to it, but several bands of adventurers intended to find out.

Owyn had laid claim to an old keep several miles east of Barrowsturm, a relic from a time when Aedrea was composed of hundreds of small territories instead of nine sprawling kingdoms. Owyn had a rare gift as far as mages went—teleportation—and some believed he could transport himself from one outpost to another, avoiding society unless absolutely necessary. He was known to enlist goblins, ogres, trolls, and other manner of dangerous creatures as his muscle because he didn't trust anyone who spoke the common tongue to assist with his personal business.

Apparently, they were loyal to the mage even in death.

Henrik stopped, admiring an arrow that protruded from a gremlin's eye socket. "Say what you will about me, but I'm a damn good shot."

Dobbin couldn't help but smile. "I've missed you."

"I know."

Around the corner, there was another long corridor. This was where shit had started to go south. Dobbin watched as his younger self crouched behind a slab of stone from a fallen wall. Vines crept in from outside. A younger Henrik knelt beside the younger Dobbin while gremlins tossed rocks and shot stone-tipped arrows.

A rock hit the barrier, narrowly missing Dobbin as he ducked, and clattered down the corridor. Gremlins screeched and cackled, eyes full of menace as they snarled at the interlopers.

Goblins were a pain in the ass, but gremlins were like their feral cousins. With bulbous eyes, pointy ears, and a mouth full of fangs, they would fight to the death with little regard for whether they lived or died. That was precisely the reason their band had partied up with a fire mage.

Who just so happened to be one of the biggest cowards Dobbin had ever met.

An errant arrow sailed down the corridor, passing through Dobbin. Even though he could touch and interact with Henrik, it seemed the scene would play out as it had regardless of their intrusion.

Dobbin's younger self grabbed the young Henrik by the arm. "This is a bad idea. We need to go back and regroup."

"You should have listened," Dobbin said coldly.

"I should have done a lot of things. But this isn't about me." He winked at Dobbin. "This is about you."

Several yards in front of them, Roswen—their rogue—slunk behind a column. She shrugged when her eyes met the younger Dobbin's.

Across from her, Gregor—the fire mage—hid behind

an overturned table. Dobbin wanted to strangle the man, to tell him that if he didn't do something, then they were all going to be in a world of shit. The bald, slender mage's arcane abilities were powerful. He could throw fireballs and incinerate entire rooms. He was supposed to be an invaluable part of the team, but he'd yet to do anything of worth.

"We need to retreat!" Younger Dobbin called above the noise.

The mage peeked his head out, and an arrow lodged in the table inches from his face. He leaned against the column, muttering to himself.

Younger Henrik shook his head. "We're so close. If we make it through this hallway, we'll be in his chambers. That's where the treasure is."

"If Gregor doesn't do something, there's no way we're making it anywhere." Younger Dobbin scowled at the table. "Look at him, he's as yellow as a daisy."

"Come on, man. We're so close." Young Henrik nudged Dobbin's side. "Come on, Gregor! We believe in you."

Young Henrik nocked an arrow, stood, and let loose. A gremlin dropped. Roswen threw one of the many daggers strapped along her ribs and thighs, taking out another.

Sweat beaded down Gregor's face. He was terrified, more so than Dobbin had even realized at the time. Flames crackled to life in his palm, and then he let them fade.

"Come on, Gregor!" Henrik shouted encouragement once again. "You've got this."

The mage took a breath, nodded to himself, and flames engulfed his palm. He stood with a momentary look of determination and unleashed a red-hot stream. The temperature in the room rocketed, and young Dobbin and Henrik dove out of the way as fire flowed down the corridor. It bounced off the far wall, consuming the gremlins.

Henrik nudged Dobbin again. "You've got to admit. That was pretty badass."

Dobbin chuckled. "At the time, I was hoping he didn't burn us all in the process."

"See, what'd I tell you?" Young Henrik slapped the mage on the back. "You've got this."

"I did it." Gregor nodded, as if surprised at himself. "I did it."

Young Henrik wrapped an arm around young Dobbin. "Just one more room to go and we'll all be sitting pretty. I can finally learn to bake, and you can sit around reading those books you love so much."

A pang of regret pierced Dobbin like a knife.

Young Dobbin kicked open the door, rushing into the room followed by young Henrik, Roswen, and then Gregor.

What happened next was seared into Dobbin's memory like a story he'd read a hundred times. There was a chest in the back of the room, guarded by a massive ogre and two banshees. Dobbin had gone after the ogre, fighting the massive monster while Henrik peppered the banshees with arrows. After the first banshee screamed, Gregor would run. Dobbin would fall to his knees from the attack, and Henrik would turn to call for the terrified mage. Then, the ogre would...

Dobbin made to follow them and witness his shame one more time.

Henrik extended his arm, barring Dobbin's way. "This is as far as you go."

"Why?"

Henrik stepped in front of Dobbin, placing a hand on each massive shoulder. "Because this isn't about what happened in there. This is about you and me. You had the right of it. We should have turned back. Gregor was afraid, and I was so blinded by the thought of one final payday that I couldn't see reason. I wanted to settle down with Isabella and start a family. This was my ticket, and it didn't matter if it was you or someone else, I wouldn't have turned back. I appreciate everything that you've done for Isabella, and for my—" Henrik's eyes glistened as he choked on the words. "—my son, but you have to know that my death isn't on your hands, Dobbin. You need to let go, because if you don't then you're no better off than I am."

Dobbin wrapped his arms around his friend and cried for the first time in seven years. He hadn't known how much he'd needed to hear those words until now. His broad frame heaved as emotion passed through him in waves. When he could cry no more, he let go. Truly let go. He felt lighter, like a gentle breeze could send him floating through the ceiling.

The banshee screamed from the other end of the hallway.

Henrik nodded in the opposite direction. "What do you say we go for a walk? You can tell me what you've been up to all these years."

They walked. They turned around and left one of Owyn the Turbulent's many outposts. They walked until they found a quiet spot in the woods and sat by a babbling stream. And then, they talked.

Dobbin didn't know if he was experiencing a true

vision or if this was all a hallucination within his own mind. It didn't matter, though, because he talked to Henrik like not a day had passed. He told the man of his adventures, of Lyra and Myrtle, and of everything he'd witnessed through the windows of Cupped Cakes. How big Henrik's son had grown and how there were always customers every time he'd stopped by.

"Will you promise me one thing before you go?" Henrik asked.

"Anything."

"Stop by and see them. They deserve to know the man who's been looking after them all these years."

Dobbin cursed under his breath, and then the world began to fade.

# 31. THERE AND BACK AGAIN

Morning sunshine breached the fissure in the wall, stirring Dobbin awake. His back throbbed from the hard surface, but he couldn't recall the last time he'd slept so peacefully. It was as if a weight he'd been carrying for years had been lifted.

He may have found peace, but that story was far from over. He still had a promise to keep, after all, but the fear and anxiety of seeing Isabella had faded.

Dobbin grimaced as he sat up, and Snort came bounding over, knocking him back to the floor. "Good morning to you, too."

Myrtle and Gru sat on the ledge, watching the lake.

The druid turned around, leaning on one arm. "How are you feeling?"

"Good." He scratched Snort under the chin, and she oinked happily. "I'm feeling good. Thanks for not letting me fall into the lake."

She chuckled. "I thought about stringing you up with vines until you promised to stay."

"I don't doubt it." Dobbin laughed. "Honestly, I wish I could stay longer, but I have other commitments to see through." He pushed Snort aside and sat up. "Thank you, though. For encouraging me to try the mushroom. It was a good thing I did."

"I'm glad. Dragons are wondrous creatures. If anyone has earned a taste of their power, it's you and not some rich lord who jingles when he walks." She stood, walking over and offering Dobbin a hand.

Her forearms flexed, but she didn't so much as grimace as she pulled Dobbin to his feet.

Damn, she was strong. "If all goes well, I'll be jingling myself soon enough."

"Just don't start asking me to call you Lord Dobbin." She smirked.

"Lord Dobbin?" He waggled his brows. "It does have a nice ring to it."

Sunlight bathed the city as they made their way toward the goblin cave. Everything seemed less gloomy. There were still specters and ghosts within the ruins, but without the wraith empowering them, Myrtle and the goblins would sort them out in time.

Moss Ears waited with her tribe beneath the apple tree outside the stairwell. Tawny swooped down, landing on the top-most branch with a soft hoot. The goblins offered Dobbin a woven basket filled with snails as a parting gift. Slime coated the basket from where the snails had wandered within.

The elder goblin spoke, and Myrtle translated.

"She says you are welcome among the tribe at any time."

"Thank you." Dobbin bowed slightly, accepting the gift

with grace and ignoring the fact that he would be repurposing it in a short while.

Shadowmane led them out of the crag and into the valley. Fog lingered in the morning light, but it was a normal fog he'd seen a thousand times on his travels, nothing like the blanket that had persisted for five hundred years. In the distance, sunlight bathed the meadow Myrtle had grown. The wraith's presence had loomed heavily on the land for so long, but change was coming.

They stopped at the circle where they'd camped together several nights ago. For a moment, Dobbin and Myrtle stood in silence while Gru and Snort chased one another for a final time.

Myrtle placed her hands on her hips. "So, I guess this is it, huh?"

Dobbin sighed. "I guess so." He was never really good at good-byes, always preferring to disappear before anyone knew he was gone.

Myrtle crossed her arms, seemingly unsure herself. "You take care of yourself out there."

"You as well." Dobbin handed her the basket of snails. "Give these to Gru for me."

He then removed Brightblade from his waist and offered it to Myrtle.

She frowned. "What's this?"

"There are still specters roaming the crag." He held the sword across both hands. "You might need this more than I do."

Myrtle pushed the sword away. "Dobbin, I can't accept this. I know how important swords are to adventurers."

"Consider it a loan." He smiled. "Keep it safe until I return."

She took the sword and stepped forward, wrapping her arms around Dobbin's massive frame and squeezing. He hugged her in return.

"You take care of yourself out there," she said again. Her eyes glistened as she clutched the sword to her chest. Snort came over and sniffed at the basket of snails. "You too, little one."

Dobbin wrapped an arm around Myrtle's shoulder and squeezed one more time. "Try not to destroy the place while I'm gone."

<hr />

As Dobbin left Hells' Crag, there was a hollowness in his chest that he hadn't felt for quite some time. Loneliness. It had settled on him like a weight in the aftermath of Henrik's death, but this was different. This wasn't a loneliness born of loss but of fortune.

While he'd set out in search of gold and glory, he'd found something else. Friendship and understanding. The world was full of people in it for themselves. Myrtle chose the difficult path simply because it was the right thing to do. She'd challenged Dobbin's notions on kobolds and goblins, and she had encouraged him to take chances.

The mushrooms in his cloak weren't the only treasure he'd found in the ruins.

Every so often, Snort would stop and turn back, looking in the direction of the crag. Dobbin wasn't alone in his emotions. She was no doubt missing her friend as well.

"We'll see them again, girl. I promise you that."

Their journey was long and mostly uneventful, for which Dobbin was grateful. When they arrived in the Arenian forest, some of the trees were beginning to turn with the first signs of fall. They ate well whenever they passed through a town or village, and Snort was now nearly double the size she'd been when he'd first found her. Tusks had started to come in on her lower jaw, and a bristly mohawk had sprouted down her spine.

One evening, they made camp by a stream and a family of horned rabbits appeared on the other side. The creatures were supposed to be a sign of good luck. The adults both had a creamy coat like toasted marshmallows and an opalescent horn protruding from their foreheads. The kits each had tiny white nubs.

The rabbits drank from the stream. When Snort noticed, she charged after them and they scattered through the forest. She paraded along the bank, head held high as she huffed and kicked up dirt.

Aside from a run-in with a direbear, they passed through the woods without issue. In Arenia, they stopped by The Golden Tankard for a night, where Dobbin once again regaled the patrons with tales of his adventures, though nothing from his childhood.

Soon after, they were on the long stretch of road that led toward Eastborne. A thousand moths fluttered within Dobbin's stomach in anticipation of what awaited. In a week, he would be back in the city and would finally have to face what he'd put off for the last seven years.

# 32. PROMISES

The midday sun shone down on the harbor when Dobbin finally arrived at the gates of Eastborne. He inhaled the salty air as he took in the tiered city. A powerful storm had rolled through in his absence. Wracked ships lined the harbor, and more were in a state of disrepair. Scaffolding ran along the Warehouse District, where a large section of buildings were being rebuilt.

Dobbin pulled Shadowmane to a stop next to one of the guards. "Must have been some storm to do all this." He gestured toward the wreckage.

The guard shook his head. "Wasn't a storm. A bloody kraken attacked the city a few weeks ago. I've never seen something so terrifying in my life."

"A kraken?" Dobbin arched his brows.

"That's not even the craziest part." The guard left his post and stepped into the street, clearly excited to share the story with a newcomer. "There was a blood mage. Apparently, he's been living in the city for months and running a tavern. Can you believe that? All the way down here."

Dobbin frowned. "A blood mage this far south? You've got to be pulling my—"

Wait, it couldn't be… He recalled the umbral elf he'd met at the tavern months ago on his way to meet with Lord Ferant. Rhoren, was it? The elf said he'd retired from service in the Northern Guard. Was there truth to this guard's story? Every blood mage in the realm was conscripted to serve in the Guard because they were the only ones capable of defending against behemoths.

"What happened with the blood mage?" Dobbin asked.

"He defeated the kraken, if you can believe it. The most powerful mages in the city were trying to fight it off, but they were losing ground. And then this blood mage comes out of nowhere." He shook his head as if he still couldn't believe it himself. "Thank Ahteus that he did, though, because I hate to say what the state of the city would be without him. They said he slept for three days after the attack."

"You happen to know the name of the tavern?"

The frowned. "Hmmm, Cursed Cocktails, I believe."

"Son of a banshee." Dobbin grinned. It had been him. He made a mental note to stop by at some point. It seemed they both had stories to share over a strong drink.

He made his way across the river, where his small shack had miraculously survived. After dropping off his belongings and checking Shadowmane and Snort into the stables, he hired a cart to take him to the Council District.

It was time to get paid.

By the time Dobbin arrived at the Council District, dusk had settled over the city. The streets this far up had been untouched by the kraken's presence and were as meticulously well-kept as ever.

Outside of Lord Ferant's mansion, Dobbin took a deep breath. He'd considered stopping for a drink beforehand, anything to ease the headache he knew was coming, but thought it best to collect his fee and be done with it. In the light of the glowlamp, he was strongly reconsidering.

"You've stood outside the lair of a wraith. You slept beside goblins." Dobbin talked himself up. "You can survive thirty minutes with a noble."

He stood a little straighter and pounded the heavy golden knocker against the door. The golden ram head stared at him until a young man wearing a black tunic emblazoned with the Ferant crest opened the door.

"How may I help you, sir?" the man asked.

"I'm here to see Lord Ferant about the completion of a quest."

The young man nodded. "One moment."

He shut the door and returned a few minutes later, welcoming Dobbin inside. "May I take your cloak, sir?"

"No, thanks."

The man fidgeted before composing himself. "Very well, Lord Ferant will be waiting for you in the sitting room. Please, if you'll follow me."

He led Dobbin through the foyer, which now had the addition of an ebony statue of a ram, complete with gilded horns and bull ring. The statue was polished to perfection, and Dobbin caught his travel-weary self in the reflection. They passed the marble staircase that led to the second and third stories before moving down an arched hallway filled with paintings that stretched from floor to ceiling.

Lord Ferant waited in the sitting room, swirling a glass of red wine. He stood when Dobbin entered, smiling broadly. He wore a fine tunic, black with a ram head elaborately stitched in gold thread.

"My boy, my boy!" Lord Ferant grinned. "You have missed a spectacle while you were away. If you have not dined on kraken, let me assure you, it is divine!" He kissed his fingers and then swirled his wine. "Would you care for a drink?"

"Oh, would I." Anything to take the edge off as Ferant grated on him for the next hour or so.

Lord Ferant snapped his fingers and a servant poured Dobbin a glass.

"So, tell me, were you able to locate the dragonfire mushroom?"

Dobbin nodded his thanks to the servant and took the wine. He swirled it once and took a sip. The wine was like velvet in his mouth, silky smooth and ripe with flavor. Dark fruit and a hint of pepper played on his tongue as he closed his eyes, savoring the moment of silence. Lord Ferant might be insufferable, but the man knew his wine.

"Gods, that is good." He set the glass on the table and reached into his cloak, pulling out the vial of mushrooms. "I had to defeat a wraith to find them."

Lord Ferant spat out his wine. "A wraith? My boy, did you say a wraith?"

Dobbin smirked. "Like I told you, I always get the job done."

A servant rushed over to clean the spewed wine, and Lord Ferant stood, pacing in front of the large fireplace.

"That you do, my boy. That you do." He sat on another sofa closer to Dobbin. "Tell me all about it."

Sometimes, Dobbin wondered if Lord Ferant got as much enjoyment from listening to the recounting of the adventure as he did eating the rare meats. This time, though, there would be no speculation on the magical properties of the item he procured. Dobbin had firsthand experience of the mushroom's potency.

After Dobbin finished the story, he handed the vial to Lord Ferant.

"So, this is it, then? Your adventuring days are over?" The man looked upon the vial with wonder. "I don't blame you, not after this reward, but we will certainly miss your services."

"My questing days are over." Dobbin stood. "But there's still plenty of time for adventure."

Lord Ferant scribbled on a piece of parchment and then stamped it with a wax seal. "Take this to the Bank of Aedrea tomorrow and they will settle the accounts." He handed the letter to Dobbin. "Take care of yourself, my b —" He paused, then extended a hand to shake. "Take care of yourself, Dobbin."

The hour was late by the time Dobbin left, so he headed home for the night. Tomorrow, he would make good on his promise to Henrik.

***

The next morning, Dobbin stopped by the Bank of Aedrea, facilitating the biggest transfer of his adventuring career. There would be no grand ceremony of his achievement. The Eastborne Dinner Cult prided itself on discretion, and so had Dobbin, for the most part. It was why he'd been in their constant employment for the last few years.

Only those closest to him would even believe the story. There was no head to mount or trophy to display from his time in the crag. But Dobbin had never done it for the accolades.

After years of work, he'd finally looted the dragon's den, and he promptly deposited twenty-five percent into the account of Isabella Hargrave.

Now, he paced in the alley across from Cupped Cakes. He'd been there for an hour already, long enough for the morning rush to pass, but he still hadn't gathered the courage to go inside. A customer left, and the storefront was empty for the first time all day.

An older lady passed by and clutched her bag closer when she spotted Dobbin lurking in the alley.

"Come on, Dobbin." He took a deep breath, flexed his fingers several times, and walked across the street.

The door jingled as he entered.

"Be right with you," Isabella called. Her back faced him as she finished decorating a pastry on the far counter.

For a moment, he almost turned back, but then he remembered Henrik's words. *They deserve to know the man who's been looking after them all these years.*

Her son, *Henrik's son,* peeked out from behind the counter. "You're big."

"Henry, that's not how we talk to people." Isabella turned around. "Sir, I apologize for my son's—"

The spoon fell to the floor, and icing shot across the room. She stared at Dobbin with a shocked expression.

Dobbin smiled. "Henry, is it?"

The boy nodded. He was the spitting image of his father. Slender frame, curly brown hair. Even at such a young age, his eyes were as alert as Henrik's had ever been. He would grow into a handsome man.

Isabella's mouth hung open, her brow furrowed, and she just stared. "Dobbin, is that you?"

"Yeah, it's me." His gaze drifted to the floor for a moment and then he met her eyes. "Sorry it took me so long to come around. I just…" He wasn't sure what to say. How to explain that he'd blamed himself for Henrik's death for all these years.

Her face softened. "Yeah, we just, too."

They locked eyes for a moment, and Dobbin wondered what he'd ever been so afraid of. She'd been his friend, too. If anything, there was a comfort in knowing they'd both lost someone dear to them.

"You dropped the spoon, Mommy." Henry pointed at the splatter of icing on the floor.

"You're right. Do you want to help Mommy clean it up?"

The boy nodded and disappeared into the backroom, returning a moment later with a towel.

"This is Dobbin. He was a friend of your father's. His best friend, in fact." She gestured at a stool in front of the display. "Come, have a seat."

Dobbin hesitated. "Are you sure?"

"No offense, Dobbin, but I'm afraid if I let you walk out that door, I may never see you again."

Dobbin chuckled. "You always did have a good read on people. It was one of the things Henrik loved most about you."

She took a pastry from the display and placed it on a

plate in front of him. It looked like a paw drizzled with icing and sprinkled with almonds. "Here, try this. It's a new recipe I've been working on. I call it a bear paw."

He took a bite of the fluffy pastry and groaned. The inside was filled with a sweet, almond paste, and the glaze on top was decadent. The almond sprinkles added a crunch to each bite.

"Wow. That's good."

"I know, right." She grinned. "So, tell me. What have you been up to all these years?"

Dobbin lost himself in thought as memories flashed before his eyes. Seven years of defining moments filled with adventure, anger, pain, growth, and now healing. He licked the glaze off his fingers and placed the pastry on the plate. "You wouldn't believe me if I told you."

Yet, part of him knew that she would.

# EPILOGUE

Dobbin took a sip of his drink, keenly aware of the eyes on him as he carefully placed it back on the table. The bar was focused on him, even the two bartenders. The story had started as a tale among friends, but as more tables turned their attention toward him, he let his voice carry across the room. He had the floor, and like any good storyteller, he milked it for all it was worth.

"So, there I am, frozen in place, the call of the wraith raging in my mind like the pull of a heavy tide, beckoning me to come down. My will is strong, but I've never felt something so all-encompassing. I knew that if I lifted my boot, if I tried to take another step, there was no way I was making it out of there alive." A soft hand caressed his forearm, and his body tingled. He glanced at Lyra, placing his hand over hers. She'd heard the tale a half-dozen times since she'd arrived in Eastborne, and yet she always listened like it was the first time.

The two of them had settled into a nice room at the Seaside Inn for the past week. A shack by the docks was hardly fit for someone they called the Glamour Mage, so he'd booked a room with a balcony overlooking the ocean. They had barely left but to eat and check on the animals.

Lyra had been content to stay down by the docks, across from the rowdy patrons of the tavern down the street and the tolling bells of ships as they entered the harbor, but Dobbin had insisted.

What was the point of having coin if he couldn't spend it on those he cared for?

Across from him, Isabella had her fingers pressed together. She waited anxiously with the rest of the tavern for the tale to continue. Dobbin had stopped by to visit her and Henry several times a week since he'd returned, but this was her first time hearing the full story of what had happened with the wraith.

Henry sat in front of the hearth playing with Jinx, the giant cat that roamed the bar of Cursed Cocktails.

To Dobbin's left, Alina rolled her eyes. She'd just returned from her own adventure somewhere in Revelia. "Get on with it already."

He grinned and continued. "The next thing I know, Myrtle reaches into a pouch and pulls out this greenish-purple powder, blowing it straight into my face. I still don't know what it was, but it lifted the wraith's hold, and I could finally think straight. We rushed up the stairwell, and then the elder goblin showed her full power."

The crowd was so enraptured by his performance of the specters, ghosts, and Moss Ears's magic that the tavern was eerily silent aside from the occasional glass returning to the table. He didn't tell the full story, leaving out the part about the dragonfire mushrooms and his vision of Henrik. That part would only be heard by those closest to him.

When he finished, there was a round of applause.

A raven-haired man took to the stage with his lute. He was broad-shouldered with thick thighs and looked like he'd fit in better at the Adventurer's Guild than the Bard College.

The man brushed shaggy black hair from his eyes and strummed his lute, chuckling. "Nobody warned me I was going to have to follow that."

Chatter returned to the bar as he played, and soon the elven bartender stopped by the table carrying a tray of shots. "Good to see you again. Dobbin, right? I brought you a little something for a tale well told. It's a sample of the new cocktail my partner is working on." The man with the silver beard waved from behind the bar, and the elf acknowledged the others sitting with Dobbin. "I'm Rhoren, the owner of this little hole in the wall. Thanks for stopping by tonight."

"That's nice of you, Rhoren." Dobbin raised a hand in acknowledgment to the other bartender. "You have some of the best drinks in the city. Though I hear you have quite the story yourself."

Rhoren laughed. "Stop by some other time and I'll tell you all about it."

He returned to the bar, and Dobbin passed out the drinks. They were bright yellow and served with a spiral of lemon peel.

Dobbin raised his glass, toasting to Alina and Isabella. "To old friends."

"And new lovers." Alina gave him a devilish smile, and her gold tooth gleamed in the candlelight.

"And new lovers," Dobbin echoed as he turned his attention to Lyra.

She bit her lower lip, and his insides burned with passion. The fact that she'd traveled all the way to Eastborne just to see him was a testament to what they were building. Their night together had been more than just a one-night stand. He held her gaze as he downed the drink.

The cocktail was refreshingly tart with a hint of honey. Not too sweet and not too citrusy.

"Gods, that is good." Alina rubbed her tattooed hands together. "So, what's next for you two?"

"We were thinking of getting out of the city for a bit," Lyra answered. She squeezed Dobbin's hand. "I think he's earned a little break, don't you?"

Isabella nodded. "You've got to make time for the important things in life." She turned to Dobbin. "Before it's too late."

Dobbin reached across the table and patted her hand.

"There's a big difference between what we think and what he'll do." Alina raised a brow. "Has the mighty Dobbin finally decided to put pleasure before business?"

"Something like that." He smiled. "We're planning to return to Hells' Crag. Snort's not a little pig anymore, and I think the open space would do her good. I was hoping you might come with us."

"Me? Hells' Crag?" Alina arched both brows. "Whatever for?"

It was his turn to smirk. "There's someone I want you to meet."

# ACKNOWLEDGMENTS

**Thank you for reading *Sword & Thistle*!** If you enjoyed traveling across Aedrea, please consider rating, reviewing, and sharing your thoughts on social media using the hashtag #SwordandThistle. Word of mouth is the best way to support indie authors like myself.

---

*Sword & Thistle* was a fun book to write. Growing up, *The Hobbit* was my gateway into epic fantasy, and with this book, I wanted to capture some of the wonder that I had while reading that adventure for the first time. Not just the epic quest and wondrous world, but the found family and cozy moments that have left a lasting impression on many readers over the years.

For me, creating a novel is more than just putting words on a page. Numerous people have played a part in this novel's creation, either directly or indirectly. I would be remiss if I didn't give them proper acknowledgment.

Cindy Koepp, thank you for being the first set of eyes on the unedited drivel I like to call writing.

And to Caroline, thank you for your constant support. When the days are long, or the words aren't flowing, I can always count on you to lift me up.

Thank you CartographyBird for designing the map of Aedrea and Lucian for creating such a beautiful cover.

Thank you to my amazing team of beta readers: Paul Tuson, Jordan Mellor, Sean Flint, Greg Trotti, Andrea Tessito, Tom Nemes, Loren Foster, Cindy Koepp, Chris Ostrowski, and Evan Fleischer.

I would also like to thank all of my patrons on Patreon.

**Platinum Tier:** Joel Southard

**Gold Tier:** Michael Percell, Robert Schaefer

**Silver Tier:** Nicholas Kelly, Rickie Brookes, Sam Taylor

Until next time…

# ABOUT THE AUTHOR

**S.L. Rowland** is a cozy fantasy and LitRPG author known for crafting immersive worlds filled with adventure, heart, and a touch of humor. A lifelong gamer and fantasy enthusiast, he draws inspiration from tabletop RPGs, video games, and the fantastical. When he's not writing, he enjoys weightlifting, hiking with his Shiba Inu, and enduring the heartbreak of being an Atlanta sports fan.

SLRowland.com

Patreon-For signed paperbacks, advanced chapters, exclusive short stories, art, merch, and more.

<u>Newsletter:</u> For updates on new releases, sales, and behind the scenes content!

<u>Email:</u> slrowlandauthor@gmail.com

Find out more at https://linktr.ee/SLRowland